ᴴᴱʀBERT ERNEST BATES (1905–1974) woʀᴋᴇᴅ as a journalist and clerk on a local newspaper before publishing his first book, *The Two Sisters*. His most famous work of fiction is the bestselling *Fair Stood the Wind for France* (1944). Other well-known novels include *Purple Plain* (1947), *Jacaranda Tree* (1949), *Scarlet Sword* (1950) and *Love for Lydia* (1952). *The Darling Buds of May*, the first of the popular Larkin family novels, was followed by *A Breath of French Air* (1959), *When the Green Woods Laugh* (1960) *Oh, To Be in England!* (1963) and *A Little of What You Fancy* (1970). His last works included the novel *The Triple Echo* (1971) and a collection of short stories, *The Song of the Wren* (1972).

H. E. BATES

Fair Stood the Wind for France

Fair stood the wind for France
When we our sails advance,
Nor now to prove our chance
Longer will tarry.
Michael Drayton, 1563–1631

PENGUIN BOOKS

PENGUIN CLASSICS

Published by the Penguin Group
Penguin Books Ltd, 80 Strand, London WC2R 0RL, England
Penguin Group (USA) Inc., 375 Hudson Street, New York, New York 10014, USA
Penguin Group (Canada), 10 Alcorn Avenue, Toronto, Ontario, Canada M4V 3B2
(a division of Pearson Penguin Canada Inc.)
Penguin Ireland, 25 St Stephen's Green, Dublin 2, Ireland (a division of Penguin Books Ltd)
Penguin Group (Australia), 250 Camberwell Road, Camberwell, Victoria 3124,
Australia (a division of Pearson Australia Group Pty Ltd)
Penguin Books India Pvt Ltd, 11 Community Centre,
Panchsheel Park, New Delhi – 110 017, India
Penguin Group (NZ), cnr Airborne and Rosedale Roads, Albany,
Auckland 1310, New Zealand (a division of Pearson New Zealand Ltd)
Penguin Books (South Africa) (Pty) Ltd, 24 Sturdee Avenue, Rosebank 2196, South Africa

Penguin Books Ltd, Registered Offices: 80 Strand, London WC2R 0RL, England

www.penguin.com

First published by Michael Joseph 1944
Published in Penguin Books 1958
Published in Penguin Classics 2005

012

Printed in England by Clays Ltd, St Ives plc

978–0–141–18816–4

www.greenpenguin.co.uk

SOMETIMES the Alps lying below in the moonlight had the appearance of crisp folds of crumpled cloth. The glacial valleys were alternately shadowy and white as starch in the blank glare of the full moon; and then in the distances, in all directions, as far as it was possible to see, the high snow peaks were fluid and glistening as crests of misty water. Somewhere below, in peacetime, at Domo d'ossola, Franklin remembered he had once waited for a train for England.

He held the mouthpiece of the intercomm. to his mouth, dry now after all the hours of flying across France, across the Alps, and into Italy and called his crew.

'All set for France,' he said. 'Any complaints?'

'Home is where I long to be,' the sergeant rear-gunner said, 'before I bust with boredom. What year is it?'

'We're Hannibal crossing the Alps,' Sandy said. 'The year is 218 B.C.'

'It could be,' Godwin said. 'It's all right for Connie. He just sits and plays patience.'

'Patience hell,' O'Connor said. 'I'm dying of excitement now.'

Franklin listened rather dully, his mind flat with strain, to the talk of the crew. It was August and the papers were beginning to use once again, with slight agitation, the word offensive. It did not mean very much to him. All through the winter the offensive had been mounted against Germany and had gone on, with some breaks in the late winter because of weather, into the third summer of the war. The New Year had come in again, as it had done the previous year and the year before that, with snow, and the spring had followed with bitter dry winds in May. There had been much east wind and sometimes that summer, with things going wrong again in Egypt and the summer seeming as if it would never come, people everywhere had seemed ill-tempered. Now with what the newspapers called the rising tide of war he could feel in himself, delayed and arid, his own impatience at the war. If he kept flying until October he would have been actively operational, with the same crew with the exception of Sanders, the wireless operator who had joined them in late spring, a whole year. He would have completed the first three hundred hours. From the first trips over Bremen, where he wore his belt so tight that it was like a warm knife laid curved and sharp over the sour cushion of his stomach, to the new long trips to Italy that had now begun in the late summer, it did not seem as if he had been flying a very long time. But the trips themselves, immensely long over the dull terrain of France, spectacular over the Alps, not yet violent over Italy, now began to seem longer in themselves than all his previous hours together. On the earlier trips he had learned very quickly the habit of flying relaxed and of fore-shortening the focus of his mind: so that he never looked forward beyond the next moment of darkness. He learned never to anticipate the flak, the searchlights, the exciting terror of the target, the long journey home. In this way the trips had never seemed long; the hell had been broken up into endurable fragments. Now he had begun to be cautiously aware of being tired.

He was aware, too, that below him the Alps were receding very fast. Folded snow distances that had seemed infinite were already broken at the northern edges by the darker shadows of lower mountains, below the snow-line, as a clear sky is darkly broken in the distance by storm. He was glad of the change. These mountains began to take on, as the aircraft flew fast towards them, the crusty appearance of old bark, grey and fissured under the moon. He fancied he saw beyond them, the light was so strong and white and clear, the beginnings of the French plain. As he stared at the changes on the forward horizon, feeling for them with his eyes, he fought away with the edges of his mind the beginnings of tiredness. In a few moments the two things became one. His eyes and his mind were flickering mentally against the distances of fatigue as they groped physically for the new horizons beyond the last of the mountains.

He shook himself out of a momentary doze and began to think of the crew again. They were silent now; he did not care for talking. He took very seriously the business of flying four other people over long hostile distances. In a year his affection for the four men had stiffened rather than grown. He measured

6

it now not so much by what they were, but by his fears of whatever changes the absence of one of them might bring. All four were sergeants. None of them ever called him 'sir' now, and he never thought of any differences, service or social, between himself and them. In flying jackets the distinctions of the ground disappeared. From the beginning he had felt also, being the only officer, that it must be for him to go over to them, rather than that they, four of them and equal, should come over to him. To be accepted by the sergeants, to feel their unified confidence in him growing and opening wide at last to acceptance, was a great thing. It had given him something higher than fear; the firm knowledge, never expressed, that if anything should happen they would be together, for each other and of each other, in whatever sort of end there might be.

The mountains of the distance had now become the mountains, huge and dark blue and wrinkled, of the country immediately below. The port wing of the Wellington seemed to mow across them like the black and slightly shining blade of an enormous scythe. As it cut over them and they were gone, their place was taken smoothly by the inward and backward flow of earth that seemed to have no more life, from that height and in the dead glare of the moon, than a relief map on a table. As Franklin looked at it he felt boredom once more fight through the edges of his tiredness, and he looked at his watch, surprised to find it earlier than he had thought. The time was ten minutes to two.

'My watch must be wrong,' he said into the intercomm. 'What time do you make it?'

One by one the four sergeants told him the time. Sandy counted the seconds for him, coming up to the minute. 'Five, six, seven, eight, nine,' and Franklin automatically turned the hands of his watch, making an alteration of less than three seconds. The time by all watches was ten to two. He thanked them and heard Taylor, in the rear turret, say that he could still see the Alps and that they still looked very wonderful from there. The moon was going down a little now, and the great glare that had lain over the snow-peaks had already diminished and was touched with amber. In this weak and more beautiful light the distances northward became shorter. France seemed for

7

some time longer a country of placid yellow patterns smoothed out of sight by both wings of the aircraft, and then there were more mountains on the port side, not very high but sharp with abrupt shadow where the lowering angle of the moon struck them. He did not yet know the Italian trip as he knew the trips to Bremen and Cologne, and he did not know which mountains they might be. He remembered them vaguely from an earlier trip, ten days before, and he calculated by them that he was well into France. He calculated he might be home by four.

The mountains had already slipped away and the boredom of new stretches of placid French country to the north was already eating into his mind again, making him slightly sleepy, when the trouble in the port engine began. It was as if the engine ejected something violently. It seemed to lose suddenly part of its weight. The whole aircraft skewed violently to port and took a sideways and downward slip. The level skimming of the wings that had remained constant now for so long was broken in a second. The violence of the dive took him by surprise and he had lost about five hundred feet before his reactions became clear again and he began to take any action. His own confusion, together with the confused shouts of the crew over the inter-comm. did not last more than a second or two. Shock cleared his mind of fright, leaving it wonderfully awake, so that all the possible reasons for everything drove brightly and swiftly through it. In this moment of alert realization, a second before his hands and feet began to do the instinctive things, he felt the whole aircraft pull up, give a sort of gigantic double shudder and flatten out again. This in itself was over so suddenly that he felt for one second longer that they might, after all, have hit nothing but an air-pocket and that all was well. Then he felt rather than heard, and instinctively rather than consciously, the change in depth of the sound of the engines. It seemed suddenly to have become shallow.

'Christ, Frankie,' O'Connor said. 'What happened? What the hell happened?'

For a second or two they were all talking together. They were excited by shock. He did not listen. He was listening only to the sound of the engines: in reality, as he now knew quite well, to the sound of one engine. He knew quite well that the port had gone

8

'God, what was it?' Taylor said. 'I felt like something in a catapult.'

Franklin did not answer. The reasons for it all, the reasons that had raced clearly through his mind, now came back in reverse order, more slowly and more clearly and more forcibly. He felt his hands sweating slightly on the stick. He felt one part of him struggling to accept the easy reasons, the other rejecting them. He tried to reason that it could be a short, that it couldn't be overheating, that it couldn't be the delayed result of flak, since the Italian stuff had been too light to touch them. He tried to reason that it could be just one of those things, inexplicable and apparently causeless, that may suddenly affect an engine anywhere, and then finally his fears and reasons were abruptly crystallized by the voice of Sandy.

'You could get that same effect, skip,' he said, 'by breaking an air-screw.'

Franklin was silent for a few moments longer. He looked in those moments at the altimeter and his speed. The air speed was already down and was falling in irregular jerks on the dial. The altimeter showed a little less than sixteen thousand. It fell as he looked at it. In those few moments the situation cleared itself finally of doubt. They had plenty of height and he was not afraid. They would lose more height, but it would, he hoped, be smooth and over a period of time. He rejected quite calmly first, the thought of getting home, and then, directly afterwards, the thought of baling out. In those few moments, making his decisions, he felt very alone and finally assured. If he had any other emotion of comparable strength it was a moment of anger: anger that a cause beyond his control and perhaps beyond his explanation should affect and change his life with violence and perhaps catastrophe.

The altimeter was down below fifteen thousand when he spoke again to the crew.

'It is the air-screw,' he said.

'Well, for Christ's sake,' O'Connor said. 'Just like that.'

'Just like that,' he said, 'and we won't make it.'

They did not answer now. He felt the moment of silence deeply. It was their confidence and did not need to be spoken. He had forgotten utterly now about the Alps, the moonlight,

9

the boredom, and even about the air-screw. A few moments of the immediate future were all that mattered. They were a division, a gap, in the lives of all of them, and it was his business to take them through it. They were waiting for what he had to say.

'Listen,' he said. 'I'm going to land within the next five or ten minutes. Roughly where are we, Sandy?'

'About west-north-west of the Vosges. Away south of Paris.'

'Occupied or Unoccupied?'

'Unless you turn back it'll be Occupied. I'm not sure of the line.'

'What's it matter?' O'Connor said. 'They're all crooks.'

'You're going to find that out,' Franklin said.

He went on slowly and calmly telling them what to do, watching his height and his speed at the same time. The situation in these few minutes, as he reminded the crew of maps and emergency rations and the details of landing, did not once seem desperate.

'Don't do anything cock-eyed,' he said. 'If anything happens to anybody do your best for him. Take away identification marks. Bust the kite up as much as you can and then start walking. Go south-west. Walk at night and go through the towns about dusk. Remember what you've been told. O.K.?'

'O.K.' They answered him one by one. 'O.K.'

'O.K.,' he said. 'Pack your bags and take up stations for landing.'

The face of the land in the moonlight began to show clear patterns of gold and shadow and white straight intersections of road as he put the nose of the Wellington down. The land, perhaps because of the lower angle of the deeper moon, seemed everywhere of a possible and easy flatness. Coming lower, he saw here and there the white and black cube of a house in the moon. The transitory landscape stopped being dead. It became real and alive with fields and roads and houses, and here and there, as he came lower still, he could see in the whiter fields the rows of shocked corn.

He came in to land with the moon low and heavily gold on his right hand. His speed was lower than he would have liked, but the pale yellow landscape seemed to come up towards him at a furious slant. The tail did not seem to go down well and he pressed with all the strength of his legs on the rudder bar until he knew at last, as the trees began to tear past underneath him like fragments of wreckage torn up by a tornado, that it was successfully down. Then he saw before him the clear spaces of earth, almost beautifully rectangular and free of obstruction and smooth as asphalt, that he had all this time been seeking out. Until that moment all that had been happening and had happened was clear and right and uncomplicated. The light earth came up to him very fast, and after the first bumping moments of contact became, as it were, secured to the aircraft. Then a second later he knew that something was wrong. The ground was too soft and the moon for a few seconds jolted wildly about the sky. The Wellington did a ground loop, about three-quarters circle, and Franklin could not hold it. He was aware of being thrown violently forward and of his sickness knotting in his stomach and then rising and bursting and breaking acidly, with the smell of fuel and oil, in his mouth. He was aware of all the sound of the world smashing forward towards him, exploding his brain, and of his arms striking violently upward, free of the controls. For a moment he seemed to blackout entirely and then the moon, hurling towards him, full force, smashed itself against his eyes and woke him brutally to a moment of crazy terror. In that moment he put up his hands. He felt his left arm strike something sharp, with sickening force, and then the moon break again in his face with the bloody and glassy splinters in a moment beyond which there was no remembering.

CHAPTER 2

WHEN he opened his eyes the moon was full on his face. He could smell his own sickness on his flying jacket and he could feel, in a way that pained and troubled him, the beat of aircraft engines pumping and thundering in his left arm. This arm was also wet and hot. The terrible thump of engines beating down the arteries seemed as if they must finally sever the arm from the shoulder.

'It's O.K., Frankie,' Sandy said.

He could not speak in answer. He knew that he was lying on his back. He could see Sandy's head moving across the line of the moon. He wondered what had happened to the rest.

'It's all right,' Sandy said. 'Everybody is all right.'

'What happened?'

'Everything was lovely, except the ground was too soft. We just looped and wrapped up. That's all. We're in a sort of marsh.'

The thump of engines pulling the socket of his arm with sickening pain began to increase as his consciousness came back. There was no blood in his lips and his face felt intensely cold and drawn.

'Where are the rest?'

'They're in the kite,' Sandy said. 'Collecting things. What are we going to do? Burn it?'

'I don't know. I don't think so.'

'The whole neighbourhood will have seen us come down. If there is a neighbourhood. Perhaps it's luck we came down in this marsh. Are you all right?'

'Jesus,' he said. 'I don't know.'

More and more the pain of his arm was sucking away his strength. He felt himself dragged down, helpless, through a cold wet descent of darkness. With his free arm he dug his nails into the earth and made a great effort and kept himself, cold and weak, on the edge of consciousness.

'Jesus, it's my arm.'

12

'I'll get your jacket off. Roll over a bit,' Sandy said, 'can you?'

He rolled over on his right side and Sandy zipped the Irwin jacket open. He pulled out his right arm and then Sandy took the sleeve of his left arm and pulled it gently down. The pain of this slow movement crawled up his arm, beating against the downward flow of blood, until it reached the socket. The sleeve came slowly off and with it, as it came free, all the returning pain and blood and sickness of his arm. He felt for a moment so weak that he could not even look at the moon. He looked down at his arm instead. And in that moment, as his jacket came free, he saw the spurt of his own blood spewed upward from the vein, vicious and thick, pumped irregularly from the wound.

'For Christ's sake,' Sandy said. 'Can you hold it up? Can you lift it? I've got to get a tourniquet on.'

He raised his hand, and then the wrist a little, but it made no difference. The flow of blood was changed but not lessened. The pain of it was still sucking and thumping from the socket to the fingers.

Suddenly he felt the pressure of Sandy's thumbs on the arm. The two thumbs were big and violent at the first pressure. Then as they held the pressure he felt the pull of blood lessen. He thought of a test-tube under heat. The liquid pumped high in the test-tube, and then you took the heat away and suddenly the liquid fell and quietened.

He was slipping away down the slope of cold darkness again when he heard Sandy call. All this time he had not seen the aircraft. Now as Sandy called O'Connor, the voice no more than a tiny whisper, and he heard O'Connor answer from a few feet away, he realized that the Wellington was somewhere just behind his head. He heard Sandy say something about the first-aid box, and then he saw O'Connor come into the light of the moon. He heard the lid of the first-aid box open, and then O'Connor was twisting the tourniquet on his arm. In the next few vague moments all he knew was the grip of the tourniquet cutting down through his flesh, and that soon it was as if he had no arm below the elbow.

'It's O.K., Frankie,' O'Connor said. 'It's stopped.'

13

He tried to say something, but there seemed to be some dislocation between his tongue, very bloodless and cold still, and his brain. This is bloody silly, he thought. He tried to get up. Too weak to lift his head he lay back and shut his eyes, and instantly the danger of the moment, the fact of the aircraft undestroyed, the parachutes, the position of all of them, struck him with terrifying force.

'Sandy,' he said. 'Sandy. We must get moving.'

'Can you move?'

'I don't know. I think if you get me up I could move. What's happening about the kite? You've got to get those parachutes hidden.'

'Taylor and Goddy are doing it. They're nearly finished now.'

'What are they doing?'

'Busting the inside up. Trying to get the parachutes hidden.'

'How long have we been here?'

'About half an hour. Perhaps a bit more.'

'But Jesus,' he said, 'any moment now we'll be done for. We've got to get moving. We've got to.'

'O.K.,' Sandy said, 'as soon as you feel you can move.'

He knew that this was the important thing. Somehow he had to move. The moon was still too bright, and he knew that everything, at the moment, was against them. Everything depended on whether he could move.

'Get me up,' he said.

'I'll hold the arm,' O'Connor said. 'I've got you.'

He stood up between them. He stood up and then knew, at once, that if they let go of him he would fall down. His body seemed empty. It was empty of blood and warmth and the elementary means of strength. Some time previously he had been sick down his jacket and shirt, and now the smell of it revolted him again.

'Just hold me,' he said.

'Have a little rum,' Sandy said. 'It probably isn't the right thing, but it might help.'

'We've got to get out somehow.'

'Sit down again until I come back,' Sandy said.

'No,' he said. 'I can stand.'

Sandy went away and he stood lop-sided, leaning against

O'Connor, who in turn held the tourniquet on his arm. 'This is just bloody silly,' he said, 'but I can't stand straight.'

'You were out cold,' O'Connor said. 'You were gone at least ten minutes.'

'It could have been years,' he said.

He took a lot of the rum when Sandy came back. He drank it quickly, spilling it, feeling it beating sweetly against the sickness still acid in his throat. He was very anxious. With enormous effort he forced himself to feel better. He certainly felt warmer. The rum drove hot down his chest and seemed, in a few seconds, to stimulate the heart.

'By the time they've finished in the kite,' he said, 'I think I could go.'

'Are you cold?' Sandy said. 'What about your jacket?'

'Just put it over my shoulders. Without the sleeves.'

Sandy put his flying jacket over his shoulders and then went away, leaving him with O'Connor. He called after Sandy that they must hurry up. It was important to get away.

'Are you sure you can do it?' O'Connor said.

'You can do anything you've got to. I only wish to hell I knew exactly where we were.'

He felt slightly stronger by the time Sandy came back. With O'Connor holding his arm he stood for a minute by himself, his legs wide apart, hard on the ground, his teeth set, forcing himself into the new responsibility. He had to go forward now, he thought, whatever happened, and not back.

'They're about ready,' Sandy said.

'Have they done everything? Got everything? We want all the maps, compass, logs. Don't leave anything. Have they let the petrol out?'

'They left it till last. It's going now. Are you all right?'

'I'm O.K.,' he said. 'We ought to get going, though. We've got to get going.'

A few seconds later Godwin and Taylor came, carrying rations, maps, old gear from the aircraft. Now he could hear the petrol slopping and dribbling into its own pool in the ground, and could smell the odour of it in the air. He noticed the moon was already down a lot, and he was glad of the darker sky.

'All right,' he said. 'You're sure you've got everything? All the rations? We may lay up for days.'

'Everything we can,' Godwin said.

'All right. The point is we must start walking. We must. What's the time?'

'It's now three thirty-four,' Sandy said. 'Exactly.'

'O.K., we can walk for an hour. We can walk till just before sunrise. Then we'll lay up for the day. We'll try to walk roughly west, straight into the moon. That's as good a guide as we have. Everybody O.K.?'

'O.K.,' they said.

Sandy and Godwin and Taylor began to walk across the flat ground, marshy in spots and broken up by patches of sedge, where the aircraft had come down. It was necessary for Franklin to walk with O'Connor. Before moving he put his left arm in the half-closed front of his Irwin jacket while O'Connor held his shoulders. Turning, he took his first and last look at the Wellington, the big curved tail up against the light sky, the nose a little further down than normal against the earth. His conscience was quite clear. The land was so bare and open that it had seemed dangerous to him, from the very first moment of consciousness, to fire the aircraft. It seemed to him, if there must be a choice between firing it and escape, that escape was the better thing. He looked at the Wellington for about ten seconds, thinking all this, thinking very swiftly how good the kite had been and how much a part of his life she had been for so long, and then turned to walk away.

The pumping had now ceased in his arm, and the warmth had begun to flow back, slightly but positively, into his lips and face. But now when he came to walk his legs were bloodless. They seemed hollow, and when they met the earth it was as if he had pins and needles. The lack of reaction and pressure was in itself a new and stupid pain. His movements forward, across the marshy ground, were those of a man coming out of a sickbed, and they made him feel foolish and angry. All the time he could see the three sergeants about a hundred yards ahead, their flying jackets brown in the light of the moon.

'We've got to keep them in sight,' he said. 'The sod of it is I can't feel my feet.'

16

'You lost a lot of blood,' O'Connor said. 'Take it steady.'

He went across the marsh in painful stops and starts, leaning very slightly on O'Connor, very conscious of the foolishness, the pain and the inevitable weakness of his position. As he groped forward he made up his mind not to be silly about it one way or the other. He was very weak. He would go steady. At the same time, they had to get away. So he could keep going, foreshortening his view as he had learned to do when flying, not anticipating things, never reaching beyond the next moment.

In this way he covered, with O'Connor, two hundred yards without a break. He could see, always, the three flying-jackets in the moonlight ahead. They were light against the black earth of the marsh, itself intersected at intervals with small shallow dykes, about two feet wide, partly filled with water. Now and then the sedge thickened into large hummocks over which he could not lift his feet. When he stumbled, his big flying-boots slopping in the marsh water, O'Connor held him up. Away to the right of him, the grey leaves bright in the moon and stirring now in the silence with the first movement of wind he had detected since landing, he could see a plantation of osiers, about ten feet high, and felt himself lucky to have missed them. After they ended, the marsh went on again unbroken except for clumps of sedge and shallow intersecting dykes. All the time the moon was going down, bigger and deeper in colour, until he judged that only a little more than half an hour of light remained before dawn began to break the other way.

They walked on for twenty minutes before they saw the three flying-jackets motionless ahead. In a few moments they caught up with them.

'There seems to be some sort of road ahead,' Sandy noted.

'O.K. Take a look,' Franklin said.

'Have a rest while I'm gone.' Sandy said. 'Take a little more rum.'

'I'm all right,' he replied.

The words came to him automatically. Standing still, he felt extraordinarily weak again. The thump of blood in his arm had begun again, either because the tourniquet was too tight or too loose, just below the elbow. Below that his arm was dead. And for the first time, standing there, his legs hollow and the morning coldness drying the sweat of exertion on his neck and back, he wondered about the size of the wound. If it was large and close to the vein there was little hope, he thought, of the blood congealing. Sooner or later it would be a problem not only for him but for them all. It must affect the speed and safety with which they went on.

He was still thinking about this when Sandy came back.

'It's a kind of farm-track,' he said. 'There's a wire fence the other side.'

'All right,' Frankie said. 'Straight over.'

'The ground seems to rise a little on the other side. It's the end of the marsh.'

'That's all right. We'll keep going west,' he said. 'About another half hour.'

'You should take some more rum,' Sandy cautioned.

'No,' Franklin protested. 'The more often I take it the more I'll want it. I'm all right now.'

They went on and crossed the track. It was quite narrow and beyond the fence, where the ground rose, there was rough grass, grown thick and coarse and now burnt dry by summer. He could hear their flying-boots swishing through it as they climbed the hill. Soon, as before, the three sergeants began to go ahead, until the distance between them and himself and O'Connor was again about a hundred yards. Climbing the slope, he again began to feel unsure of himself. His legs had no substance, and the effort of putting them against the slight incline over-stimulated his heart. He could feel it knocking with immense bumps against his chest. These bumps began to reverberate in his head and then, more painfully, in his arm. He knew that he had to stop, that for a moment at least he could not go on. So he made the excuse that the bandage was loosening, and O'Connor stopped and tightened it again. As he halted Franklin felt his breath heaving up in great gasps, too loud for him to suppress, so that O'Connor heard them. 'You should take it steady,' O'Connor warned.

'I'll be all right,' he said, 'at the top of the hill.'

Walking forward again, slowly and with difficulty, he kept his eyes on the moon. By deliberate concentration, staring at the enormous butter-coloured face of the moon going down on the now hazy and darkening horizon, he forced himself upward in a series of stupefied efforts. There were moments when he did not know what he was doing. They came slowly to the top of the hill. The moon by that time had a fantastic enormity. It had begun to surge heavily forward, all gold and dazzling, into his face, and then recede, dark and eclipsed, away from the limit of his vision. At the top of the hill he was surprised to see the three sergeants already waiting. He had completely lost sight of them.

'There's a big dip of country,' Sandy said. 'A valley.'

'Yes?' He tried to go on speaking, but the words seemed swollen and could not press upward through the constriction of his throat. It was as if someone had hit him powerfully on the heart.

'Are you all right, Frankie?' O'Connor said.

'Jesus, I – I – Jesus.'

'Sit down,' Sandy said. 'You've been going strong. Sit down!'

He was silent, gathering his strength. It was like being drunk. The faculties dimmed and receded and surged back, and in a desperate moment he fought to hold them. He felt the four sergeants silently waiting while he stood helpless on the hill-top, trying to get his speech and strength again.

They came painfully back at last.

'It's no use,' he said. 'We've got to get a bit farther on and find a place to hide in. I can rest when we get there. I can rest all day.'

'You'd better have a little more rum.'

'Just a drop.'

He kept the rum in his mouth for a second or two before letting it down his throat. It drove away the dry taste of his breathlessness. It was sweet and hot, and after a few moments he felt ready to go on.

'Get ahead again,' he said, 'and see if you can't find a place to hide in. A wood if you can. Somewhere high. So that we can watch the lie of the country.'

He watched once again the three brown flying-jackets, edged white, go ahead of him and then disappear round the curved rim of the hill. He followed with O'Connor. The moon was now slightly on his right hand, so that he could not repeat the trick

19

of watching it and so blotting out the consciousness of his pain at waking. Instead he watched his feet. It comforted him unexpectedly and enormously to watch them, to see them lumping along, huge in the flying-boots, in the rustly dry grass, and in this way he went on for another ten minutes, until his steps had begun to pump the blood painfully into his face and arms again.

When he raised his face at last it was to find the moon, smoky and red, severed in half by the horizon, and the three sergeants waiting for him under a clump of trees.

'It seems all right here,' Sandy said. 'There's a wood. Plenty of undergrowth. And we can see the valley.'

'Get in then,' he advised. 'Not too far in. You've got to watch the approaches.'

He had never felt quite so unsure of himself as at that moment. He was vaguely aware of going into the wood, of the trees blacking out overhead the sky that had begun to grow as light now with dawn as it had been, for some time, with the moon. He was aware of lying down in this darkness, of earth cold against the short hairs of his neck and his free hand. He was aware of lying motionless and then of seeming slowly to move, weakly, not of his own volition, down into the old darkness of coldness and sweat. It gradually took him down and down, until he could feel even the pain of his arm no longer.

CHAPTER 3

When he woke the day was hot and calm. He could see a jagged blade of sunlight, bright and intense, slitting the black edges of the overhanging pines. His mouth was very sick. When he moved his head from side to side it was as if it were weighted with a leaden ball that rolled from one ear to the other. He came out of the stupidity of sleep and tried to turn his body; he felt the pain of his arm, and then with a slow shock he remembered it. He looked down at himself, slantwise, as he lay, and saw that his arm had been bandaged, quite skilfully, so that his elbow was free. It lay flat on his chest, so that he could not lie on it, and was suspended by a sling of bandage. Somebody had taken his flying-jacket off and had laid it over him, but now it had slipped away.

'No need to get up,' Sandy said.

'What?' he asked.

'You're all right where you are,' Sandy replied. 'We're in the wood. It's perfectly O.K. You've had ten hours' sleep or more.'

'Jesus,' he cried. 'What happened?'

'You went clean out, and then I gave you a shot. It quietened you down, and you've been sleeping ever since.'

'What time is it?'

'About twelve.'

Franklin lay looking at the sunlight jaggedly cut by the black needle edges of the pines.

'Where are the boys?' he questioned.

'They've gone on a sort of reccy,' Sandy said. 'Through the wood. It seemed a good idea to find out what sort of country it was. The wood seems pretty big. Much more like part of a forest.'

'They shouldn't have gone,' Franklin objected. He was worried. 'We should stick together.'

'I think it's all right,' Sandy said. 'O'Connor will see to that. He's an old hand at this sort of thing. He was in France for the first eight months.'

'It doesn't matter,' Franklin protested. 'What we have to find out is whether we're in Occupied or Unoccupied France. Never mind what sort of country it is.'

'I hope to Christ it's Occupied,' Sandy said.

'We'll find that out before long,' he said.

He sat up. The weight of his sickness seemed to rise as he himself rose. It gathered in his head and seemed to make him top heavy. Beyond the dark edge of woodland the brightness of the day jumped like a shutter, black and then intensely white again.

'Have you looked at the country that way?' he said.

'Only from here,' Sandy said. 'Nobody has been out.'

'Let's have a look,' he said.

They walked slowly together to within five yards of the edge of the pines. They stood each behind the trunk of a pine and looked at the open country. The slope of rough grass up which they had come in the night had been scorched by the summer to the colour of dirty straw. Beyond the depth of the slope the land was stepped up in a series of folds. On the lowest of these folds white strips of cornland were already partly bare of crops. Along the middle folds were terraces of vines, blue-green in the vertical sun.

'Can you see the telegraph poles?' Sandy said.

'No.' Franklin felt his eyes jumping up and down at the strong light of the distances. 'No. I can't see them.'

'On the top of the hill. A good way over the top of the vines. In a straight line.'

Franklin was still dazed. 'No. I can't see them.'

'They're there all right. It must be a road.'

'I don't see any houses,' Franklin said.

'If you go down to the corner of the wood,' Sandy said, 'you can see a house half-way up the slope.'

'Somebody ought to watch it,' Franklin said.

They went back into the woodland and Franklin sat down on the pine-needles, his back against a tree. He felt weak with movement and the light of the sun.

'How is your arm?' Sandy said.

'It's all right.'

'I warn you it isn't altogether good. Sooner or later you'll have to do something about it. It'll have to be stitched or there'll be trouble.'

'We can think about that later. The main thing is to get moving.'

'We can't move until dark. That's certain.'

'No. That's the hell of it,' he said.

He lay back against the pine-tree, listening to the noon silence brittle and dead all about him, the trees and the sunless air under the trees unmoved by wind. His mouth was dry, and he was worried because the three sergeants were not back.

'They shouldn't have gone,' he said. 'There's no point in it. We must keep together.'

'Your arm makes you jumpy,' Sandy said. 'They'll be careful.'

'They'd better be,' he said. 'If they're seen the whole bloody lot of us are done.'

He lay back against the tree, listening and fretting. The situation was unreal. He had not yet adjusted himself to it. The cool and apparently impregnable silence under the pines seemed dangerous. He shut his eyes.

The blood beating up into his head became the sound, after a few moments, of the three sergeants returning. He opened his eyes and felt his relief take the form of annoyance. It rose hotly inside him and he checked it. He heard the sergeants rustling the pine-needles as they walked, not talking, from the depth of the wood, and then he saw them coming, without their flying-jackets, their blue sleeves bright in the shadows. He held his annoyance down and decided to hear what they had to say.

'Hullo, how do you feel?' O'Connor said.

'Not bad. What did you find?' he said.

'Not much. I think we're lucky. We got to the edge of the trees farther down and you can see the forest stretching for miles. It would take days to search it all.'

'All right. Did you see any houses?'

'None at all.'

'Right,' he said. His annoyance had gone; he felt himself reassured by the competence of O'Connor's voice and face. O'Connor was thirty-four. His Air Force service had begun in

23

boyhood, in apprenticeship. He had fought in France, flying Battles, and had been twice wounded. His face was tough and pale and sure. It was right that Franklin should trust him.

'Where do you think we are?' he said.

'I've got a feeling we're in Occupied.'

'I hope so.'

The four sergeants were sitting down now, resting on their flying-jackets, among the pine-needles. They were full of confidence.

'I think we might eat,' Franklin said. His fear had gone.

Lounging on the dry pine-needles, they had a meal of chocolate and biscuits, with a small tot of rum. Franklin felt the sickness of shock and loss of blood still lying hot and sour all across his chest, above his heart. He was not very hungry.

'We might as well discuss what we're going to do,' he said. 'My idea is to lie up here for the rest of the day and then start walking again at twilight. We've got to find a house before it's dark.'

'That's a risk,' Taylor said.

'It's a risk you have to take,' he said. 'Anyway, a farm is fairly safe. It's a thousand to one there are no troops in isolated houses. Anyway, we have to do it. We can't go on without food.'

'Can you speak French?' O'Connor said.

'It's good enough,' he said. The chocolate he could not eat was already soft and warm in his fingers. He felt sick and now at the same time impatient. He was fretted by inertia and even though he knew it was impossible, wanted to be moving on.

'We'd all better rest this afternoon,' he said. 'Get some sleep if you can.'

'Better take it in relays,' O'Connor said.

'Yes,' he said. 'You'd better make it three resting and two off. That means one watching the inside of the wood and one the valley.'

'And if we see anyone?'

'We'll talk about that when it happens,' he said.

They rested and watched in relays all the rest of the afternoon and on into the evening. The heat began to go down a little with the sun, about six o'clock, but all afternoon the bare cornland was white with heat below the shimmering blue-green vines on the far slope of the valley. As he tried unsuccessfully to sleep under the trees he watched the sky splintered above him into sharp blue lace by the needles of the pines, and as he lay on the edge of the wood, taking his turn at watching, he occasionally saw the distant telegraph poles quivering on the blue-white horizon in the taut heat of full afternoon. Once he went along to the far edge of the wood and lay watching the farmhouse a mile or two away, a block of bare whitewash among its low cubes of newly harvested corn and a clump of high grey poplars, but no one came out of it, and the folds of the valley, beyond the vineyards, remained empty in the sun.

There began to be some sign of twilight soon after eight o'clock. The horizon beyond the vines turned purple after the heat of day, the vines glowing sharp green against the background. As Franklin went down the slope from the wood, walking a little behind the three sergeants as before, with O'Connor, he watched the line of telegraph poles, just visible like clusters of white pin-heads against the darkening sky. He knew that somehow they had to get over the road. It looked like a big road and it ran roughly south-west, the direction they wanted to go. He knew that it might be dangerous to reach it through the open cornland and the vineyards, and he knew that their only chance lay through the farm.

He was not quite sure if the farm, which lay a little west of the vines, belonged to the vineyards. To the east the vineyards curved round the slope of the hillside, out of sight. They were quite evidently very big.

The farm was quite small. Down at the foot of the slope he found himself looking up at it. The bare track coming up from the grassland, dusty after the heat of summer, went up the second slope, by a wire fence, with the vineyards on the other side, and then merged into the yard of the farm. The farmhouse was one-storeyed, washed white, with big red curling tiles on the roof. He saw two small stacks of corn and a black-brown heap of muck by the door, but there was no one in sight.

He stopped the sergeants on the slope. They looked very conspicuous and odd in their flying-jackets and he did not like it. They were about three hundred yards from the house when he stopped. He made them squat down by the vines, and as he

25

squatted down too, he could see long shadowy alleys between the vines, and grapes plump and green among the leaves.

'I'm going up to the house,' he said. 'If I don't get food we've got grapes.'

'We've got grapes, anyway,' Taylor said.

'And if you don't come back?' O'Connor said.

'I'll leave it to you. Hide all day and keep walking at night. But don't go north. Whatever you do, don't go north.'

'You'll be back all right,' O'Connor said.

'Keep in the vines, anyway,' he said.

He began to walk away up the slope steadily, watching carefully the land beyond the fence. He was very conscious of the white sling on his arm and he tucked it deeper into the opening of his jacket. He felt the wound throbbing as he walked and the blood making corresponding beats in his head. As he came to the farmyard the twilight was rapidly coming down and he could see under a big apple-tree a cluster of white chickens already roosting in the dry hollows they had scratched in the dust about the roots. They fluttered a little as he went by. Then he went on and into the farmyard and halted for a moment about ten yards from the door of the farm.

He thought afterwards that the woman must have seen him from the windows. She came running out of the house and then stopped very suddenly, about five yards from him, her body flattened upright by the act of stopping, her hands slightly uplifted. All the time they were speaking she did not come any nearer.

'I'm English,' he said.

He felt foolish. His French, normally very fair, would not come. He stood looking at her stupidly. She was a little woman, about sixty, her hair drawn tightly back in a grey knot, her yellow brown face scared and almost hostile.

'No,' she said. 'No. Not here. Not here.'

'Something to eat,' he said.

'No.' She stood arrested, more scared than himself, her very dark eyes staring.

'Is the road safe?' he said.

'I don't know. I don't know.'

'Where does it go?'

26

'I don't know.'

'It's all right. If you're alone it's all right. Don't be frightened.'

'There is no food here,' she said.

'It's all right,' he said.

'Nothing,' she said. 'Nothing. They take so much. It's not easy.'

'Can you tell me what's over the road?' he said.

'You go now,' she said.

'Over the road,' he said, 'up there – what is there?'

'You go now,' she said; and then: 'The river.'

'The river?'

'You go now. You're all right if you go now.'

'What river?' he said.

'I don't know,' she said. 'I don't know. I don't know.'

He knew suddenly that it was no use. Her eyes were large and tearful with fear. She was too scared to offer either coherence or bread. He had eaten nothing but the chocolate for twenty-four hours, but now he felt suddenly that the road and what lay beyond the road were more important than hunger.

'Thank you,' he said. 'Thank you.' He began to move away.

Transfixed, upright in her first stiff attitude of astonishment, she watched him go, not saying another word.

Five minutes later, when he came up the slope again and through the farmyard with the four sergeants, she was still standing there, flattened and upright, as if she had been shot where she stood. The twilight was deepening rapidly, but as the five went past her Franklin could see the deep scared black eyes alive in the frightened face, but she did not move except to give a little harsh sound of new astonishment as they went by. When he looked back once more, and for the last time, she was still standing there, vague but unmoved in the twilight, not watching the five men, but only the empty air of the spot where Franklin had first appeared.

At the top of the hillside they lay down in the ditch between the field and the road.

'What happened?' O'Connor said.

'She was frightened.'

'No food?'

27

'She was too scared for anything.'

'We brought some grapes,' O'Connor said. 'Will you have some? They're sour, but they quench your thirst. I like them.'

'Break a few off for me.'

He lay on his good elbow, pressing the grapes one by one into his mouth. They were good and clean and sharp on his tongue. It was almost dark now. There was no sound except the slight noise of air moving overhead in the telegraph wires, and he felt that in a few moments the road would be safe.

'Would she do anything?' O'Connor said.

'I don't think so. She was scared. I think she thought I was someone else,' he said.

'What now?'

'Somewhere farther on there's a river,' he said. 'I found that out. But I can't make up my mind whether we ought to stick to the road or go on to the river. What do you think?'

'If there was just one of us,' O'Connor said, 'if it was myself, I'd say the road. But there's five of us. We look like bloody explorers.'

'That's what I feel,' he said. 'Come on.'

The road was empty as they went over it. He just had time to see the black shine of the tyre-worn tarmac and the line of telegraph poles vanishing on either side into a falling darkness, and then to smell the warm, friendly odour of tarmac scorched by the heat of the day. Then the five of them were in the field beyond, and were walking fast across it, slightly downhill again. As they walked he remembered, for the first time since the time of the crash, that soon the moon would be up, and he could not make up his mind whether or not it would be a good thing for them. The field they were crossing was cornstubble, and their flying-boots, hitting against the sharp upright straw, made a swishing and hollow sound in the wide quietness. He judged by the position of the vines that this was the north, perhaps the north-west slope, of the hill. They were going diagonally across it, almost dead into the thin strip of orange light lying far over in the west, the last of the day.

He spat out some grape-stones. 'We ought to make twenty miles,' he said. 'Perhaps twenty-five. The moon will be up.'

'What about the river?' O'Connor said.

'There's bound to be a bridge. If there's no bridge we can swim.'

'With one arm?'

'I'll try.'

'Like hell you will,' O'Connor said. 'And I'll tell you something else. You'll have trouble with that arm if it isn't stitched soon. You've got a slit in it as long as a jack-knife. It isn't congealing much either.'

'I'm all right.'

'I'm telling you,' O'Connor said.

He knew that what O'Connor was saying was probably true. He tried not to think of it. He finished the grapes O'Connor had given him and held out his hand for more. The three sergeants were about forty or fifty yards ahead. O'Connor gave him six or seven grapes broken from the bunch, and he ate them one by one as he walked.

Down the slope, at the end of the stubble, the sergeants were waiting.

'It looks like sugar-beet in the field beyond,' Godwin said. 'Is it all right to go through?'

'Go round it,' he said. 'Going through will make a hell of a noise.'

The three sergeants moved off. Stubble came down to the edge of the sugar-beet. There was no hedge or path between and they walked on in the stubble, keeping the roots on their right hand.

They walked on for another ten minutes without speaking The night was warm, and Franklin could smell the straw of the field and then, as they went farther down the slope, the slightly cooler air, touched with dew, coming up from the valley. From the field of roots they went down into grass, long and rough and sun-scorched again, but damp now with falling dew.

'Nearly all rivers in France are navigable,' he said. He felt they were not far from the river now.

'Which might mean something,' O'Connor said.

'It might mean barges. It'll almost certainly mean guards on the bridges and locks.'

'And a bloody good width,' O'Connor said.

'It looks like a swim,' he said.

29

'Not with that arm.'

'You want me to walk it?'

'You're about as obstinate as a woman,' O'Connor said.

They came to the last flat stretch of grass running on to the river almost before Franklin was ready. He was about to be angry with the sergeants for going too far ahead, when he and O'Connor stumbled on them in the grass. 'We thought we'd better wait,' Taylor said. 'The river bank is about thirty yards ahead.'

'Does it look all right?'

'It seems clear.'

'Go and look,' he said.

Taylor was very young, about nineteen or twenty. He was a very good gunner: so good that Franklin sometimes wondered if he knew, in a war not of his own making, anything of what it was all about. He had seen Taylor sometimes a little drunk after a big spell of ops., with gaiety swimming on his face, and with his eyes bright through the smeared glassiness of long strain, and had wondered how old you needed to be before fear stopped being half-conscious, and emerged from the embryo of mere excitement and became, at last, a harder and clearer pain.

He did not know why he was thinking of this, except perhaps to remind himself that what had happened so far, easy and lucky and in a way adventurous, was only the beginning. All the time he was trying to measure the possible distance they had to go with the capacity of all of them to go on. He did not doubt this. It only seemed to him wise to keep his alertness cool and clear, and as he lay in the grass, waiting for Taylor to come back, he realized that his fear and his alertness were one.

When Taylor came back he caught the sound of new responsibility in his voice, and was glad now that he had sent him.

'It's about sixty yards wide and it looks deep,' he said.

'Any bridge?'

'I can't see anything. There's a big bend farther up-stream,' he said.

'We might follow the bank,' Godwin said, 'and cross lower down.'

'I don't see the point of it,' Franklin said. 'Bridges are always dangerous, and the moon will be up, anyway.'

30

'Must we cross it?' Taylor said.

'We'll be better away from it, that's all,' he said. 'And away on that side.'

He slipped his good arm out of his Irwin jacket.

'Somebody take this off,' he said. 'Careful.'

'Look,' O'Connor said, 'you're being a bloody fool.'

'You can all swim, can't you?'

'All except you.'

'I can swim with two fingers.'

'You can't swim with that arm,' O'Connor said, 'and what's more, you're not going to.'

'We've got to get over.'

'Quite apart from the fact that you can't move it, the bandage will soak and slip off and be no good. You'll probably break the wound open again and lose a hell of a sight more blood. It's tough tit, Frankie, but you can't do it.'

He knew all at once that he was being obstinate, and suddenly he did not care.

'All right, what then?' he said.

'I'll tow you over,' O'Connor said.

He did not answer.

'I swam two rivers in France in 1940,' O'Connor said. 'It's easy, if you do it right. Now you do it in relays, see? You strip and you take your clothes over, a few at a time. It means more swimming but you keep your clothes dry. It's better than rushing like a bull.'

Frankie knew that O'Connor was right. 'O.K., you do it your way,' he said.

'I'm going over with my clothes on,' Sandy said.

'Do as you like,' O'Connor said, 'but I'm going first.'

O'Connor took off his flying-jacket and then began to undress. He took the braces off his trousers and then rolled his trousers, shirt, underpants and sweater into his flying-jacket, making a bulky bundle which he finally tied with his braces. 'You see, you got your boots, too. You can't swim in your boots. The best way is to swim on your back. Swim with your legs and keep your clothes above water.'

The edge of the stream was firm and sandy, where the river had risen and receded and river-sand had dried white in the sun.

It was almost dark now, but there was a faint light on the sand and a reflection of fainter light on the water. O'Connor, naked and carrying the bundle of clothes, went into the water up to his knees, then crouched and then rolled over. The splash of his going under was muffled like the splash of a water rat. The water was broken for a moment, then smoothed and then broken again as O'Connor turned on his back and began to swim. The three sergeants and Franklin watched him swim across, his upraised arms pale against the black water, his legs always more under the water than out of it, his movements making hardly a sound. He went across slowly and easily, always in sight, and finally they saw him standing on the far bank, just visible in the darkness, and heard his call.

'Piece of cake,' he said. 'O.K.'

'The three of you go,' Franklin said. 'Keep your boots and socks dry if nothing else. And shout like hell if you can't make it.'

Noisier than O'Connor, splashing heavily by the bank, so that Franklin felt momentarily nervous, the three sergeants swam the river. Alone on the bank, watching them, Franklin took off his boots. It was awkward with one arm; he felt lop-sided. And now, for the first time that night, his arm was painful again. He could feel the cut made by the tourniquet as if it were a second wound. He tried to buckle the flying-boots together, but with one hand it was no use, and he felt a fool and realized how helpless he was. As he crouched on the bank waiting for O'Connor, he caught the odour of water-mint, strong and astringent, crushed by somebody's feet on the river edge. Then he heard O'Connor's flop into the water on the far side and saw the white break of his arms in the black water as they made the natural strokes. He slipped down his trousers and undid his shirt. He tried to pull the shirt over his head, but the blood had come through the bandage, sticking one to the other. He decided to wait for O'Connor. And while he waited, watching O'Connor coming across the stream, he felt the oddity of the moment less than any potential peril. He felt comic and lonely and awkward standing there in his shirt.

O'Connor, breathing hard, came out of the river, wiping his face and hair with his hands.

'O.K.?' Franklin said.

'Lovely. I feel a man and a half. Fit?'

'Not quite. My shirt's sticking to the bandage. I can't get it over my head.'

'Hold hard,' O'Connor said. 'Can you straighten your arm?'

He tried to straighten his arm; the elbow joint seemed locked and would not move. The skin of all his arm seemed tight, as if, when he bent it, the wound must split again. A wave of cold weakness, more than pain, came up from his feet and washed over his whole body.

'I'm not surprised you can't bend it,' O'Connor said. 'Hold on.'

He began to rip the shirt up from the cuff. He peeled it off from the dried blood of the bandage and it came away crackling and dry like paper ripped from a wall. When finally it was free, O'Connor pulled the shirt over Franklin's head.

Franklin heard a sound. 'What's that?'

'It's Sandy. He's coming to fetch the boots. In five minutes we'll be clear.'

'I think it's best like this, don't you?' he said. 'Better than trying a bridge.'

'Better? I'm just in my bloody element,' O'Connor said.

They waited for Sandy to come over, and while they waited O'Connor tied Franklin's things into a bundle, and then buckled the boots, two pairs, together. Sandy had swum across without his flying-jacket. He stood on the bank, jumping up and down, blowing water, and wiping his hair. As they stood there, the three of them, waiting for the moment to go, Franklin felt keenly, more even than at any moment when flying, their interdependence, profound and clear and inexpressibly tense, and the trust he had in them.

The moment was broken by O'Connor's voice. 'Sit in the bloody water,' he said.

'Sit in it?'

'Squat down. Haven't you ever been baptized?'

'I'm C. of E.,' he said.

'You are? Well, now you're going to see how the Baptists do it.'

He went down into the water, gripping the sloping sand with

33

his feet. It was cold and the shock surged up into his throat. He crouched down, holding the bundle of his clothes against his chest, high under his chin. 'Don't do a damn thing,' O'Connor said, 'except just lie still.' A moment later he felt O'Connor pull him backwards into the water. He had for one second a spasm of panic, but he held all of himself tight against it, holding his breath, and then he felt O'Connor's hand under his chin. A moment later he felt the motion of O'Connor swimming, and held his wounded arm up in the air and the clothes tight against his chest with the other arm, and he felt the water going past him, smooth and cold and easy. He came to accept this motion, and the sure buoyancy of his own body, so much that he became aware, in the last minute of crossing, of something else. The great glow of moonlight was spreading fast in the east, the moon still invisible but the light expanding, pale orange, all over the sky above the river. And in the last moments of going across the river he saw the moon bursting like ripe orange fruit beyond the black straight clumps of distant poplars far upstream. It rode smoothly up into view at the moment he himself sailed smoothly into the bank, drawn right up into the sharp dry sand like a boat by O'Connor's arms.

'Get your arm wet?' O'Connor said.

'No, I'm O.K., I think. Thanks,' he said. He remembered suddenly the rations, the maps, the first-aid kit. He asked if anyone brought them.

'Sandy brought them the first time,' Taylor said.

'Is Sandy O.K.?'

'Just coming into port,' Godwin said.

'All right' he said. 'Goddy, get the rum and get a tot for everybody.'

Sandy came up the bank, blowing water again. The moon was coming up fast, the red quarter deepening beyond the far black trees, the glow spreading across the sky and gradually down now, liquid and pure, on the smooth dark water. The three flying-jackets and the white figures of himself and O'Connor began to seem very conspicuous as they stood there, and he felt now that it was dangerous to be waiting.

'We've got to get on,' he said.

'I'll rub you down,' O'Connor said. 'How's your arm?'

34

'Rub O'Connor down,' he said to Taylor. 'The arm's as right as rain.'

'At home you'd be in hospital,' O'Connor said.

'Don't talk cock,' he said.

Five minutes later they began to move away, the three sergeants ahead as before. In the water and before dressing, Franklin had felt cold. Now, after the rum and with his body dry again, he felt warm and light and buoyant, as if he could walk for miles. His arm did not pain him much except for the dull ache of the stiffness, and it was always warm against the inner wool of his flying-jacket.

He did not remember much else about that night except their walking on, in what he knew, by the rising moon, was a roughly westward direction. He remembered the moon always very white in the clear summer night sky, and the same crops repeating themselves, roots and corn and potatoes and sometimes a slope of vines, over the successive folds of the bright land. He remembered a small road and how they crossed it into the same repeated pattern of fields, and how he was alternately glad and uneasy about the moon, so clear that he could see the colour of a few late potato flowers in one field as they passed and the brown of the three flying-jackets always half a field away.

They came at last to a place, a slight hill, where the three sergeants had stopped and waited for them. The sergeants were out of the moonlight, near a group of beeches.

'Look down there,' Sandy said.

'Jesus,' he said.

Looking down into the valley, where divisions of many fields were stencilled dark against the flat whiteness of moon-white land, he saw the river, broader now and bright as chromium between the dark banks of reeds, curving in a deep arc below the hill.

'See the house?' Sandy said.

'Yes.' He could see a house, tall and squarish, dustily white in the moonlight on the curve of the river, down below his right hand. Nearer, up the slope, he could see a little orchard and then a strip of vines, about ten rows deep, across the middle of the hill. 'It's a mill,' he said.

'What do we do?' Sandy said.

35

'Another swim,' O'Connor said.

'No,' he said. 'We'll get down in the vines for the night. We'll get cover there, and some more grapes, and a rest, and then in the morning I'll go down.'

'To the house?' Godwin said.

'We've got to get help,' he said.

They walked down the slope, keeping close together, until they came to the vines. They broke off a few clusters of grapes and sat in the shadows of the terraces, eating them. They lay among the vines for the rest of the night. The moon went down across the broad flat land below them, and in the early morning the coldness came up from the river, settling on the slope with dew.

It must have been about six o'clock when Franklin looked down and saw a black flutter of hens on the grass about the fruit trees, and then the white apron of a girl as she followed them. She was about three hundred yards away, below the vines, but he could see quite clearly the black of her hair above the white apron, and the wide motion of her brown arm, as she threw, from a brown bowl, the food to the hens. He could hear her voice, too, as she called them, spasmodically, repeating the call in the high, clipped, imperative French way. Then he saw the hens feeding, their red-black heads hammering the grass, and then the girl walking a few steps up the slope, her head up towards the sun, as if she had just got up and were breathing in the day.

'I'm going down,' he said. 'If I don't come back you know what to do.'

He went boldly out of the vines without another word, and down the sharp dry path that went through the fruit trees to where the girl stood. The blood was pumping heavily into his chest with the excitement of the moment. He walked fast, thinking, 'This is it. One way or the other, this is it.' His arm was aching and his mouth was very dry, and he thought, 'Give me a dozen Bremen trips before this. Anything before this. Christ, if only she doesn't run.'

She did not run. She went on idly standing among the hens, her head up, as she still looked at the rising day.

And then suddenly she saw him coming down.

CHAPTER 4

SHE did not move. She held the smooth brown wooden bowl with both hands, tight against her body, just under her breast, crinkling the pinafore into shadow. She was very dark, and her eyes, big and bright and black, did not move either. She held them level against the sun.

'I'm English,' he said.

Once again it was all he could remember to say. Once again it seemed very foolish and pantomimic: not at all what he had wanted to say. She did not speak, and he was struck in an extraordinary way by her silence and her motionlessness. There was nothing passive about them. They were strong and definite and he knew that she was not afraid.

'Can you help, please?' he said. 'Please.'

'Only you?' she said.

'No,' he said. 'No. There are five of us.'

'Where?'

'In the vines.' He waved his hand towards the hill.

'I wondered why the dog cried in the night,' she said.

She said it quite calmly, as if she had always expected it. She did not even look up the hill. She clasped the bowl tight to her chest and kept her eyes levelly fixed at him.

'You had better call them down,' she said.

'It is all right?' he said.

'Yes,' she said. 'It is all right.'

He knew the four sergeants were watching from the vines. He turned and waved his hand, not shouting, and in a second or two he saw the four flying-jackets on the path coming down from the terraces.

'Is this Occupied territory?' he said to the girl.

'It is Occupied,' she said. 'Are you glad?'

'I'm very glad.'

'Have you heard about us?'

'A lot.'

37

'Then I'm glad, too,' she said.

'And where is this?' he said.

'This? It is in Occupied France.'

'Yes, but what place?'

'Your friends are coming,' she said.

The four sergeants came down past the fruit trees to where Franklin and the girl were standing. 'Bonjour,' O'Connor said. The girl smiled. O'Connor grinned and Franklin saw the four of them as a stranger might see them, tired-eyed and unshaven and embarrassed, and he said, 'It's all right. It's O.K.'

'You had better come in,' the girl said.

Franklin began to walk ahead with her down the slope, towards the mill. The path widened and became a stone-slabbed cartway that went between the big stone mill on the right-hand side and the house, also of stone, but smaller, on the left. He could just see the cartway going on towards the river and opening out still further there into a stone jetty. The river was calm and low beyond. He could hear the water rushing down with an ascending and powerful sound in the sluice somewhere on the other side of the mill and he could smell the old smell of water and the smell of sun-dried water-weed on stone, strong as seaweed in the sun, and then the summery smell of corn-dust, dry in the cool air of the still morning. As the girl went a few paces ahead of him over the threshold of the kitchen he saw her legs bare and brown in the sun. They were slim and strong and the brownness was smooth and a little deeper than the natural sallow of the skin of someone very dark, and her neck had the same beautiful brownness below the short black hair.

The five of them followed her into the kitchen. It was very big. Copper utensils shone on the whitewashed wall above the fire, and he smelt the old but not stale odour of cooking, and saw, at a long central wooden table, an old woman in black cutting a stick of bread.

'My God, my God,' she said. She stood up.

'Where is father?' the girl said.

'My God. English? Upstairs.'

'Fetch him down.'

As the old woman went out of the room, excitedly, the girl turned to Franklin, calm as before.

'You'd better take off your flying-jackets,' she said, 'and give them to me.'

'I want to show you my papers,' he said.

'Yes.'

'She wants your jackets,' he said.

He took out his wallet from his hip pocket with his good arm and flapped it open. His pass was inside, but with only one arm to use it was hard to get it out. The girl stood watching him, looking at the bandaged arm. He was very afraid she would try to help him, but she did not move, and suddenly he realized that she was not helping because she knew, quite calmly and quite surely, that he felt like that. Finally he laid the wallet on the table and held it down with his thumb while he pulled out the pass with two fingers. She was calm and serious as he gave her the pass to see.

'What were you flying?' she said.

'A Wellington. We had been to Italy.'

'Did you jump?'

'No,' he said. 'I brought the aircraft down.'

'What kind of country was it?'

He told her about the marsh and the forest and then the river, and how the five of them had walked for some part of a day.

'Where are we now?' he said.

'This is the same river you crossed,' she said.

He knew suddenly that she was not going to tell him where they were and that perhaps she never would tell him, and he knew now that it was the right thing.

'Are you the captain?' she said. 'Or is it just that you speak French?'

'I'm the captain,' he said.

'What about your arm?' She spoke of it for the first time.

'I hurt it when we crashed.'

'You lost a lot of blood?' she said.

'A little,' he said.

'It will have to be properly dressed,' she said.

The four sergeants had taken off their flying-jackets and laid them on the long wooden table. Franklin had begun to undo his own when the father came into the room. He was followed by the old woman, who gathered up the flying-jackets in her

39

arms and went out again. Then the father came over and stood by the girl, and Franklin said 'Good morning'. The man was tall and thin. with dark hair, and the same sallow skin as the girl, and with deep fissures, like cuts, below his high brown cheek-bones. He held out his hand and Franklin took it and shook hands.

'I do not know how long it will be possible to stay,' he said.

'It will help if we can rest,' Franklin said.

'You aim to get to Spain?'

'If possible.'

'The situation is not easy,' the man said. 'There have been rumours about labour orders. All sorts of rumours. Farther north they have taken hostages. The situation is increasingly bad. Everywhere.'

'I don't want you to take risks for us,' Franklin said.

'In France everything is a risk now,' the man said. 'That is the way of it. It is what we have come to.'

'I'm sorry. We know,' Franklin said.

'You will want to eat,' the man said. 'Perhaps you will go upstairs first. Have you the necessary things to shave with?'

'My friend here has a razor,' he said, pointing to O'Connor. 'He is always the man of emergency.'

'Then please go up. My daughter will take you.'

'Thank you,' Franklin said. 'Thank you, indeed. Very much.'

The girl went out of the room the way the old woman had gone, and Franklin and the four sergeants followed her. She took them through the house and then up wooden, carpetless stairs to a first landing, and then up a second flight of narrower stairs to a room at the top. The room had a single window that looked down-river, across the valley. There was a single bed, with a bare straw mattress, and a china ewer and basin on a washstand in one corner, and a mirror on the wall.

The sergeants stood awkwardly in the room, tired and nervous with the strain of what had happened. Franklin stood back from the window and looked down at the mill and the yard below.

'There's a man down there,' he said.

'Only Pierre,' she said.

'Your brother?'

40

'No. He would be helping my father in the mill if the mill were working.'

'Will he know about us?'

'He will know, and it will be all right.'

He did not say any more. The strain of things, of walking without food and sleep, of his wound and the loss of blood, of the final moments of wondering if the girl could be trusted, and now of relief, came rushing up through his body in a spasm of cold weakness, faint and stupid. He checked it and held it down. And in that moment he looked at the girl, alert and dark and supremely assured, in the doorway. Her black eyes had not flickered for a moment since he had first surprised her among the hens. But now there was a faint smile on her face, her lips not quite parted, and she looked like the calmest, surest person he had ever known.

CHAPTER 5

O'CONNOR was old in the game and carried a razor, shaving cream, toothbrush, soap, nail-scissors, and a revolver and twenty rounds. Using the razor in turn, the four sergeants and Franklin washed and shaved in the bedroom, taking about an hour. When they had finished Franklin went alone downstairs. He found the girl and the old woman waiting for him on the first landing.

'We have finished,' he said.

'Now,' the girl said, 'there are only four of us. This is my grandmother. My father's mother.'

'Madame,' he said. He bowed slightly. The old lady, who looked more than seventy, had a big silver crucifix on her chest. She looked eternal and old and scared, and did not say anything.

'Then there's Pierre and my father and myself.'

'Yes,' he said.

'That's all. Just the four of us,' she said. 'There is a bridge about two miles down the river, and if anybody else comes it will be that way. But if anybody comes it probably will not be any good. Somebody may come. If you see a man like my father, taller, rather like him, it will be my uncle. He may come.'

'Yes.'

'We are going to put you in the mill. You will have to be there all the time and not come out. My father and Pierre are getting it ready now. You can only come out at night, and then only one at a time.'

'Yes.'

'It is all right for you to come down now to eat.'

'Thank you.'

'Do you like eels?'

'I never ate them.'

'You will have to begin. It will probably be all eels until we can arrange otherwise. I am sorry about it, but they will be very good.'

42

'We could eat anything,' he said.

'There will be eggs anyway this morning,' she said.

He went upstairs and called the sergeants, and together they went down into the kitchen. The old woman had begun to boil the eggs over the fire, and there were plates of sliced bread on the table, small squares of butter, and round sections of fresh soft white cheese. There was a bowl of apples, and the girl, putting glasses on the table, asked what they would drink.

'There is no coffee,' she said. 'There is milk. Or there is wine. Perhaps it is a little early for wine.'

'I think milk,' he said. 'Perhaps some wine later. If we may?'

'There is always milk and wine,' she said. 'We are lucky.'

'We are very grateful,' he said.

Through the open door, as he ate the breakfast of boiled eggs and cheese and bread and apples and drank the cold thick milk, he could look up the slope, beyond the fruit trees and the vines, to the crest of the hill over which he and the four sergeants had come. The sun was strong and white and slanted full on the vines. He could see how the heat of the day would gather on the hillside with the turning sun, full on the swelling grapes green on the low trained vines. As he looked at it, he felt that the world of the crashed Wellington, the trip above the Alps, his fatigue, the walking in the moonlight, and the swimming of the river were part of a confused and remote reality. Still farther beyond, real with the same sense of isolation, the world of the Mess, the Wellingtons lined up on the black perimeter and on the brown-green grass of the drome, all the functional reality of camouflaged station buildings and the lonely reality of the broad runway spreading away, empty and flat, before the nose of the plane, and then the final and absolute reality of operational darkness broken only by the red stars of light on the station; all of that part of his life now seemed to be pressed farther and farther away, beyond the curtain of a dream.

He must have dreamed a few seconds longer than he realized, and the voice of the girl startled him. She, too, had been watching the door.

'I think it would be better now if you got into a safer place.'

'Yes,' he said. 'We want to do whatever you think best.'

43

She went out of the kitchen and stood outside, on the white stones of the yard, in the sun, looking up and down. As she stood there he told the four sergeants what she had said. One by one they got up from the table. The old woman stood away from the table, the smile of pleasure, touched with fear, fixed on her face, her eyes bright and uneasy, her arms folded below her breast. O'Connor, getting up from the table last, looked at her and grinned and said :

'Merci beaucoup, madame, merci beaucoup.'

He grinned at Franklin, too.

'My French is quite good!'

'Monsieur is very welcome,' the old woman said.

'What's she say?'

'She says you are very welcome,' Franklin said.

'Bon!' O'Connor said. 'Bon! Merci!'

The old woman smiled again, and as she smiled O'Connor remembered something. He put his hand in the pocket of his flying-jacket and took out a slab of chocolate. He walked to the end of the table where the old lady stood, and he held the chocolate out to her. 'Perhaps you don't get much chocolate, madame,' he said. She did not move. She stood with eyes steadfastly fixed on O'Connor. 'Go on,' he said. 'Please, madame. I don't want it. I got plenty. Go on.' She still did not move, and suddenly he pushed the chocolate forward and into her hands. She did not move even then. She held the chocolate loose in her bone-white hands, against her dress. Then suddenly she did move. She let her head fall suddenly down, her chin on her breast, crying bitterly as she tightened her hands.

'Oh, blimey!' O'Connor said. 'Did I do wrong?'

'You did all right,' Franklin said.

'Oh! I'm sorry,' O'Connor said. 'Madame, I'm sorry.'

'No need to be sorry,' Franklin said.

'Did I say something she didn't like?'

'No, I think she likes it,' Franklin said.

As they were speaking the girl came in from the yard. The old woman had moved at last and had begun to pack up the plates on the table. Her tears were wet on her face, and the girl saw them and Franklin explained. O'Connor looked very embarrassed and the girl smiled. 'We had better go now,' she said.

She walked out into the sunshine again, the two youngest sergeants, then Sandy, then Franklin following her. As O'Connor followed Franklin he turned and looked back at the old woman, still packing the dishes with one hand and holding the chocolate with the other, the tears still wet on her face. 'Au revoir. madame,' he said, pronouncing it in the English way.

'Au revoir, m'sieu,' she said, and smiled.

The four sergeants and Franklin followed the girl across the yard and into the mill on the opposite side. At the foot of the wooden stairs inside Franklin waited for the four sergeants to go up. As he followed them he could smell he dry, ageless odour of the dust of corn and then, deep behind it, dead cold and slightly fusty, the smell of water. The flying-boots of the men were muffled on the planks of the stairs and the upstairs floor. At the head of the first stairs was a wide wooden floor, bare except for a flat pile of empty corn-sacks in one corner. The girl led them across it and then up a shorter flight of stairs into a smaller room beyond. She stood in the centre of the room and waited until Franklin had climbed the stairs and shut the door.

'If you stay here it will be all right,' she said. 'But as long as you have your flying clothes you must stay here.'

'Yes,' Franklin said. 'And if anything happens?'

'If anything happens,' she said, 'you can go down here.'

The room was about fifteen feet square, with a second door opposite the first. The girl unbolted the door and showed Franklin another flight of steps going down inside.

'You can go down to the bottom and then down below the wheel-shaft. There may be some water. but there is room for all of you.'

'Is anything likely to happen?' he said.

'One can't tell.'

'But you would know? Probably?'

'Very probably. But it is important you don't go out. In daylight at least. And in the dark only singly.'

She stood alert and assured and upright among the five men, not nervous, as if she had thought it all out and the pre-conception of it all had long since become real and fixed in her mind. Franklin looked at the wide clear forehead under the black hair, and the smooth sun-sallow skin of her face and arms and neck, and wondered how old she was.

'We shall try to bring your food up here,' she said. 'And we will try to get you better clothes. You will need other clothes when you leave.'

She had spoken all the time to Franklin, but as if in a general way, not looking straight at him. Now she looked clearly at him.

'What about your arm?' she said. 'How bad is it?'

'I don't know.'

'Has it been dressed?'

'It was dressed when it happened. But not since. I haven't seen it yet.'

'I think at least we should look at it here,' she said.

'Yes,' he said. He knew that it was no use being silly about the arm. Sometimes when the pain came on it felt as if a lump of lead on a taut slow wire were being pulled slowly down the main artery of his arm, making it ache from the socket to the ball of his thumb. Occasionally when he stood still after sudden movement the lump of lead seemed to be jerked heavily into his forehead, to knock there with a sort of sullen sickness between his eyes. He knew that the arm might, if it got worse, complicate the whole business of escape for them all.

'Perhaps it would be better if we looked at it at once,' she said.

'It is very kind,' he said.

'Do the others understand?' she said. 'About remaining here?'

'I will make it clear,' he said. He told the four sergeants what the girl had said. 'You know what to do if anything happens,' he said. 'O'Connor is in charge.'

'O.K.,' O'Connor said.

The girl waited. 'They are quite clear?' she said.

'Quite clear,' he said.

She went out of the room at once, and Franklin followed her down through the floors and stairs of the mill and across the yard, through the space of sun that was now like a hot bar between the two walls of shade. She went straight through the kitchen, calling to the old woman as she went, and then into

46

the living-room beyond. There was a heavy mahogany round table in the centre of the room, with a brass lamp on it. She took the lamp off and set it in one of the chairs. Then she began to take off Franklin's flying-jacket, slipping the good arm out of the sleeve and pulling the jacket slowly over his head. Immediately he felt the sudden pain swing up from his arm into his forehead, beating at his eyes. She seemed at once to know how he felt and said, 'You had better sit down,' and as he sat down, resting his injured arm on the smooth cold mahogany, the old woman came in with a big basin of hot water and a towel over her arm. She put the basin on the table and then locked the door.

'Now,' the girl said.

She unknotted the bandage and began to unroll it. Blood had soaked through the bandage in a huge brown patch, darker as the successive folds of bandage came off, until it was almost black in the centre. He felt the bandage sticking and heard the slight crackle of it as the dried blood gave way. As he looked at his arm he saw how the bandage had bitten into the flesh, and how the rim had slightly swollen beyond the taut brown fringe. Then he knew what was coming: the folds of bandage that no longer pulled at each other, but pulled, deep and raw and harsh, at the live tissue of the wound below. He sat waiting for it. He saw the girl pick up the towel and soak it in hot water and begin to bathe the bandage free. He felt her pull the fold of bandage away, tautly and tenderly. The pain did not increase much, but he felt the bandage pulling against the flesh, as if it would pull the lips of the wound open. Then as he looked down at his arm he saw the blood clotted in a black lump in the centre of the bandage, and then, beyond the fringes of the bandage, the extreme fine edges of the wound. It looked about six inches long.

'Did you lose much blood?' the girl said.

'I think quite a lot.'

'I'm afraid if I take the bandage off it will bleed again and I won't be able to stop it.'

'It will probably be all right with a fresh bandage over the old.'

'It could never be,' she said. 'A wound that size needs stitching.'

47

'It will be all right,' he said.

The girl did not answer. He knew that it was not all right; that what he said did not mean anything. He knew that the arm was bad and that it would be better not to be foolish about it. He thought again of the sergeants and how it must complicate the business of escaping.

'It must be stitched,' the girl said.

'That's a problem,' he said.

'It would not be possible for a doctor to come up here,' she said.

'Then what?'

'We must take you to a doctor.'

She said it quite fearlessly, and he knew at once how dangerous it might be.

'That means great risk for you,' he said.

'The whole thing is a risk,' she said simply.

'That's what I'm afraid of,' he said.

She looked at him with shining black eyes in which there was a sort of startled determination but no sort of fear at all, and there was nothing he could say.

'It's quite simple,' she said. 'The arm needs a doctor, and there is a doctor in the town. So we must go down into the town. There's nothing very difficult about that.'

He did not speak.

'If the arm gets very bad, you know what it will mean,' she said.

'Yes?'

'It will mean hospital. It will mean you will have to give yourself up. The situation will be unpleasant for everybody.'

'Then we had better go into the town.'

'It is the obvious thing,' she said.

The old woman had brought in a jam-jar of ointment. It looked like yellow lard. Now the girl took a lump of it in her fingers and spread it thickly along the line of the wound, slightly over the edge of the bandage. Then she took a towel and damped it and, from above and below the wound, washed away the blood that had run down the arm. Then she dried the arm with another corner of the towel and began to wind the bandage over the wound again, pressing down the ointment. As the pressure squeezed it out, she smeared it back over the new fold of bandage with her fingers.

'You need some sleep,' she said.

'Yes. But don't we go into the town to-day?'

'Not to-day. I hope to-morrow. We have to arrange it.'

'It will be very difficult?'

'I don't think so. Once we have got the chicken it will not be difficult.'

'The chicken?'

She smiled. 'With a chicken you can do most things,' she said. 'With two chickens you can do anything.'

The smile remained on her face, luminous and beautifully clear and fearless, while she finished the bandaging of his arm. When it was done the old woman took away the bowl and the towel and the ointment, and for a few moments Franklin and the girl were alone in the room. She picked up his flying-jacket and put it over his shoulders, leaving the sleeves loose. Then she looked at him with fearlessly clear, calm, dark eyes and said, quite simply, 'There is no need for you to be afraid.'

'Afraid?' he said. 'Good God!'

'Yes,' she said. 'You have been afraid all morning. But there is no need to be.'

'Afraid? Why should I be?'

'You have been afraid of someone coming. You have been afraid for the others. You have been afraid of us. And just now you said you were afraid for us.'

For a moment he did not answer. What she said was true. He had had the jitters all morning; he was afraid of all the things she said. Not consciously afraid, but with a slight wateriness of the stomach. He looked at her and saw once again how clear and untroubled her face was. Its clarity was almost a state of excitement. She looked like someone who had waited for something for a long time; almost like someone who had prayed for something a long time. It seemed almost like the fulfilment of some dangerous devotion.

'You are naturally worried because you are tired,' she said.

'It is natural I should be worried,' he said. 'It is my responsibility.'

'You know what *grand'mère* says? Go to sleep and trust in God. Isn't that very sensible?'

'It is very sensible,' he said.

'Then you go now and get some sleep,' she said.

'All right,' he said. 'Thank you for doing my arm.'

She smiled and did not say anything. He stood at the door.

'What is your name?' he said.

'Françoise.' She waited a moment. 'What is yours?'

'My name is John,' he said. 'They call me Frankie.'

'To make it difficult?'

'No,' he said. 'My name is John Franklin. My mother calls me John. But everyone else calls me Frankie. It is a diminutive. Do you understand?'

'No,' she said.

'It is a diminutive of my father's name.'

'What was your father's name?'

'He was called Henry. But it has nothing to do with it.'

'You said it had.' She looked bewildered and did not understand. And in that moment, as she stood there, slightly puzzled, her lips slightly parted, he had the first full picture of her: young and fearless in her devotion to the dangerous moment, now troubled by the simple contradiction of his name. As he looked at her, she still trying to work out the small stupid problem of what he was called, he felt her wonderful coolness break down and the warmth of her simplicity take its place. And he knew in that moment that if he had been afraid of anything he had been afraid of her. He had been afraid simply of that immense assurance, frightening because it was so clear and unequivocal and young. And now as he saw her troubled by the confusion of his name he was no longer afraid or even perturbed for her. For the first time he felt nearer to her, and could talk to her like an ordinary girl. 'It would be simpler if you called me John,' he said.

'John is better,' she said. She pronounced it in the French way.

'Good,' he said. 'I am going to sleep now.'

'You can sleep all day,' she said. 'I will see you across the yard.'

She stood at the door of the kitchen and looked out, her dark

50

head leaning forward and turning in the sun. She called that it was all right and as she spoke the hens came running down from the orchard at the sound of her voice. He crossed the yard as they came running down, and then as he went out of the hot sun into the cold shade of the mill, into the dusty petrified air, he heard her voice turning them back, voluble and high and clear, in the French way: a repetition of the first moment he had seen her in the morning sun.

Up in the room on the second floor the four sergeants were already lying down, eyes closed, on beds made up of sacks and straw, their flying-jackets rolled up as pillows. They had made him a bed in one corner.

O'Connor opened his eyes. 'Arm O.K.'

'Pretty well,' he said.

He folded his flying-jacket as best he could with one hand, and then put it on the straw and lay down. He lay for a moment with eyes open, looking at the sky very blue beyond the small window in the wall. Then he closed them, and felt the blood and the darkness and the bright light beating together in his mind.

CHAPTER 6

FRANKLIN, the girl, and Pierre drove into the town on the following morning, starting about nine o'clock.

The girl sat holding two chickens, tied in brown paper, on the broad seat in the front of the low cart. Pierre was driving the cart and Franklin, wearing black trousers with a faint pin-stripe and a black jacket and striped blue shirt, sat between Pierre and the girl. The jacket was buttoned up so that his injured arm, tucked into the shirt, was not visible. The land, flat and white in the hot sun with many clear patches of corn-stubble beyond the river, began to rise after the first few miles into a country of more vineyards. All along the roadside the grasses and the leaves of beet and potatoes, and then, on the higher land, the leaves of the vines, were white with the dust of summer.

'How far is the town?' Franklin said.

'It's about six kilometres,' the girl said.

'What town is it?'

'It is a market town. There is a market to-day.'

He knew that she did not want to tell him the name of the town, and he decided not to ask again. He decided that even if he saw it or heard it mentioned he would never convey to her that he knew it. He would use it solely as a means of orientating their position on the map. He did not know at all what plans she had for their escape but he had decided that, whatever they were, he would work out alternative plans of his own. He knew that these plans depended on his fixing their position on the map, and he knew, too, that these plans, and perhaps still more her own, depended entirely on his arm.

It struck him as they drove along that he had already got fully into the habit, begun the day before, of regarding the girl as completely in charge of things. It struck him as curious that, from the first, he had put all his faith in her. He had scarcely thought of Pierre, the old woman, or the father, and now he suddenly remembered that he had not seen the father since the previous day. 'I haven't seen your father to-day,' he said. 'Has he gone away?'

'For a short time.'

'Is your grandmother alone at the mill?'

'For a few hours, yes.'

'Supposing something happens?'

'Well, it will happen.'

'And if somebody comes?'

'She has lived in three wars,' the girl said. 'She knows better than I what to do.'

'You have great trust in her.'

'No,' the girl said. 'I have great trust in God.'

They drove on for a long time after that without speaking; he felt once again that he could not argue beyond the simple finality of her words. The road was very straight now, with double lines of tall poplars that threw diagonal brushes of shade across the white stubble and the dust-whitened patches of roots and potatoes. In some parts of the road, dust had gathered as thick as white sand on the edge of a river and lay deep and unblown because there was little traffic to blow it away. A few bicycles came along the road and a few peasants walking, but there were no cars. Once he heard the high sustained hooting of a horn, and two army trucks came fast from behind them, not slowing down to pass the cart, blowing great clouds of dust and raising a wind that went rattling down the avenue of big flat poplar trees. They were two-ton trucks of the German army. The second truck was fitted with breakdown gear, and he saw two German troopers lying asleep on the floor of the lorry by the crane.

They were the first Germans he had seen; he felt it was time to talk again.

'What is the procedure in the town?' he said. 'Shall we be stopped?'

'There is no procedure,' the girl said. 'Some days they stop you, and some days they don't stop you. That's all.'

'What do we do?'

'We drive straight in.'

'It seems very obvious.'

53

'It is better to do the obvious thing. Better than trying to be clever.'

Now the avenue of poplars had ended and beyond them he could see groups of red and white houses. In a few moments the road turned and began to go uphill. On each side of the hill ran the beginnings of a sidewalk, seedy and dusty and unrepaired.

As the road went uphill into the town the sand of the sidewalk gave way to stones, roughly embedded like cobbles, and then the stones to slabs of broken paving, split and uplifted by the roots of the street trees. Little red and white houses at the foot of the hill gave way in time to larger villas standing back from the road; seedy and unpainted and shuttered against the sun. In the gardens in front of them stood occasional groups of yuccas, the stalks of the flowers creamy-brown and dead, the sword-flat leaves grey with dust blown in from the rainless road. Sometimes the larger houses were enclosed by high walls of stone smeared over with plaster. Beyond the walls were strips of trees and you could see sometimes the white scrapings of bootmarks on the wall-plaster where someone had climbed the wall to break the branches of a fig tree. Between the high walls, on the hillside, the heat of the sun was caught and held, dusty and flat and arid as the air of decay.

Pierre drove the cart on into the centre of the town, the horse always walking, the villas giving way gradually to shops, the dusty broken sidewalk to a pavement without trees. There were cafés now among the shops and all the awnings were down against the sun. Most of the tables were empty, and outside one café Franklin saw a waiter sprinkling the pavement beyond the empty tables with a carafe of water. He could see how he held his thumb in the mouth of the carafe and then released it in jerks, swinging the carafe so that the water made a sprinkled arc in the sun. Then the shops and the cafés became larger, and there were more people, both on foot and in carts and on bicycles. Franklin saw an occasional queue of women outside a shop, and in the windows of the pâtisserie shops trays of bread. The bread was underbaked and grey, and there were no pâtisseries. Then he began to look for Germans, and discovered as he did so that he was holding himself very tense. He was

54

pressing his feet hard against the floor of the cart, tightening the muscles of his legs. Then suddenly he saw his first Germans. They were two troopers, and they were coming along the pavement towards the cart. They were men of thirty-five or so, and the elder of them had grey hair. Suddenly they stopped on the edge of the pavement, looking up and down the street. Franklin looked straight ahead, seeing nothing but the blur of people and traffic in the sun, the moving head of the horse and the two troopers waiting. This is the bloodiest business I was ever in, he thought. He saw the Germans out of the corner of his eye and thought in that moment of all that he had ever heard of people escaping through France; how they went at night and avoided towns and kept away from trouble, in secret, walking, hiding, and not being seen. And here he was in broad daylight, with a wounded arm stuck up for anyone to see. And in that moment too, as the cart came abreast of the troopers, he remembered the girl. Even if she isn't scared, he thought, I am. This is worse than the bloodiest trip I ever did. He half looked at her. She was looking straight ahead, not tensely or proudly, but simply and negatively, and she was holding the chickens lightly and indifferently but firmly in her hands. And suddenly as he looked at her it seemed that her hands, brown and firm and unexcited, had all the assurance in the world.

When he looked up from her hands again the cart had passed the troopers and it was all over. He felt the pressure of his feet relax, becoming fully aware of how great it had been. The cart was coming now to a central square, with fruit-stalls along three of the four sides and country carts parked in three or four rows by a fountain in the centre. The fountain was not playing, but on the stone steps, on the shady side, a few old men sat with their heads leaned back, half asleep against the cool stone. On the fruit-stalls there were heaps of small greenred peaches and small green grapes and yellow summer pears. On the fourth side of the square, where there were no stalls, there was a big church. The front was wide and ornate, with two spires, and there were wide steps leading up to a single central door.

Pierre drove the cart into the centre of the square and during the last few yards of the journey, as the wheels bumped over the heavy flags, the girl began to talk to Franklin, telling him what to do.

'You see the church,' she said. 'To the right of the church is the rue St Honoré. It is the first street on the right. You see?' she said. 'The street where the two men on bicycles are just going in?'

'I see it,' he said.

'Go down the rue St Honoré and take the first turning on the right. It is a little street and it is called rue Richer. Is it clear?'

'It is quite clear,' he said.

'Go to Number 9,' she said. 'Ring the bell twice and say I have brought the chickens.'

'Is that all?'

'That is all. My father has arranged it. The doctor and he are friends.'

'Is that where your father has been?'

'Partly. Partly he has been arranging other things.'

'For us?'

'Yes, I hope so. We shall know what he has done when we get back home.'

'I am very grateful,' he said. He tried to put into his voice a feeling deeper than gratitude. His French seemed stiff and formal. 'I am most truly grateful,' he said. 'I understand and I am truly grateful.'

She was smiling a little as he spoke. She laid the chickens on his knees as she smiled, and the cart came to a halt in the middle of the square.

'Where will you be?' he said.

'I shall be in the church,' she said.

'However long I am?'

'However long you are.'

'Shall I come back to you there?'

'Yes, you had better come back there,' she said. 'If you don't come back there I shall know that something has happened.'

'And Pierre?'

'Pierre will wait somewhere here.'

'By the fountain,' Pierre said.

Franklin got down from the cart and held the chickens under

56

his good arm. He had brown canvas shoes on, and as his feet touched the ground, light and soft, he felt unexpectedly sure and free.

'Don't hurry,' the girl said. 'Walk as if it did not matter.'

In another moment he was walking away across the market square. He did not look back. He walked quite slowly, his feet light and soundless in the canvas shoes. He came in about fifteen seconds to the rue St Honoré: he saw the blue and white nameplate on the corner of the street as he turned in. It was a long street, fairly narrow and quite straight, with four-storeyed business premises and houses and a few shops on either side. A few people were going down it. There was a café at the corner. Walking into the street, out of the unbroken sunlight of the square, out of the morning heat into the empty shade, he felt suddenly washed out of the war. He was in any French provincial town, on a hot morning in late summer, and no one knew who he was. Walking in the brown canvas shoes, in the strange clothes and down the strange street of the strange town, he was himself no longer. He remembered as he walked what the newspapers in England had said about the rising tide of war, and how, only a day or two ago, he did not feel part of that tide. Well, he thought, I am part of it now. The tide had washed him down into the marsh when the Wellington had crashed, across the moonlit countryside and across the river and the field to where the vineyards lay above the mill; it had washed him into the moment when he had seen the girl feeding the hens in the morning sun under the fruit trees and it had washed him forward now, alone, apart from the girl, apart from Sandy and O'Connor and Godwin and Taylor, utterly apart from his flying and all the life of operational war, to the moment when he was walking out of the rue St Honoré into the rue Richer, out of the shade once more into the sun, detached from everybody and everything, no longer afraid.

The rue Richer was about a hundred yards long, and it was numbered from the end at which he had come. He was walking on the side with the even numbers, and he crossed to Number 9. He went up the steps without waiting or looking round, and rang the bell. He heard the bell ringing deep in the house.

He held the chickens ready and listened for the sound of

feet. He looked up and down the street as he waited. Outside a café at the corner, leaning against the pole that kept up a red-and-white-striped awning, a waiter was looking out across the street, staring idly at Franklin. Under the edge of the awning a row of short evergreen shrubs, in boxes, divided the tables from the street. The waiter, his cloth under one arm, was breaking off the leaves of the shrubs and idly destroying them with his fingers. Franklin could plainly see the dark fragments of leaves falling, and then the waiter's hand reaching out, his head not turning, as he broke off another leaf to destroy.

The door of the house opened as he was looking at the waiter. He turned, feeling his heart beat heavily, and saw a woman of sixty or so, dressed in black, with a white starched apron, like a nurse. She stood with her body half behind the door.

'Good morning.'

'Good morning,' Franklin said. 'I have brought the chickens.'

'Come in,' she said. Stiffly she held open the door an inch or two wider and Franklin went into the house. Uneasy, he wondered how little or how much the woman knew.

She shut the door behind him and led him down the passage without another word. The passage was quite dark, and it seemed suddenly like a trap. It was not real, and it seemed so fantastic that he did not feel himself. Then he remembered the girl in the church; he remembered the reality of the little cart; and he felt calm again.

'Wait here,' the woman said. She opened a door at the end of the passage and he walked into the room beyond. The room was square, with big French windows. One window was open and there was a high surgical chest, with small drawers, along one wall and a plain wooden table in the centre. Above the table was a single electric bulb, with an adjustable fitting.

The doctor came in almost at once; a tall man with a short black-red beard. He was wearing a white coat. He switched on the electric light and said 'Good morning', and then shut the French windows and pulled the dark green curtains across them. 'It is all right,' he said to Franklin. 'Take your coat off.'

The doctor went out of the room by another door, and Franklin heard the sound of running water in the ante-room.

In about a minute the doctor was back, standing in the door, wiping his hands on a towel. Franklin had struggled out of his coat and now stood with his arm crooked, slightly away from his body. In the bright electric light he noticed suddenly how dirty the bandages were. 'How long since you did this?' the doctor said, and Franklin, in the few seconds before answering, could not remember what day it was, and felt that half his life lay in the few days since the Wellington had come down in the marsh. 'Two or three days,' he said. The doctor did not say anything. He went back into the ante-room and came out again immediately, his sleeves rolled up above his dry, white hairy forearms.

'Lie on the table,' he said.

Franklin lay flat on the table and stared upwards. The impact of light on his eyes, shrill and harsh, centralized itself and pierced his eyes with brilliant pain as he felt the doctor un-knotting the bandage on his arm.

'An English aviator?' the doctor said.

'Yes.' He was very guarded now.

'My son was an aviator.'

'In this war?'

'He flew Morane 406s at the front until 1940.'

'Fighters.'

'You know them?'

'No. I know of them.'

'You were not in France?'

'No, I was not in France,' he said.

He heard the dried blood of the bandages crackling on his arm. The doctor gave each successive fold of bandage a little rip, diagonally, until it came free.

'My son shot down four planes and had four probably destroyed,' the doctor said. 'You bled a great deal.'

'Yes.'

'He was himself shot down on May 31st,' the doctor said. 'Just before the end. It was bad luck. He was taken prisoner.'

'It was very bad luck.'

'Almost at the same time Henri was also shot down."

'Henri?'

'Françoise's brother. Has the bandage been off before?'

59

'No.'

'One moment,' he said.

The doctor went away to the ante-room and Franklin raised his head and looked at his arm. The bandage was down to the last two folds. They were black with blood. He lay back and closed his eyes against the light, thinking briefly of Françoise and the brother. The fact seemed suddenly to illuminate all that she did.

'We have practically no anaesthetics,' the doctor said. 'I am sorry. It is symptomatic of the conditions of France to-day.'

'I brought morphia and anti-tetanus and gentian ointment from the aircraft,' Franklin said. 'Please have them. They are in the pocket of my coat.'

'I am grateful,' the doctor said. He stood under the arc of light, thin and tall and tired, hands upraised. 'I am grateful and humiliated.'

'There is no need to be humiliated.' He felt the strength of the word to be out of place, too emotional for a simple thing.

'I am humiliated because of France,' the doctor said. 'A country that has no anaesthetics leaves one humiliated.'

Suddenly, without warning, he took the bandage and with a short diagonal rip pulled it with skilful savagery off the arm. Franklin felt the raw tissues pulled up with the bandage in a violent second or two of pain. He felt the lips of the wound broken again, the congealed blood split, and the new blood, warm and sickening, force its way through the cracks and run down his arm. The impact, not so much pain as nausea, surged up in his throat, and filled his mouth with hot sourness. He wanted to spit it out. Then before he could think again the cool swab of antiseptic came down on his arm and then up and then down again, the coolness changing suddenly to burning as the antiseptic bit down into the flesh. He felt that all his arm lay open, slit and raw, to a wind of acid blowing fiercely down on the naked veins, cauterizing and shrivelling them up. Then it seemed to him that the hands of the doctor were pulling the flesh apart. The sourness was drained from his mouth, and in its place was the dry air of faintness, rising into his face and condensing on his forehead in sweat. The flesh of his arm was broken apart, and then, in a few moments of confusion when

60

pain and faintness and the light on his eyeballs beat him back into waves of colder and colder darkness, came together again. It was held together with a new pain, metallic and tight and unrelenting. The edges of his flesh gnawed at each other and were fused before the wet swab of antiseptic, cool and then burning, came down for the last time.

After that he heard the doctor go away. He heard the sound of running water. He lay alone. His arm was flat and taut, as if wired through every vein, and pain beat through these veins in uneven throbs transmitted in waves to his shoulder.

The doctor came back at last. He stood over Franklin, wiping his hands again with the towel.

'The best I can do is to put on clips,' he said. 'With an arm like that you should go to hospital.'

'Which is the equivalent of prison.'

'Exactly. You are all right now?'

'I am all right.'

'Good. One moment,' he said.

He went over to the door and pushed a bell-button by the light switch. 'You had better put on your coat,' he said. He picked up the coat, holding it by the shoulders. Franklin slid slowly off the table, the angle of the floor at once steepened, like the horizon seen from an aircraft, and then slowly straightened again as his feet touched the floor. His sickness followed these movements, sinking and slipping and settling again, and his arms seemed light and fragile as he held them out for the sleeves of the coat. He put his good arm into the first sleeve and then swung slowly round while the doctor eased the second sleeve over the bandages of the other arm. There was no pain in his arm to worry him; only the emptiness of his face and body as the sickness rose again and drained away. Then the door opened and the woman dressed like a nurse came in.

'He is ready to go now,' the doctor said. 'It is all right?'

'Yes,' the woman said. 'As far as one can judge it is all right.'

'Where are you going now?' the doctor said.

'Back to Françoise. In the church,' Franklin said.

'That's all right,' the doctor said. 'Act simply and don't hurry. It is all right to do as Françoise says.'

He held out his hand. The woman stood holding the door

61

slightly ajar, ready to go. Franklin took the doctor's hand and shook it and not knowing quite what to say, stood looking at the dark, tiredly alert face.

'Good-bye.' The doctor spoke the word in English, smiling as he spoke. 'Good luck,' he said.

'Good-bye.' Franklin, too, spoke the word in English, feeling the deeper intimacy of the moment by the change in language. 'I can't thank you enough. I know how it is for you.'

'It is a pleasure to do something which is a positive help.'

'I know it must be,' Franklin said. 'But I am aware of the risk for you.'

'We shouldn't exaggerate the risk,' the doctor said. 'It is relative.'

'To what?'

'To the whole condition of France: which is a second revolution. If anything, more important. If anything, more unhappy.' He stopped suddenly, smiled slightly, and put his arm on Franklin's shoulder, turning him towards the door. 'But this is not the time to talk of that. I think you had better go while you can.'

The woman held the door fully open, and the doctor and Franklin went past her into the passage beyond. All three stopped in the half-darkness by the outer door.

'And the arm?' Franklin said. 'What about that? Is there anything else I can do?'

'Try to be quiet. Drink as much liquid as you can. At the moment it is more your condition, the fatigue and so on, than the arm.'

'Thank you,' Franklin said. 'I am very grateful. Good-bye.'

'Good-bye,' the doctor said.

The woman opened the door and Franklin walked out of the house, straight out of the darkness of the passage into the white wall of sunlight outside. He walked fast, without realizing it, and then suddenly he remembered it and felt the sickness weak in his legs, and halfway across the street he slowed down. He did not look back, but as he crossed the street he knew that someone was watching him, and in a moment, out of the corner of his eye, he saw the waiter outside the café, leaning against a pole of the awning by the empty tables. He was looking at Franklin steadily, emptily, without emotion. It was the most

negative thing Franklin had ever seen: the stare into the sunlight at a figure passing across the line of vision, the hands picking at the leaves of the shrubs and letting them fall on the dust
of the pavement. For a moment or two Franklin held himself
rigid, wondering what it meant, and then he turned his head
and looked at the waiter. And he saw then how the eyes did not
move to follow him beyond the narrow frontal line of vision.
He saw that they were looking not at him but at nothing in
particular: at nothing, out of nothing, and for nothing but the
empty habit of looking.

He felt the fear and surprise and uneasiness of this moment
creep up behind him, like a person following, as he turned into
the rue St Honoré, and out of that street into the square
beyond. At the corner of the square he looked back, as if he
expected to see someone behind him, but the street was almost
empty except for a few casual shabby pedestrians and a cart at
the far end. All the time he kept his injured arm in his trousers
pocket, feeling the bandage tightly restricting the elbow and the
blood beating thickly and painfully now in the lower arm and
hand.

He walked slowly up the steps of the church, out of the flat
heat of the square, into the brown dead shade of the western
porch. Inside, he stood in the nave for a moment, looking for
Françoise. A few women were kneeling in the back rows of
chairs and he felt for a moment frightened, not seeing her
among them. Then he walked forward, his feet quiet on the
long strip of dusty matting running up the stones of the aisle,
and suddenly he saw her alone, about halfway to the altar,
kneeling with her head on her hands.

He went quietly and sat beside her without saying anything.
She did not lift her head, but he saw her open eye like a black
cherry held against the partly opened fingers, and he knew she
had been watching him.

'Is it all right?' she said.

'It is all right,' he said. 'Quite all right.'

'You had better kneel down,' she said, 'and put your head on
your hands. Did anything happen?'

'Nothing happened.'

He slipped forward on his knees, kneeling on the hassock,

and putting his good hand and then his head on the chair in front of him. He was very close to her and felt the intimacy of the moment. When she spoke her voice was so low that he could hardly catch the words in French, and after a moment he moved his head so that he could see again her flickering black eye and her lips moving against her brown hands as they spoke the words.

'I'm sorry I was long,' he said.

'You were not long,' she said.

'It is very good of you to wait.'

'I have been praying for you,' she said. 'For all of you. Do you belong to the Church?'

'Not to your Church.'

'To what Church?' she said.

'The Church of England,' he said.

'Does it differ very much?'

'Not very much.' He raised his eyes and looked at the fabric of the church, the half-light on the pillars, the few large and small candles burning up against the image of the Virgin. 'In outward respects hardly at all. It is simpler, that's all. It rests less on the ritual expression of faith.'

He saw her dark eye flicker against her hand.

'It is a proper thing to have faith,' she said.

'Very proper.'

'I had faith you would come back this morning and you came back.'

He did not speak.

'I have faith that you will get away safely, and I know that it can happen. I have prayed very hard for that.'

He did not know what to say. He felt small because of her simplicity and the great assurance behind the simplicity. She did not speak for a moment or two either. He knelt there looking at her sideways, watching her black hair curl against her face, and the lips firmly and quietly set in the shadow of her hands. As he knelt watching her the feeling of being watched and followed by someone no longer meant anything. It slipped away and seemed ridiculous. The hard tangle of events was smoothed away, too, with his fear.

'Is your arm going to be all right?' she said.

64

'Yes.'

'Do you feel all right yourself? Now?'

'Yes.'

'You looked very white when you came in. It is better to rest if you don't feel strong enough.'

'No,' he said. 'I am ready whenever you want to go.'

She turned her head, and now, for the first time, he saw her two eyes, level and black and shining. She looked at him very steadfastly for a moment or two, and suddenly as she looked at him she seemed so young and calm that he was horrified. He saw all the horror of the situation clearly and for the first time. He remembered with a sickening shock all that it meant, in France, to help someone like himself. He did not remember the rumours, the propaganda, the atrocity stories, but only the simple fact: the rule that it was treason for her to help him. His sickness rose and turned sour in his throat and he swallowed it acidly, but the horror remained and suddenly he felt the urgency of the situation. He felt now that they must get away and go on by themselves, he and the four sergeants, away from the risks and the complications of hiding, so that if anything disastrous should happen it would happen only to themselves, and not to the girl.

'Do you think we can go on to-night?' he said.

'No,' she said. She was firm and she did not seem surprised.

'We ought to go on now as soon as possible.'

'When it is possible: yes. But it isn't yet possible.'

'But it must be soon. It's a great risk for you. It must be possible. Will it be possible to-morrow?'

She looked at him without moving her eyes.

'There is no need to be afraid for us.'

'I am afraid for you.'

'There is no need. It has been done before. If you have faith it can be done again.'

'Have you done it before?' he said.

'No,' she said. 'But others have done it. It is a question of patience and faith. You have only to trust us. That's all.'

He suddenly put his free hand up against hers, touching her hair and then holding her finger-tips closely with his flat hand.

'I will trust you,' he said. 'But in turn will you trust me?'

'In what way?' she said.

'In this way,' he said, 'that if you feel at any time that the risk is too great, you will tell me and let us go. It would be better and we shall understand.'

'I will trust you in everything,' she said. 'Shall we go now?'

'When you like,' he said.

She did not answer and he saw that her eyes were closed. He waited for perhaps half a minute while she said her last prayer, and then he saw her cross herself swiftly but with proper humility, her head still slightly bowed as she got to her feet.

'Don't hurry and don't look back,' she said. 'Don't imagine things. We are going to buy some peaches.'

He followed her out of the church and once again, as when he had come out of the house, the sunlight was like a blinding white curtain beyond the door. It struck down on his head with a bright ache of heat as he and the girl walked across the shining flagstones past the fountain to the far side of the square. As they went past the cart he saw Pierre sitting down on the shady side of it, propped up by the wheel, his eyes closed. The girl spoke as they went past, but the eyes did not open and Franklin and the girl went on as if nothing happened until they came to the fruit-stalls. There were six or seven stalls, and under the grey-green awnings were laid out the perishable produce of the late summer that could not be transported: small green-pink peaches, sweet green grapes, soft early pears, a few apples. The girl stopped at one stall and picked up a peach and pressed it with her thumb and fingers. She put it down again and he saw the mark of her thumb like a bruise on the pink skin of the fruit. He stood for a moment or two watching it, fascinated, as if expecting to see it disappear like the dent made by a child in a rubber ball, and then he turned and the girl was no longer there.

His heart shot up in his throat in alarm. He caught his breath and tasted for a moment all the hot sweet smell of ripe fruit in the thick air. He looked wildly round, and then knew in the same moment that he had no need to be alarmed. He could see her standing two stalls away, bargaining for the fruit and again picking up the peaches and pressing them with her fingers.

He walked up to her.

'I thought you had gone.'

'Don't be frightened,' she said.

'I'm not frightened.'

'It looks better if I walk away sometimes. It looks as if we know each other well.'

He felt sick and stupid.

'I promised to trust you,' he said, 'and now I don't trust you.'

'Don't talk much,' she said. 'Have a peach. It will stop you talking.'

She gave him six or seven of the small peaches, in ones or twos, because he could only use one hand, and he put them into his pocket. He waited for her to pay the woman in charge of the stall, and then she, too, filled her hands and they walked slowly back across the square. He ate the last peach she had given him, gnawing the stiff flesh like an apple. It was cool and juicy, and he thought immediately of the four sergeants in the dusty room in the mill, wondering about him. He thought of O'Connor, smiling and crafty; of Sandy, bald and rather correct; and of the two young sergeants, tense and too eager. They're probably more scared than I am, Franklin thought, and, thinking it, he knew he was no longer scared. He was eating a peach in the sunlight of a strange French square, walking naturally as any Frenchman might walk with a country girl, a stranger in a strange town. He was far away from the war; from the bombs dropped by people like himself; from the shrivelled life of war-time England and the drabness and dustiness of bombed places, and above all from the tension and smell and exclusiveness of flying. If you look at it simply, he thought, it is simple. We have to get out of France, that's all.

He was still eating the peach when he saw Pierre coming across the square with the cart. As it stopped by them the girl said again, 'How is your arm?' and he said, 'I'd forgotten it,' telling the lie quickly because he did not want the complication of more questions. She looked at him swiftly: her eyes an odd mixture of doubt and pity and amused tenderness, as if she knew quite well what he felt and why he was saying it.

'All right,' she said. 'We will go now. You sit between us, where your arm isn't noticed. As you did when we came.'

He got up into the cart, and then the girl after him. Pierre looked at him and grinned, but did not speak. Then as the cart moved forward Franklin remembered something.

'What town is this?' he said. If he had the name of the town he could orientate his position from the map. With Sandy doing the navigation the rest would be easy.

'There is no need for you to know,' the girl said.

'I would like to know.'

'It would be better if you didn't know.'

'It is important for me to know,' he said.

'It is very important for us that you shouldn't know,' she said.

Suddenly he felt cheap and small and humiliated. It was as if he had been given food in a strange house and had said, 'I must know how much it costs. I can't eat it otherwise,' and he felt sick and bitter through his own stupidity.

'Forgive me,' he said. 'Please forgive me.' He put his good hand on her two hands which lay crossed in her lap. He felt the intimacy of touching her and he knew that she felt it too. She did not move her hands and did not speak, but he knew that her silence and her motionlessness were signs that she understood what he felt.

They drove on in silence, in the hot sun, out of the town and across the flat land, the way they had come, towards the ridge below which the mill lay on the river. All the time the sun beat down on his head with the same bright aching power he had first noticed in the street behind the square. As they came near the end of the journey he felt as if a knife had been laid edge-wise across his skull and that every motion of the cart bounced it jaggedly up and down.

When they came to the mill-yard and he got down from the cart, the force of his feet striking the ground seemed to rock his head from side to side on his shoulders.

'Go straight up,' the girl said. 'We will bring you something to eat.'

'And to drink,' he said. 'I must drink a great deal.'

'Yes. But go up,' she said.

Climbing slowly up the wooden stairs inside the mill, the shadow cool on his eyes after the pain of the sun, he heard the sergeants' voices long before he opened the door of the room.

They were all very excited, and the voices burst together at him as he opened the door.

'God, Frankie, thank Christ you're back. We were scared to hell about you, Frankie boy, we thought it was all over.'

'All over?' he said. 'What happened?'

He stood in the middle of the room, swaying slightly on his feet, looking vaguely at the excited, scared faces of the four sergeants.

'The Jerries were here,' O'Connor said. 'That's what. The Jerries were here.'

CHAPTER 7

HE could not eat the soup and bread brought up by the old woman half an hour later, but there was milk to drink and he half-lay in a corner of the room, sipping it, eyes almost closed, while the sergeants ate and told him what had happened.

'After you'd gone,' O'Connor said, 'we decided to keep watch. In relays. Half an hour each. I took the first, Goddy took the second. Goddy and Sandy were just changing over when Goddy says, "Hell, I haven't seen him before," and we all rushed to the window and there was a Jerry, walking up towards the grape-vines.'

'Alone?'

'No: with the old man. The girl's father.'

'What did they do?'

'They walked up to the grape-vines, stopped, had a bit of a conflab, and then went into the grape-vines.'

'It might be nothing,' he said.

'They were in the grape-vines bloody near half an hour,' O'Connor said. 'When they came out again the old man was grim as hell. You can guess how we felt, watching them came down that path. That wasn't funny.'

'What else?'

'That's the damn funny thing,' O'Connor said, 'nothing else. They stood downstairs another twenty minutes, talking. We could hear them. Then the Jerry went. Walking. Walking, mind you. That means he couldn't have come from far away.'

'It might,' Franklin said.

He set the glass of milk on the bare floor and thoughtfully held it with his hand, staring at it. He tried to think calmly, but all he had ever heard about treachery in France began to break in on his calmness, complicating it. With his head beating heavily as if someone were striking the wall with immense blows behind him, it was difficult to take his thoughts one by one and piece them together into a convincing pattern of sense. He wanted no more hasty conclusions.

70

'Sandy,' he said, 'what do you think?'

'I think we should start walking,' Sandy said. He was very quiet.

'You're telling me,' O'Connor said. 'I could start walking now.'

Godwin and Taylor laughed and said 'Yes,' looking at O'Connor. Franklin knew suddenly that all four of them had talked it out, that all four of them were thinking the same way.

'Let's take the thing calmly,' he said.

'Never mind about calmly,' O'Connor said. 'Let's get going. It isn't healthy.'

'What sort of town was it?' Sandy said. 'Did you find out the name of it?'

'No.'

'If you could find out I could get our position,' Sandy said. 'The rest would be simple. We've got all the maps.'

'Did you ask the girl?' O'Connor said.

Franklin hesitated. He knew that it was going to be difficult to explain this. In his absence he felt that the interdependence of the crew, as far as he was concerned, had broken. They had made up their minds together, seeing everything as a simple black and white picture of danger and treachery. He himself, after the two journeys with the girl, the few moments in the church and the talk with the doctor, was some experiences ahead of them. There were some things it would be better not to try to explain.

'They would rather we didn't know the name of the town,' he said. 'That's all.'

'Thinking of themselves,' O'Connor said. 'Just like the bloody French. Thinking of themselves.'

'And what the hell are we doing?' Franklin said. His anger broke in his head like a painful echo of thunder. 'Have some sense. Nobody is going to cut your bloody head off if you're caught. Or set you up against a wall and shoot you. But that's the risk they run. For you.'

'If they don't sell us out!' O'Connor said.

'We'll never get anywhere if we don't trust them,' Franklin said. 'That's certain.'

71

'Well, I don't trust them,' O'Connor said. 'I saw the French in '40, and I don't trust them. Not again.'

'All right, you don't trust them!' Franklin said with new anger. 'All right! But perhaps you can trust me?'

O'Connor did not speak again, and there was a short awkward silence, during which Franklin lifted the glass of milk and drank a little and then set it down hard on the floor. His anger thumped viciously in his head as he sat in silence watching the smoky film of milk clear smoothly from the sides of the glass.

It was Taylor who spoke at last.

'Does the name of the town matter?' he said. 'We got here without the names of any towns.'

'That's the first sensible remark I've heard since I came back,' Franklin said. 'If we have to get out of here alone we can. If we have help it may mean waiting a couple of days. But with help we can do it twice as quickly. Now are you satisfied?'

He waited for a second for someone to answer him and then got up.

'All right,' he said. He felt his anger flatten into hostility. He was very tired, and the milk, cool at first but clammy after the first drink or two, seemed to lie heavy and curdled in his throat. 'All right. Just to satisfy you I'll go down and find out what this Jerry business was all about. That's the simplest way.'

He went out of the room without another word and downstairs and straight across the yard. His anger was still thumping painfully in his forehead when he came to the threshold of the kitchen and saw the girl.

'You shouldn't be here,' she said. 'You shouldn't come down here.'

She came and shut the door quickly behind him, and he was out of the sunlight and in the shadow, the shock of the change rippling in dark and light before his eyes.

'There was someone here,' he said.

'Yes,' she said. 'A German.'

'Is it all right?'

'Quite all right,' she said. She stood straight up, young and clear and rather defiant, her back against the kitchen table where the men had breakfasted. 'Quite all right.'

'We wondered —'

72

Before he could finish speaking the girl's father came into the room. It seemed to Franklin that he looked tired and rather strained. The craggy taut lines of his neck were tightened as he raised his head.

'Something the matter?'

'No, no,' Franklin said.

'The German,' the girl said.

'He was here about the vines,' the father said. 'Only about the vines. That's all. Don't worry.'

'You think he suspected anything?' Franklin said.

'Impossible to say. I don't think so. He is too interested in the grape-crop. He was here to assess the grape-crop. That's all. You have no need to worry.'

'I am not worried,' Franklin said. He tried again to be natural and polite. 'The presence of the German was disconcerting to the others. That's all.'

'Naturally.'

'Have you any idea when we might go? We are very anxious to go. We do not underestimate the risk for you.'

'There is no risk. Except the risk brought about by impatience.'

'That is my feeling.'

'The first five days are very dangerous,' the father said. 'Also, you must have papers. It is very necessary to have papers. They must be prepared. It takes time.'

'I understand,' Franklin said. 'Please forgive my impatience.'

'It is very natural.'

Franklin leaned against the table. He noticed for the first time that the girl had drawn slightly away from them. She stood by the big kitchen dresser, upright, her brown hand flat on her thighs, watching him but not speaking. It struck him that she was remembering his promise to trust her. He looked at her and looked away again.

'How is your arm?' the father said.

'Much better,' he said. He remembered the doctor. 'The doctor sent his remembrances to you.'

'Thank you.'

'He talked about your son. I understand how you feel,' Franklin said.

73

'Thank you,' the father said. 'Thank you.' He looked quickly at the floor and then raised his face again. Franklin could see that his eyes were wet with tears, and he knew that from that moment, for him, no matter what the rest might feel, there would be no more doubt.

'I will go back now.' He looked swiftly round at the girl, who stood in the same attitude, watchful and, he thought, half doubtful of him. 'You think it better if we don't come down?'

He addressed the remark partly to the girl, hoping she would answer, but she did not answer. 'Yes, it is better,' the father said. 'By day at least. By night it will not much matter so much. One of you may come down at a time.'

'Thank you,' Franklin said. He stood by the door, ready to open it, hoping the girl would break the long silence of her stare at him, but she did not speak. Her eyes were fixed on him brightly, but now, he thought, with a kind of critical passion, and when finally he wrenched open the door and went out, the sunlight hitting once again too brightly after the shadow, she was still standing there, erect and immobile, not having spoken another word.

All that afternoon he lay upstairs in the mill, on the bare floor, feeling as if all the heavy old-fashioned mechanism of the mill had been set to work beneath him, beating the water into a thundering cataract just below his head. At intervals he felt himself go off into a daze, more stupor than sleep, from which he would emerge to see one of the four sergeants standing at the window. The rest were lying on the floor, and not another word, except of his own explanation of the German and the vines, had yet been spoken about their leaving. He could still detect the slight hostility of the four men against him, but it did not trouble him now. All that worried him was the face of the girl as he had last seen it: hostile, too, he thought, but troubled as if he had hurt her very much by seeming to take away the trust he had put in her. And as he lay there, hot and stupid with the pain of his arm that in turn pumped the recurrent feverish pain into his head, he was surprised that in one day his feelings about a person could become so sharp, so perplexing and some-times so painful themselves. No matter what he thought that afternoon, or how much pain became confused with thought, the face of the girl, beautifully trustful and simple with only the one black cherry of her eye visible in the church, doubtful and troubled in the kitchen, would rise up in his mind and reproach him. He knew that somehow he had to talk to her again.

Late in the afternoon he went to sleep and yet remained aware, in a dream-conscious way, of where he was. His head seemed very large and hollow, and not tightly connected with his shoulders. He did not wake till about seven o'clock. He rolled over and lay on his back and looked at the brown wooden rafters above him and tried to gauge the angle of the sun. The pain had now slipped down between his eyes, and he was very thirsty. When a shadow moved across the room he looked up and saw that it was Sandy, whose face, held sideways and above him, seemed troubled.

'All right?' Sandy said.

'It's hot in here.' He did not want to talk much.

'The old lady came up with some food about five,' Sandy said. 'But we didn't wake you.'

'That's all right. I don't want to eat. I'm thirsty, though.'

'There was some milk left.'

'I don't want it. It makes me thirstier.'

'The choice was wine or milk,' Sandy said. 'I thought the wine would pump up your temperature.'

'What temperature?'

'Your temperature. I took it while you were asleep. We've got a thermometer – just another of those things O'Connor carries.'

'What was it?'

'It's O.K.,' Sandy said. 'A degree and a half above normal.'

Franklin looked at Sandy sharply, not knowing whether to believe him or not, and then suddenly realized that the room, except for themselves, was empty. He felt alarmed and angry again.

'Where the hell are the others?'

'It's all right. Upstairs. They found there was another floor above. The old lady said it was safe, so they went up to keep a better look-out. They can talk up there without disturbing you. And walk about a bit.'

'Is that what keeps bumping?' he said.

75

'Nothing's bumping,' Sandy said. 'You can hardly hear the water up here.'

Franklin lay back and did not speak. He could see the sky, blue and hot and without cloud, beyond the windows. There was nothing by which he could judge the wind, and there was, as Sandy said, no sound. It all seemed confused and odd.

'Sandy,' he said, 'did I fly off the handle too much this morning?'

'You flew off the handle, but not too much.'

'We can't go yet. You see that, don't you?'

'Well —'

'We've got to trust them, Sandy. Having got into it, we've got to act as they think best.'

'I know. You've got to convince O'Connor of that.'

'O'Connor is just an insular bloody Englishman. He's got an Irish name and he's pigheaded like the worst English and hotheaded like the worst Irish. Then he lumps the whole French nation together and says they're rotten right through. That's just silly.'

'I shouldn't worry about it,' Sandy said. 'You're the skipper, anyway. You can always order him to shut up.'

'I never ordered this crew to do anything,' he said. 'You know that.'

'Don't worry about it,' Sandy said. 'Take it easy and rest. Will you drink some of the milk if I put some rum in it?'

'Yes,' he said.

He propped himself up against the wall, his eyes blacking out with sickening heaviness for a moment until his body recovered from the movement.

Sandy brought the rum and milk in a glass.

'Thanks,' Franklin said. He took the glass and drank a little, feeling the sweet rum taste with his tongue below the smooth cool milk. For the first time he realized how thick his tongue was, the milk furring on it like crust.

'You remember Davies of 7 Squadron?' he said. 'He waited a month in a farmhouse just a bit south of Paris before he could get away.'

'It's been done in three days, too,' Sandy said.

'Three days or three months,' he said, 'the thing is to do it.'

76

'Yes,' Sandy said.

'I'm glad you see it my way.'

He drank a little more of the rum and milk, his tongue thickening again, so that suddenly he no longer wanted to talk. 'What's the time?' he said. He gave the glass to Sandy and slipped his body flat on the floor again.

'About seven. She said there'd be food about half-past.'

'I think I'll get some sleep again.'

'Shall I wake you when it comes?'

'No. Wake me if anything happens.'

He flattened his face sideways against the floor and, trying to sleep, went off again into the doze of pain and stupor, his forehead thumping heavily and his mind sickeningly bright with reproachful pictures of the girl standing by the dresser, looking at him but never speaking. Some time later he heard the three sergeants come in and begin talking, their voices loud and then quietening, but he did not open his eyes. As the sunlight lessened he found it more restful to sleep, and he slipped away at last on a long murmur of voices.

When he woke again it was so dark that he sat up with a start, leaning on one elbow. Somebody had covered him over with a blanket. He could feel how the sweat and heat of his body had been kept in by it, until now it was like steam.

'Everybody here?' he said.

'It's O.K.,' Sandy said. He came across the room. He had taken off his shoes. 'We're taking it in turns for a breath of air. O'Connor and Goddy have been. Taylor's down now.'

'Anything happen?'

'Not a thing. You want to go down?'

'Yes,' he said. 'I'll go now.'

He got to his feet and stood for a moment rocking slightly, shaky, glad of the darkness because of his weakness. He wiped the sleep film off his face with his good hand and then suddenly stopped. He could see something in the darkness. It was the crimson end of a cigarette.

'Who's smoking?' he said.

'It's me,' said O'Connor.

'Put the bloody thing out,' he said.

'Why?'

'I said put it out!' he said madly. 'Put it out! You dumb, silly bastard, put it out!'

'I don't see —'

'For Christ's sake!' he said. 'Put it out!'

He saw the crimson spot disappear in the darkness. The moment was final: the moment of unanswerable blinding anger through which he somehow struggled as if he were half drunk towards the door. As he opened it and went down the stairway through the mill he felt very sick with heat and temper and the discomfort of moving for the first time since noon. He came down into the air with great relief, suddenly smelling the night, clean but still warm, faint with the sweetness of corn-straw and more thickly faint with the odour of water and water-washed stone after the heat of the day. He stood for a moment against the outside wall of the mill, sick within himself and sick of himself, and took heavy clean breaths of air with opened mouth, as if they were food.

He had been standing there for two or three minutes when he heard voices. They seemed to come from the direction of the river. They seemed to be talking in French. He walked down the stone roadway between the house and the mill until he could see the water shining beyond the jetty under the not quite dark sky.

He first heard the voice of the girl; and then the other voice deeper and slower, but also speaking in French, struck him as being very familiar. In a moment he knew it was Taylor's voice. He stopped in the roadway and listened. Taylor seemed to have no difficulty with French at all.

He went on and there, by the jetty, Taylor and the girl were standing talking. Franklin walked towards them as if he were going to walk into the river. He felt impelled by the same violent anger as when he had discovered O'Connor smoking the cigarette. He knew there was no reason for it, but he had no strength to check it. It seemed to spew up from the inside of him, as if he were being emotionally sick.

'Hullo,' he said.

'Hullo, sir,' Taylor said. The official politeness seemed strained and suspicious. 'I was just talking to Françoise.'

'I didn't know you spoke French,' Franklin said.

78

'Yes, I do.'

'I asked if anyone spoke French and you didn't say anything.'

'I knew you did. I felt it didn't matter.'

'It may matter.' His voice was hard and stiff. He felt that he hated Taylor. He did not know why, but knew only that he was behaving strangely and, by all his normal standards, badly. 'You'd better get back,' he said. It was like giving an order. He saw the boy, very tall, move in the darkness away from the motionless figure of the girl. 'There's no sense standing talking here.' He hated himself more and more, and yet there was nothing he could do.

'All right,' Taylor said. As he moved away he looked back at the girl. He's just a kid, Franklin thought. It's all perfectly natural, and there's nothing to it. Why am I behaving like this? What the hell is the matter with me?

He stood stiff and critical, waiting for Taylor finally to turn and go.

'Bon soir,' Taylor said. The French was excellent, smoother by far than his own. The intimacy of its excellence made him mad. 'Bon soir, mademoiselle. Bon soir.'

'Bon soir,' she said.

Taylor turned abruptly and went, and as he turned Franklin felt as if he were deliberately left between them, Taylor walking quickly away towards the mill, the girl now slowly turning and going towards the river.

He walked after the girl and then, walking with her, he felt suddenly very cheap and, underneath the inexplicable anger, humiliated.

'I'm sorry,' he said.

'Do you feel better after your sleep?' she said.

'I'm better,' he said. 'I didn't sleep much.'

'Grandmother will give you something that will help you to sleep,' she said. 'It will bring the temperature down.'

So she knew all about the sleep and the temperature, he thought. She knew everything. He did not speak. She walked slowly and now they were away from the mill, behind the house, where the garden came down to the water. She was wearing a dark coat and she seemed to him all of piece of darkness, except for the pale shape of her face lowered slightly as she looked at the path. The fence enclosing the garden ran by the river edge, a path beside it, and then clumps of apple trees overhanging it at the far end. The girl leaned against the fence under the apple trees and he stopped, too. He could smell now the over-ripe fragrance of apples, fallen and perhaps crushed in the grass, like the smell of new wine, stronger than the smell of water and corn. He took a long breath and knew suddenly that what he had to say must be said now or never at all.

'I wanted to tell you how it was I came down into the kitchen,' he said.

'It no longer matters.'

'It was the others who did not trust you. After the German came. Not myself. I trust you. I trust you completely,' he said. 'I trust you all. How could I do otherwise?'

He put his good arm on her shoulder. She did not come towards him. She did not speak either, but presently he felt some of his complicated anger smooth itself out, the moment growing through quietness and hesitation into ease and tenderness.

'Please,' he said.

He moved his arm very slightly, pressing her shoulder, and she came towards him a little.

'Forgive me if it seemed that I doubted you,' he said.

'Some doubt on both sides is natural.'

'At first,' he said. 'But not after a time. Not now.'

'I have no doubt,' she said.

He leaned his face towards her, feeling her cheek smooth and so much cooler than his own. All his anger had gone now, replaced by the simple ache of his own sickness. As he touched her she came very slightly towards him, and he was at once tired and grateful with slight exultation at the same time. He put his hand on her neck and drew her towards him, but he did not say anything. There were many things he would want to talk to her about in time, he thought. He would want to talk about France, her brother, the escape, the war from their two points of view. But he was occupied now only with the transition of his feelings from anger to humiliation, and now from humiliation to the simple tenderness, so like the moment in the church, of holding her and not speaking to her in the darkness.

80

He held her like this for some moments, and he was very glad all the time because she was young and warm and because, though French, she was close to his own world: the world of being young on the edge of danger, the experience of running your finger along the thread holding things together and not knowing if or how soon the thread would break. As he held her he looked across the river, over the dark fields. The stars in the summer sky were repeated in the smooth flow of water, and there was no sound, and he thought of the countryside at home, in England, when leave took him to Worcestershire and the valleys were heavy with blossom or fruit and the war was a separate and unreal experience. It seemed unreal to him now as he looked at the river and held the girl with his one good arm, her face cool against his weariness. Then all the unreality of it became real as he turned his face and put his lips against her throat and kissed her. It became real because the stupidity of the one thing was sharpened by the naturalness of the other, and suddenly it was all he wanted: to hold her there by the river, under the dark trees, and not care about time.

'You're tired,' she said.

She lifted her face. Her voice was very tender, and he was startled.

'How should you know?'

'The way you kissed me is tired.'

'Do you want me to kiss you in a way that is not tired?' he said.

'If you like,' she said.

He waited for a few seconds and then she turned her body and he kissed her full on the mouth. Her lips were warm and soft and he felt all the former intimacy of the day in the way she let the kiss go on, unprotesting and seriously tender.

She broke away when she was breathless and he laughed slightly and said, 'I am not very good with one arm,' but she was very serious and did not even smile in the darkness.

'Listen,' she said. 'Your arm.'

'What about it?'

'You want to go, don't you? From here?'

'I must go.' Now he was sure that he did not want to go.

'Whether you go or not depends on your arm. If you have a

81

little temperature to-night there will be more in the morning. You have to take great care.'

'You want me to go now?'

'No,' she said. She suddenly put her face against his shoulder. 'No. But the arm is dangerous. You look sick.'

'I feel sick.' Suddenly he admitted it. It seemed useless to keep any part of himself from her now.

'If the arm gets worse it will be very complicated for all of us.'

She took his good arm and began to walk back along the path towards the mill. He knew now the cause of his anger against O'Connor, of his feeling against Taylor. His sickness had gone down to his feet. He could hardly set them on the path and he was glad when he and the girl stood by the mill again.

'Good night now,' she said. 'You must go up.'

'Good night,' he said. 'Where is your father?'

'There is a possibility of getting passes for you. For at least two of you. He will be back to-night.'

'I can't thank you enough,' he said.

He stood close to her and put his good arm across her shoulder. He could not lift his other arm and he tried awkwardly to draw her to him. He saw the slightest light in her dark eyes as she lifted her face.

'Will you kiss me again?' he said.

She kissed him again without even troubling to speak and the moment was fixed for ever for him by the light in her black eyes, the silence and the breaking of the silence, by the noise of a train, far off, out of another world, across the hillside beyond the invisible vines.

CHAPTER 8

THE night was a repetition of the late afternoon and evening; and the morning, when he woke, a repetition of the night. His head seemed to have swollen strangely. His tongue was thick and sour in his terribly thirsty mouth. Above all he did not want to move.

The sergeants had covered him over with blankets, and when he first opened his eyes he saw all four were sitting on the floor, looking at the navigation map spread out by Sandy. He watched them for some time, not moving, his view odd and horizontal. The sun was well up, and he could see the sky blue already with morning heat through the little window. He could feel the sweat of himself like steam under his blankets and slowly, as his mind cleared to the sun, he became aware of his arm. It was as if someone had bound it to his side and the hot swollen flesh of it was trying to pulse itself free. The blood hammered continuously with sickening force through the choked tight veins.

At the same time the faces of the four sergeants did not mean anything. He discovered that he bore none of them the slightest ill-will. And though they were talking he did not follow what they were saying, and did not care.

Then Sandy looked up and saw him and came over.

'Hullo, Skip. All right?' He knelt down.

'I feel lousy,' he said. 'What goes on?'

'The father has been up. He wanted to talk to you. You were asleep and we wouldn't wake you. You look all in.'

'What was it about?'

'Taylor talked to him. He says there will be two passes by tonight. It seems odd, only two.'

'No. It isn't odd. We'd be lucky if we all five got away together. Why the map?'

'I've been going over the nav. again. Trying to check all the rivers. Just to see where we might be.'

'It doesn't matter where we are,' Franklin said. 'This room matters. Getting out matters. Nothing else.'

He suddenly felt the effort of talking. His words seemed to run away from him and he was too tired to catch them.

'O'Connor wanted to say something to you,' Sandy said.

'O.K.,' he said.

He shut his eyes for a second or two, and then, when he looked up again, O'Connor was there in the place of Sandy.

'How do you feel, Skip?' O'Connor said.

'Bloody awful.'

'I'm sorry,' O'Connor said. 'I'm sorry about yesterday, too.'

'It's all right. My fault,' he said. 'It was the arm. Then the strain of driving through that town full of Jerries and then when I got back everybody mad because I couldn't find its name.'

He stopped talking suddenly, tired again.

'It seems there's going to be two passes,' O'Connor said. 'I don't want to go. Not yet. Let the two kids go.'

'All right,' Franklin said. 'We'll see about it when it comes.'

He looked at O'Connor and grinned. He liked the feeling of friendliness, stronger in renewal. O'Connor, tough and common and warm as a brick, grinned back.

'Want me to shave you?' he said. 'It's cold water. But you'll feel fresher.'

'It would be damn nice.'

O'Connor fetched shaving-cream and razor and water in a cup, while Franklin tried to prop himself up against the wall.

'No need to get up,' O'Connor said. 'Lie down. Have it done in state. It's easier for me.'

He lay back and shut his eyes and felt the water very cool on his face as O'Connor rubbed it on, and after it the cream, with his fingers. He had no energy or desire to speak until Sandy began to pull his leg gently, his voice mocking quietly. 'Nice weather for the time of year, sir. How are your onions looking?' He heard Taylor and Goddy laughing. He grinned and felt the safety razor, flat and smooth, drawn down his cheek.

'Stop nattering,' he said, 'and have a look at this arm. The bandage has tightened up like hell.'

'It's tough tit, this arm,' O'Connor said.

'What do you mean, tough tit?'

84

'I wouldn't want it, that's all,' O'Connor said. 'I hate being sewn up.'

'On with your job, barber,' he said.

The four sergeants laughed, but he did not open his eyes. He did not even open them when Sandy came to undo the pins of the bandage and unfold it. He simply lay midway between the sensation of the pleasant pull of the razor and the fretful tender pull of the bandage unrolling from the arm. As the bandage came away he felt the air cool on the hot arm, and at last he could resist it no longer. He opened his eyes and looked down at himself and saw the arm swollen and fiery far up the fleshy part towards the shoulder.

'The arm's putting on weight,' he said.

Sandy did not say anything. He began to roll the bandage back very loosely, pinning it finally with a pin. O'Connor had finished shaving, and now he, too, was looking at the arm.

'We got to get that arm well,' he said.

'What do you mean?' he said. 'A doctor saw it yesterday. It is well.'

Neither O'Connor nor Sandy said anything, and he knew that if it was possible to fool himself it was no use for them. O'Connor wiped his face with a small damp towel. 'All right?' he said.

'Thanks,' Franklin said. 'It feels wonderful.'

'Want something to eat?'

'No, no thanks,' he said.

'Some drink?'

'I could drink and drink,' he said. 'Pints and pints of cold light ale. Pints and pints and pints.'

'The girl brought a big jug of water,' O'Connor said.

The memory of all that had happened, of the night and the girl and the intimate moment by the river, suddenly came back for the first time. The pleasure of it broke through the difficult mist of his consciousness like light. He shut his eyes. All his mind became immediately clear and happy, fresh with recollection, his surprise as great as if he had suddenly had an enormous piece of good luck. Then O'Connor brought the water in a glass jug and made as if to pour it out, but Franklin said, 'No, give me the jug,' and drank straight out of it, spilling some of the water on his shirt. Its cold cleanness had on his body the same effect as the memory of the girl had on his mind. It was like cool light in the dark heat at the back of his throat. He took a second drink and then sat with the jug between his knees, looking at the little remaining water in the jug and then at his face in the water, and then remembering, through the reflection, the face of the girl simply and seriously lifted up to him in the darkness.

When O'Connor had taken the jug away again he lay down. The remembered image of the girl did not retreat. It was to remain fixed in his mind all day, whether she was there or not, cool and clear.

And suddenly he wanted her there. The image was not enough, and in any case, he thought, we have to be rational. There are still five men who have to escape from here.

'Is the girl coming up again?' he said.

'She said someone was to go down if you wanted her,' Sandy said.

'I wanted to talk to her.'

'Taylor will go,' Sandy said.

'No,' he said, 'you go.'

After Sandy had gone downstairs he spoke to O'Connor. He deliberately did not want to speak to Taylor. The two boys stood looking out of the window. They looked very young and no longer tired in the sun.

'Take Goddy and Taylor upstairs,' he said. 'Keep your eye on the roads. And put the map away.'

He shut his eyes so that he should not look at Taylor. His jealousy against him was like a small gritty seed of irritation. The very unreasonableness of it fascinated him. He kept himself close to it, knowing now that it was part of his affection.

When he looked up again the room was empty. Alone, in the emptiness, he realized now that he felt very ill. The separate pain of his arm and head and throat became one acceptable piece of thought, the expression of his entire self, unpleasant but final. He knew that he was slipping towards the point when he would no longer care what happened.

The girl came in with Sandy very quietly, a moment or two later. She was dressed in a short green skirt and a white blouse.

86

The blouse was of some shining thin material that showed the shape of her breasts, and above the white collar of it her brown face looked darker still. He saw her wholly, then as it were fragment by fragment: the black eyes, the clear breasts under the blouse, the brown bare legs below the green skirt.

'Françoise,' he said.

He smiled at her and she came over to him, and for the first time he realized that he had never attempted to get up. 'Jesus, I must be ill,' he thought.

'How is your arm?' she said.

'All right. The bandage became tight in the night. It's better now.'

He looked over her shoulder for Sandy. He was not in the room.

'They said something about passes,' he said.

'Two.'

'Is it safe?'

'There were two aircraft came down,' she said. 'They know about one, but not the other. Not about yours. So it is safe.'

'What kind of aircraft?'

'I don't know,' she said. 'It was north-east of here. You must have come north-west.'

He watched her as she spoke, not caring much what she said. She was kneeling on the floor, her skirt pulled tight across her knees and her hands smoothing it. He wanted to kiss her again, and he felt the excitement of the moment grow bigger than the feeling of illness. He reached forward and pulled her down towards him, and she came without any of the hesitation of the previous night, as if it were all very natural and right and part of the whole ordained pattern of hiding and war and escape. When he had kissed her once she turned her face, and then he held it for a moment with his good hand.

'This is no time,' she said.

'It's the only possible time,' he said.

'There are serious things to talk about.'

'This is serious,' he said.

He said it without thinking, and in a second he saw the light of pain and wonder jump sharply into her face, and he thought, Oh God! I mean it and she isn't sure. Oh hell! he thought, she

87

wants me to mean it and I do mean it, and she isn't sure. It is serious. Jesus, it is serious! 'Please,' he said, 'please.' He looked at her steadily and she looked back, calm and clear, the black eyes so seriously tender again that he knew there was no need to speak any more.

It was she who was rational again at last.

'It will be possible for two to go to-night,' she said. 'Pierre will take them the first part of the way. My father has the papers. It is possible they will go to Paris.'

'To Paris?' he said. It did not seem credible. 'That's back from where we came.'

'You mustn't argue about it.' She took hold of his good hand and held it flattened between her own, the flattened, smooth fingers cool as leaves. 'It's all right. Everything will be all right. It's you we have to look after. Your hands are very hot.'

He smiled. 'It's a hot day.'

'Be frank with me.'

It was no use. His pose seemed suddenly idiotic. I feel ill, he thought. Oh hell! why don't I admit it? I feel bloody and terribly ill. She knows how I feel, and it's stupid to try to fool her any more.

'Be frank with me,' she said. 'The arm is bad, isn't it?'

'It seems very swollen.'

'If it doesn't get any better something will have to be done.'

'I'll try to sleep.'

'If it gets worse sleep won't be enough,' she said.

He lay back. It seemed better once again not to talk about it. Talk seemed only to clip at the edges of reality, made up now of the pain of his body and the pleasure of looking at her. Outside these things it was all unreal, and the clipping frayed his nerves.

'Listen,' she said. 'Don't talk any more. There is no need to talk. I have the two sets of papers here. Don't talk. Just listen. I'll explain what has to be done.'

'Yes,' he said.

'The papers are for Jean Joubert and Michel Lebrun. They are going to Marseilles. To hospital.'

'Hospital!' he said.

'Don't talk.'

'But why hospital?'

88

'They are deaf and dumb.'

The whole thing is mad, he thought. He looked at her, oddly, but did not speak.

'It is very simple,' she said. 'The papers say they are deaf and dumb. In that way there are no questions. If they go to the right people there will be no difficulty. In the same way you can all go.'

He nodded.

'I must go,' she said. 'Who are the two to go to-night?'

'The two young ones. They have always been friends together.'

'Then the ages and descriptions must be filled in.'

'I've got a pen,' he said.

He unscrewed his fountain pen and gave it to her and, with his head lying back, told her what to write. While he watched her writing the description of Taylor and Godwin on the papers he saw the black eyes at intervals raised up to him. They were very beautiful, and once again he was seized by the awful fear that she was too young, too lovely, and too fine to have any part of it all. But the calm supreme assurance of her eyes finally repelled his fear. He decided it was better to take each situation how and when it came.

'They had better get to know the papers,' he said. 'Confidence is everything.'

'Yes.'

'I'm going now.' She laid the papers on his blankets. 'Shall you sleep?'

'I'll try to sleep.'

'Tell the others to sleep, too. They will be travelling all night.'

She bent down and held her face over him. The moment before he touched her had the reality of a dream re-dreamed and joined, finally, to a moment of waking. As if I've been here before, he thought, or as if the vines and the mill and all of it were part of some other life that once happened to me. She kissed him and he discovered that he had hardly the strength to kiss her back. 'Try to sleep,' she said.

'Come back again,' he said.

She smiled and he saw her figure go past the window and then he shut his eyes. Alone, he felt more tired than ever. His eyes began to be beaten with slow recurrent waves of pain, and he had no thought of getting up.

He did not know how long it was before the sergeants came downstairs. They walked quietly and he knew they thought him asleep. He let them come in and then opened his eyes.

'Here, all of you,' he said.

They came and stood by him. It was an effort for him to look up.

'Papers for two,' he said, 'For you and Goddy.' He handed the papers up to Taylor.

Taylor took the papers, read them, and burst out laughing.

'We always knew you and Goddy were dumb,' Franklin said. It did not seem, after all, very funny. 'Now it says so in the papers.'

'Deaf and dumb, Goddy,' Taylor said. 'Deaf and dumb!'

'You're pulling my leg.'

'No, Goddy, it says so!' Taylor said.

'And it means so,' Franklin said. 'It means exactly that. Nothing else. So don't go forgetting it.'

'When do they go?' Sandy said.

'To-night.' Franklin felt terribly sick. His words seemed to be at the far end of a chasm. He groped for them heavily and the sound of them reverberated wildly in his head. 'They'll give you all the final instructions. Memorize the papers and don't do anything they don't tell you. Is that straight?'

'Yes,' Taylor said.

'And remember your own instructions,' he said. Why must I go on talking? he thought. They know this. They've heard it a hundred times. Then he stopped talking. He could not find the words he wanted to say. His mind was chasmic and empty, and a wave of sickness was coming up into his throat.

The four sergeants waited.

At last he found what he had to say. 'If you're caught be bloody careful. However innocent the questions sound make sure they're not. Everything's a trap to get your squadron number, your type of aircraft, your station. So don't answer a damn thing. Just your name and rank and number.'

'In fact, be deaf and dumb,' Goddy said.

They all laughed at that. His eyes were open as the four sergeants laughed, and the sight of their laughing faces, bright against the hot blue square of window and the dark wooden walls, were the last fully coherent and tangible things he remembered. There was nothing else to the day except the increase of pain and sickness and the sweat of his body under the blankets, and whenever he opened his eyes the glaring square of sun, and whenever he shut them the image of the girl steady and bright in the dark confusion of fever.

CHAPTER 9

O'CONNOR roused him a little after eight in the evening. It was not yet dark. The two sergeants were ready to go.

'The Frenchie is here, too,' O'Connor said. 'Pierre.'

'M'sieu,' Pierre said. He stood stiff in the middle of the room. He had his best Sunday black cap in his hands. Franklin saw his hands picking the material of the peak, and thought he looked nervous. 'Everything is ready?' Franklin said.

'Everything is quite ready.'

'Where do you go?'

'Over the hill. There is a short walk and then we pick up the car. It will be dark by then.'

'The taller of the two sergeants speaks French,' Franklin said. 'It will be easy to explain to him.'

'It is all arranged,' Pierre said.

'Good.' Again he did not want to talk. He was sick of himself and the hardness of the floor-boards and the smell of his sweat. His arm now had swollen still more and was tight as a blown-up tyre under the bandages.

'Anything else you wanted to say?'

He looked up and it was Taylor. He was wearing a dark blue beret, and a blue sweater tucked into a pair of navy blue trousers. He looked very French and very young.

'No, I don't think so,' Franklin said. 'It depends on you. We'll come on as soon as we can.'

'All right. Well, we'll say good-bye.'

Franklin held up his hand. It was more of an effort than he expected. Taylor took the hand. It seemed an awkward moment, and they each said 'Good-bye'. Then Goddy came up and Franklin said, 'Good-bye, Goddy. Don't get arsing around too much. Keep your head. If anything goes wrong you can always start walking.'

'Good-bye, Frankie,' Goddy said. 'I hope your arm will be better.'

Franklin smiled. He's a good kid, he thought. A hell of a nice

92

kid. Too nice to be in a war and getting his life balled up. But he probably loves this. 'I hope you get through all right,' he said.

'Lucky sods,' O'Connor said.

Franklin heard the two young sergeants saying good-bye to Sandy and O'Connor, the voices jumbled in his head, and he himself not caring much about it, and then the final words and sounds as the two boys and Pierre went downstairs.

'We can watch them go up the hill,' he heard O'Connor say.

The two elder sergeants stood at the window. There was still some light in the sky. Franklin lay for a moment and then held the topmost blanket under his chin and got slowly up, kneeling first, then standing. He realized then, as he stood there, trusting the weight of his body to his legs and feeling this weight rise slowly up through his body to his head until his head seemed like a great iron ball on a matchstick, that he was very ill. The window was a long way off. He could never reach it. The floor-boards of the little room became suddenly enlarged and stretched away, up a slope, like part of a scenic railway. He held the blanket tight round his chin, stood for a moment, and then painfully walked up the slope to the window.

'What the hell are you out for?' O'Connor said.

'Shut up,' he said. 'Where are they?'

He clung to the window-sill with his finger-tips.

'Hang on to me,' Sandy said.

'I'm all right,' he said. His weakness flooded over him in waves, and the waves in turn folded over each other outside, as part of the increasing darkness.

'They're just going up the path.' O'Connor said. 'The way we came down.'

He looked and could see the dark area of fruit trees and grass, beyond it the lighter area of vines, and to the side of both the white path. Now he could just see the three figures, in single file, going up the path.

And then he thought that there were four figures. For a moment he was not sure. Then he stared again, and the figures dimmed and enlarged with his sickness. Then he had a moment of clarity, when the path and his head seemed to stand still, and he was sure there were four.

'Who else is there?' he said.

'It looks like the girl,' O'Connor said.

A second later he knew his hands were leaving the window-sill. He was already falling before they released their grasp: falling through the cold space of the mill, down through the dark hollows and the water and the air that had been for years without sun. He was going down for ever, baling out like a dead weight, to fall and fall until he struck his arm against the stone somewhere and broke it off like a piece of touchwood on a dead tree swollen by disease and rain.

The fall seemed to last through all the years of his life. He remembered hitting the floor, twisting himself with terror so that his arm should fall free. Then he remembered nothing else until they began to carry him downstairs, O'Connor and Sandy and the girl's father, and across the narrow roadway into the house. He remembered, too, how they carried him upstairs in the house, and how the cold sweat of his faintness lay all the time on his head, which seemed like a wizened and juiceless piece of flesh on his shoulders.

When he came round fully he saw an oil-lamp of opaque white glass burning on a table by the bedside, and the old woman moving about in the low light. This is it, was his first thought, this is it. If they come to us now there's nothing any of us can do. They'll shoot everybody: the old lady and the girl, everybody. There's no escape now. Oh Jesus! what have I gone and done?

His arm hurt like hell. 'Take the bandage off,' he said.

'Don't talk,' the old woman said.

'The bandage is too tight.'

'The bandage has already been changed,' she said.

Nothing made sense. They couldn't have changed it without my knowing, he thought. I haven't been here five minutes. It's only a minute since they carried me up.

'What time is it?' he said.

'It is past the time for talking,' she said. She came and stood in the lamplight, so that she was shadowy and seemed doubly old, her French rugged and rather fast in its half-patois that he could only just understand. 'Past midnight,' she said. 'That's what time it is.' Her shadow was huge and easy on his face.

She stood there, it seemed to him, all night, so that the light

94

should keep out of his eyes. Whenever he woke or opened his eyes the shadow was on his face, but afterwards he knew that it was the whole darkness and that the lamp had gone.

When he really came to himself it was day and the girl was in the room. He could tell by the blue of the sky above the plain, seen through one of the windows, that it was very hot and far into the day. He lay for a long time looking at a large black crucifix hanging on the wall opposite the bed and did not see the girl until she made a sound as she moved. She was sitting by a second window. When she saw him awake she came over to the bed.

She looked very tired. His gladness at seeing her was dry. It had no excitement. He was simply glad.

'What time is it?' he said.

'Three o'clock.' She smiled, but the black eyes were not bright.

'Have I been asleep all that time?'

'Part of it. Yesterday you didn't sleep much.'

'Yesterday?' he said. 'Yesterday?'

Nothing made sense. I remember yesterday, he thought. I remember Taylor and Goddy going, and being at the window, and the fall. I remember being brought here. Yesterday has nothing to do with it.

'This is the third day,' she said.

'Oh God!' he said.

There was no reasoning it out. He lay flat and without strength.

'The doctor is coming to-night,' she said.

'Doctor?'

'The same doctor. The one you saw.'

'Isn't it very dangerous? Why is he coming?'

'There is nothing for it,' she said. 'The arm doesn't get any better.'

He felt small and frightened and confused, lying in the centre of the large feather bed. Nothing was easy. The complication of things had happened without his knowing it, too fast. He couldn't grasp it all.

'There is no need for you to worry,' she said. 'The doctor

95

often comes. He will come for the fishing. No one suspects a fisherman.'

He did not speak. He remembered suddenly a story by de Maupassant, also of France, in a war, of two innocent fishermen who were shot. I'm not so sure, he thought. This is what war does. It is the very innocent who get caught up. They get destroyed.

'You are taking great risks for me,' he said.

'Some time we will talk of it,' she said. 'But not now.'

'Sit down by the bed,' he said.

'I should sit by the window,' she said. 'I can see the road as far up as the bridge from there.'

'Sit down. For a moment,' he said.

She sat down and he turned his face in the bed to look at her. The slight movement made him aware of his arm. It was like a huge flaming weight hanging from his shoulder. Through the increase in his consciousness there crept up, now, the increase of pain.

And now also the impact of pain made him remember things.

'The others!' he said. 'The two sergeants. Are they all right?'

'They want to talk to you. Do you feel strong enough?'

'Soon,' he said.

'It is possible they will go soon,' she said.

They'll have to wait for me, he thought. That means a day or two. At least a day or two. The thought of the doctor was comforting now. He had a spasm of very simple faith about the doctor. He had an idea that he was a very good doctor. He would know what to do. It would be all right.

He looked at the girl and smiled. He loved her suddenly because she was there and did what he asked. It was a lovingness without excitement. It did not seem to him to belong to the moment by the river, when he had kissed her first. It was created out of a new situation and was very gentle. There was no passion in him any longer.

'Will you speak to the sergeants?' she said.

'If I must,' he said. 'Could I drink something first?'

She got up and came round to the other side of the bed. On

the table were two glass jugs and a tumbler, covered over with a cloth. In the smaller of the jugs the liquid was a soft light green. She began to pour it out into the glass.

'What is it?' he said.

'The juice of grapes.' She held up the glass. 'We crushed the grapes for you.'

He could have cried as he heard it. All the complication and love and helplessness inside himself started up and struck with two points of pain behind his eyes. He tried to move and get up. He felt chained down to the bed. It was only when the girl set down the glass on the table and then put both arms round him and he pressed his good hand on the bed that he could get the leverage to pull himself half upright.

All the time he felt his arm dragging him down. When she gave him the tumbler he drank the grape-juice in slow regular sips. It was partly sweet and very cool. Once he did not drink but let his lips stay in the glass, so that the coolness bathed them, and finally, when he lay down again, he let the wetness remain on the cracked dry skin.

'Better,' he said. Apart from the fact that he could feel his heart thundering as if he had been running wildly upstairs it seemed very wonderful.

'Lie still,' she said.

He watched her put the glass back on the table, following her with his eyes but not moving his head. To set the glass down she picked up the cloth. And now, under the cloth, he could see the thermometer.

He did not say anything. She smiled again and put the cloth over the jug and the glasses. 'If you feel all right,' she said, 'I can go for the sergeants now.' Her eyes seemed a little brighter. 'You didn't tell me their names.'

'Sergeant O'Connor,' he said. 'And Sergeant Sanders.'

'I still don't understand your name,' she said.

'My name is John Franklin,' he said. 'I told you.'

'John.' It sounded strange and unintimate to him. No one except his mother ever called him John. 'John,' she said. She pronounced it rather in the French way.

'They call me Frankie,' he said.

'Your name is John,' she said, 'and they call you Frankie.'

97

'It is the diminutive of Franklin,' he said. 'I told you.' He knew she didn't grasp it.

'Frankie,' she said. 'John.'

He knew that she still didn't quite understand, and then he knew also why she didn't understand. It was because she was terribly tired. He knew now why her eyes were not bright. She hadn't slept. And in the moment of realizing it he felt sorry for her and put his good hand over the coverlet and she touched it, in a little gesture of tired and tender acknowledgement, as she went across the room.

Just before she went out he remembered something.

'My revolver,' he said. 'It was round my waist. What happened to it when they undressed me?'

'I think the sergeants have it.'

'Would you tell them to bring it? Please.'

'You don't need it here.'

'Oh! yes,' he said. 'This is the sort of situation I brought it for.'

She smiled back and went out of the room. After she had gone and while he waited for O'Connor and Sandy to come he worked himself up in bed on his good elbow and reached for the thermometer. I'd better face it, he thought. He put the thermometer into his mouth and held it under his tongue. As he waited he looked out of the window and saw the burning heat of the day, all the late summer heat of mid-France, blue and hard, lying cloudless above the yellow plain of the river. Then he looked at the room. It reminded him, with the faded striped wallpaper and the heavy furniture and its partly sanctified smell, of little hotel rooms on the coast of Brittany. It, too, gave him a feeling of having been there before. I feel I had to come here, he thought, and that this bloody arm had to be, and the river, and the girl. His mind could not deal with its thoughts, and he felt himself grow muddled, half-dreaming, and then forgetting the thermometer. Then all of a sudden he remembered it and took it out of his mouth.

He leaned back and tilted it against the light. He saw the mercury darken and then flash like a needle. The reading was just under a hundred and four.

'God,' he thought. 'Now I know.'

He put the thermometer back on the table and lay quickly down. He felt very sick and shaky. How did this happen? he thought. How did I get into this state so quickly? A hundred and four! It must mean that I've been worse than that. I've been a hell of a lot of trouble to them all. I'll be a hell of a lot of trouble yet.

His thoughts had no real coherence again and he let them go. He shut his eyes for a moment, and then was glad to hear O'Connor and Sandy and Françoise coming upstairs. He opened his eyes as they came into the room. The girl looked very lovely and clear and dark beside the two men, O'Connor tough and mousy, Sandy bald and fair, in their makeshift French shirts and trousers.

The two men came and stood a little away from the bed: as if, he thought rather crazily, I'm somebody having a baby in a hospital.

'You're a nice one,' O'Connor said.

'I'm sorry,' he said. 'I got you all into this mess from the first.'

'Oh! yes,' O'Connor said. 'I saw you climb out of the kite and break the bloody airscrew with your hands.'

'How do you feel?' Sandy said.

'I don't know,' he said. 'I don't know quite what day it is.'

The girl, hearing the conversation in English, was standing away at the window.

'Do you feel well enough to hear something?' O'Connor said.

'You're going,' Franklin said. 'I know.'

'That's the point,' O'Connor said. 'We're not going.'

'Don't talk cock!' he said. His anger was only a husk remaining from his earlier emotion. 'If the arrangements are for you to go, you go.'

'Let's talk sense,' O'Connor said. 'You've been bloody ill. How can we go?'

'It would look bad on us if we went,' Sandy said, 'and for some reason they found you here and you never got back.'

'That's just supposition.' Oh, hell! he thought, why must they argue?

'It's a supposition that stinks,' O'Connor said. 'We're not leaving you.'

99

He did not answer immediately. All his arguments were ready: he was too weak and stupefied to marshal them at once. Already, too, the talking had weakened him, so that the whole of his body, with the exception of his arm, felt stripped bare of strength, even the veins empty. Only the arm was fully and fiercely alive with its tight and bloated pain.

At last he said what he had to say. 'Every day you stop here means added risk for these people. One man is one risk. Five men is five times the risk. Every time we can lessen it it's a good thing. If the papers are ready you go. That's all.'

'Look, Skip,' O'Connor said.

'You go,' he said, 'and you go as soon as you can.'

'You're bloody stubborn.'

'I know I'm bloody stubborn,' he said, 'and that's why I'll be all right. Anyway, it's easier alone.'

'Can we wait till the doctor has been to-day?' Sandy said.

'You can wait,' he said, 'but it will make no difference at all.'

He lay flat in the pillows, looking at the two men who had been on so many trips with him and who had always trusted him yet never said they trusted him, and for whom he in turn had great trust and admiration and affection and yet similarly never spoke of it. His terms of dealing with them had always been service terms: the odd, boyish, sometimes silly service language that came out of their exclusive world, for nobody else to understand. Behind this language, you could take refuge from the fear and reality of the business. They were rarely outspoken. Now the three of them, O'Connor, Sandy and himself, had been more outspoken with each other in these few days in France than ever before. It struck him as an ironic possibility that they were really getting to know each other.

'Did you bring my revolver?' he said.

'Yes, I got it,' O'Connor said. He took the revolver out of the inside of his shirt and laid it on the bed. 'She's not loaded.' He took twenty rounds of ammunition from his pocket and dribbled it on the bed, too.

'Thanks,' Franklin said. 'You never know.' It all seemed a little strained and O'Connor and Sandy looked very miserable.

'Look, let's get this cleared up,' he said

100

The two men did not speak.

'I can do it alone. If I'd been a fighter boy there'd have been no question of doing it otherwise.'

'You're not a fighter boy,' O'Connor said. 'You're part of us. We're a unit. We always have been.'

'Oh! wrap up,' he said. He felt very tired and he could feel the coherence of his thoughts slipping away again. 'You're going, and that's that.'

'Is that final?' O'Connor said.

'It's final,' he said. He grinned good-naturedly at them, bearing no ill-will but rather amused, under his thick-headedness and pain, at their awkward misery.

'O.K.,' O'Connor said. 'You're the boss. But we go under bloody protest, I tell you.'

'Good old Connie,' he said.

'You'd better get some rest,' Sandy said.

'Yes,' Franklin said. 'Come and see me again before you go.'

They went out together. They looked very miserable. The interview was over; he felt like a business man who has withheld an order. He closed his eyes. The strain of talking instantly began to make itself felt, so that he seemed doubly weak and buoyant on the bed. An awful wave of sickness flew over him and he felt as if he would float away.

He wondered all the time why the girl did not come to the bed. He wanted her very much. I was rather good with the boys, he thought. I had all the arguments. I could translate for her what I said. He lay listening for her footsteps to come across the room, knowing all the time that she was there, by the window, watching the plain, and because he was so sure not even looking up. Once he stretched out his arm across the bed and said 'Françoise,' but she did not answer. His feeling for her was as clear as the square blue light of afternoon sun through the window. It was as serene and permanent as the sunlight. Beside it all the rest of him now seemed sick and tangled and hollow.

He came to himself about four hours later without having any idea of what time it was. But now the light lace curtains had been drawn over the open window, and from the plain a light wind had sprung up and was blowing the curtains irregularly to and fro. Once again he had the feeling that he had slept for a few moments, that the girl was still there, and that he was still waiting for her to come.

When he at last looked up she was not there, and his revolver was not on the bed. But he had the feeling of a presence in the room, and he saw the old woman, after a moment or two, walk across his line of vision and go out without a word.

He was confronted almost immediately, it seemed, by a question. For a second he could not remember the voice.

'What is this I hear?'

He looked up. Far away, very far away, a little out of focus, stood the doctor.

Franklin did not speak. You know how I feel, he thought. You don't expect me to speak. You've come for the fishing. I must ask you about it.

'Can you hear me?' the doctor said. 'Are you still sleepy?'

Hellish, Franklin thought. He tried to smile. He felt the smile crack his dry lips as they expanded. The light wind, blowing the curtains, blew the vague image of the doctor nearer, swaying it greyly in and out of focus.

The doctor went on speaking. Franklin realized that what he was saying was of immense importance, but he did not care. For some moments his mind did not respond in French, then it cleared and he grasped that the doctor was talking about a hospital.

'Hospital?' he said.

'I have to tell you that at this time the record of French hospitals is not good.'

'Hospital?'

'For such an arm as yours there is no course but hospital.'

Franklin did not speak. Why can't you stand still? he thought. Please stand still. Now what? What hospital?

'You yourself have to make the choice of course.'

Franklin struggled into a moment of coherent response.

'Between what?'

'Between going to the hospital as a prisoner and remaining here.'

There's only one answer to that, he thought. Why trouble to put it like that?

102

'For hiding an escaping airman the complications would be very serious?' he said.

'As you know.'

'No complications,' he said. 'Please. I want to stay here.'

It seemed a long time before the doctor spoke again.

'There is the other side of the picture,' he said at last.

'Yes?'

He saw the face of the doctor blown slowly forward into focus, out again, and then once more in towards him, this time to remain, grey and fixed and living.

'You must be fully aware of what it means to remain here.'

I am aware, he thought. No one is more aware. I know what it means for you.

'I find it difficult to tell you,' the doctor said.

'I am fully aware,' he said. 'There is no need.'

'It is not quite that,' the doctor said.

He retreated again, blown out of focus, and then came back. to be fairly steadfast once more.

'No,' he said. 'This is what you must understand.' The voice was kindly, distant, almost a whisper. 'If you remain here it will be necessary to take off the arm.'

The words hit him and then were swept far away, part of all the bad dreams of his sickness, as if blown on a wind of terror. This terror was a single violent emotion that came burning out of all his flying life. It was the biggest horror he had ever known. Jesus, he thought; please! Jesus! The terror seemed to career furiously round the whole world, like a terrific living comet of protest, and then complete its crazy circumnavigation in his face. It broke its motion against his eyes and became instantly a single and more terrible thought. 'I'll never fly again, I'll never fly again. Jesus, I'll never fly again, I'll never fly again! I'll never fly again!'

'You would like a few moments alone?' the doctor said.

'No.'

What can I do? he thought. If this is it, this is it. There's nothing for it now.

'The complications for you remain,' he said to the doctor.

'We will take care of that. A few more complications in France will hardly be noticed.'

103

'Be frank with me,' he said.

Franklin held the grey kindly face in focus, as he might have held the sight of a gun.

'I will be frank,' the doctor said. 'If you go to hospital they will take off the arm. There is no choice. If the operation is done now I have complete confidence. I will bring my brother from the hospital itself. He is a surgeon. Very competent. He needs some fishing, too.'

'When will you do it?'

'I hope to-night. There is no need to worry.'

Franklin, not answering at once, suddenly remembered Sandy and O'Connor.

'What time to-night?'

'It will probably be late. I have to get word to my brother. He has to get here. Don't worry.'

'I am not worrying for myself,' Franklin said.

'Don't worry for us, either.'

'It is the other two,' Franklin said. 'They are going to-night. I don't want them to know.'

'It will be all right,' the doctor said.

Franklin saw him recede for the final time out of focus. He felt very tired. He tried to say something to the doctor, but the words never came and, in any case, he thought, he isn't there to listen. There was nothing there at all now except the lightly blowing curtains moving in the wind coming up from the sunny evening plain, far away on the edge of the world. He wanted the girl very badly to be near him because he knew now, for a small moment of relief in a long obscure dream, that she had not really been there all the afternoon.

Her absence flung him down into a final moment of despair.

'I'll never fly again,' was all he could think now. 'Jesus! I'll never fly any more.'

CHAPTER 10

AFTER she had watched the two English sergeants disappear down the track that wound along the ridge above the vineyard, their striped shirts too blue and dangerous in the parallel bars of oak-shade and late sunlight that cut the track below the young trees, the girl took a few paces down the slope towards the house and then suddenly lay down in the rough grass, burnt brittle by summer on the unshaded part of the slope above the vines. She lay face downwards, her mouth open a little, panting. The heat of the day that had seemed to come down through glass now seemed to reflect back from the earth in a breath of solid dust. She shut her mouth and, putting her hands under her face, let her breath come in heavy gasps that sucked the flesh of her brown wrists. She was lying roughly in the place where Franklin had first stopped to look down at the mill below the vines, and now as she looked downwards and slantwise across her flattened hands she could see the same empty and silent valley, with the mill white between the orchard grass and the corn beyond. She looked down and waited, as he had done, for something to happen. All the time she could feel her heart pounding against the warm earth and the echo of it beating back against her chest. And all the time as she lay there, thinking of the blue and dangerous shirts of the two men who had gone, and of what was going to happen in the house below, and watching for something to happen that never did happen, she told herself that she was not afraid. Not very afraid.

She lay there for about twenty minutes, twice turning round on her back to watch the track between the oaks as if she half expected to see the two sergeants coming back, and once very startled by a voice shouting in the fields below. It was only a woman calling a cow somewhere beyond the river, but the sound in the dead calm air seemed to hit her heart, so that she held her hands against it, pressing down the frightened pain. She felt now as Franklin had done, but without knowing it: young and tense on the edge of danger, her finger on the thread that held the world together, and not knowing if or how soon the thread would break. She lay there for a few minutes after the voice had called, still feeling the breath of the hot earth like solid dust against her face, and then suddenly she got up and went down the path, her face firm and calm, as if she had at last made up her mind.

There was no one in the kitchen of the house when she got there, and she did not call. The little air that stirred down by the water had in it the smell of corn. She stood in the kitchen and listened, her head up, but there was no sound from upstairs. A black hat was lying on the table, and there was another, brown-grey, on the chair by the door. She knew then that the two doctors had come back. She picked up the hats and hung them on the peg on the kitchen door. Her brown feet were flat in their heel-less rubber sandals, so that when she moved she seemed to skim about the floor of the kitchen. The silence was quite strange; it was very living. It seemed to her like the silence before a baby is born. It held the house in a stretched light web that she broke for a moment by opening the cupboard under the big wooden dresser. From the cupboard she fetched down a canvas bag and two sections of a heavy bamboo fishing pole. She carried the bag and the pole in her right hand, and as she skimmed out of the kitchen the web of silence closed in on the house behind her, fine and complete again.

Beyond the mill, on the north side, under the wet stones where the sun never reached, there were always small striped worms, almost like small carmine watch-springs coiled in the clay. She spent five minutes getting enough worms to fill the tobacco-tin she carried in the bag. Then she went down to the river edge to where a boat, broad and shallow, lay tied up to the jetty chain-locked to an iron ring in the stone. As she got into the boat and unlocked the chain, and then took one of the heavy oars and pushed away from the jetty, she thought once again, but almost for the last time, of the two sergeants. Her fear about them had become a memory. She looked up the slope and thought of the bright blue shirts, and then mentally crossed herself, thinking quite simply, 'I forgot to give them a blessing. Perhaps that's why I was frightened.' She stood up in the boat and pushed the oar hard against the stone, her brown arms tightened, and felt the boat curve away on the stream with its moving buoyancy. 'The Blessing of God on you now, wherever you are,' she thought. 'And a little luck, too.'

The boat was very heavy and sluggish against the stream, and as she pulled it against the sun she felt the heat burning the back of her neck and shoulders as it came flat from the west across the water. She pulled hard for about two minutes, beyond the orchard where Franklin had first kissed her, and where the apples, from a distance, now looked like glowing russet berries in the sun. On the right bank, as she rowed, big willow trees leaned with flat branches down to the middle surface of the stream, with stretches of water-lilies, flowerless now, in the open spaces between. The water was very clear, too clear she thought, in the stiller pools between the lilies, and over it all was the smell of water, warm and thick like the distant smell of the sea after the heat of the day.

She rowed a little farther, until she could no longer see the mill beyond the big bend of the stream, and then tied up the boat on the right bank, under a line of willows. Two hundred yards upstream was an iron bridge built into concrete supports, in a single span on which, in the early days of the occupation, a sentry had waited to halt the farm traffic that never came. Now the Germans had taken him away.

She tied the boat up to the branch of a willow and began to fit together the two sections of the rod. The whole rod was about fourteen feet long. She threaded about thirty feet of line through the rings and then tied it, without a reel, to the thicker end. She had made a float from a goose-quill, and she fixed that, with a rather large hook, to the free end of the line. She nicked a worm on the end of the hook and then swung the line, in a low cast, across the stream. When the float stood straight the flow of the stream took it away to the full curve of the line so that it circled down beyond the bows of the boat and back again until it rested just clear of a ring of lily leaves. The girl tightened the line and rested the rod in a rowlock of the boat.

The sun had fallen quite rapidly in the time it had taken her to row up the river, and now the light was falling so that the roots of the willow, now in shadow, were losing their look of scarlet hair. They flowed with the motion of the stream like

107

tawny strands of seaweed, darkening every time the girl looked into the depth of the stream.

She sat there for a long time watching the willow-roots and the float and the sun moving away from the water before the fish began to rise downstream beyond the lilies. She sat quite silent, only once moving to take off her sandals and rest her sun-striped feet on the edge of the boat. The blankness of the sunless water seemed to create, in turn, a blankness across her eyes. She could not feel her heart. The water seemed to have made it tranquil, too.

When the fish began to rise, ringing the water and even flopping out of it, she moved to the bows of the boat and cast the line farther downstream. In another hour it would be dark. She tried not to think about Franklin. She was not quite sure what was going to happen back in the house. She knew quite well, with two doctors, that the situation was now very serious. She knew quite well how dangerous it was. But she had no thought to bring to it, as if she knew quite well that thought alone could not change it, any more than thought could help her to catch fish. At the back of her mind there was instead a continuous and unsteady flow of prayer. It was continuous because it was made up of her own patience and faith, and unsteady because its words were nothing but emotions. There were no words that could possibly have the strength of her emotions. Her emotions rose out of her body and became transposed into terms of natural prayer before she could guide or stop them.

The tension of her face that was fixed but tranquil broke when the float went down. She saw it disappear below the lily-pads with eyes that did not seem to be conscious of looking. She struck light but firm, and felt the fish draw the line from her fingers like the gut of a catapult. When she pulled it in it was a perch of about a pound. She laid it on the bottom of the boat and pressed it with her bare knee, covering the back spines, while she took the hook out of its mouth. The hook was really too long and had bitten deeply in, and when she had it free there was a little blood on her hands.

The fish flopped about in the bottom of the boat as she baited the hook and threw it in again. The sun was almost down. She put one of her sandals on the fish and then her foot on the sandal to keep it quiet. The perch would bite fast now. She would be able to go back and tell the two doctors of the new good place. The perch, too, would be good after the eels which Pierre caught in the trap below the mill, and which had begun to sicken her now after months and months of the occupation. She sat immovable, her dark eyes on the float. When it jigged and went down again her eyes did not flicker. She pulled in the line and unhooked the fish, a perch a little larger than the first, the hook coming free of its own accord, so that there was no blood on her hands. Her heart was beating a little faster now because of the excitement of the fish, but her eyes still did not move. They had all the steadfast and wonderful assurance, if anything a little brighter, that Franklin had first seen in the morning sun.

The twilight seemed to come down very rapidly with the next three fish. The doctors will eat two each, she thought. I must have ten. The goose-quill was white, almost luminous, in the oil-green water, and the little wind that stirred the lily leaves had in it the first coolness of the entire day. She would not see much longer now. She waited, watching the float with her dark bright eyes. She waited for about ten minutes, but nothing happened, and finally she shut her eyes and immediately, as it had always done when she was a child, prayer involuntarily slid through her mind: just one more, Holy Mother, just one, not a very big one but big enough, Holy Mother, please. Only about half a pound. Just one more, please. Just one. She opened her eyes and looked at the float. Nothing had happened. She shut them again. If I have faith can there be one? I have faith. I have great faith. Let there be just one more. My faith is eternal.

She kept her eyes closed for about a minute longer, and then slowly opened them. Her heart came thumping up into her throat as she saw the float no longer there, and she forgot all about her faith and began to pull in the line. It seemed very heavy and the fish made big swirls in the water, breaking the surface at last. She held the line very tight and swung the fish into the boat. Its spines pricked up like a hedgehog, but she held them down with her knee and then began to take the hook out of its mouth. The bait had been gorged and the hook was far down. The fish was about two pounds, and in her excitement she was clumsy and pulled too hard on the hook, so that it came away bloody, tearing the lip, the blood running over her hands. And in that moment, as the hook tore the flesh of the fish and the blood spewed scarlet on her brown hands, in the twilight, she knew for the first time what they were going to do to Franklin.

She felt very weak and sick as she began to row slowly back downstream. The fish flopped about in the bottom of the boat and she did not trouble to put on her shoes. She rowed with her eyes on the water. They were troubled with new light. It was the first time since Franklin had walked down through the orchard that morning that she had felt anything like terror. She had never been really afraid: only excited. Only very, very excited so that her excitement was itself an exultation that could not help, in turn, giving her that air of sublime assurance that was sometimes, to Franklin, quite unreal. She had always felt very much as if anything that had happened had been bound to happen. She had always wanted it to happen. She did not understand much about the war, at least about the intricacies of war, but what she understood was very clear and simple. She understood that the war was not finished. She understood that the war could be carried on in France, without arms, and that, by the Grace of God, it must be carried on. She was very young, but the war had a way of making her feel very old, and sometimes she felt that Franklin had come by the Grace of God, too.

She felt very old, her sickness cold and sour, as she pulled the heavy boat downstream. It was almost dark now, and the little light on the water was splintered by the boat like delicate glass. As she rowed by the orchard she remembered the moment there with Franklin, under the apple trees. It was a very wonderful moment, and it, too, had seemed inevitable. She had known that it had to happen. And now as she remembered it she was struck by the terror that it would never happen again. It was no longer a simple affair of hiding and escape. There were many people in it now, and soon someone would say too much. Franklin would be taken and in turn, she thought in terror, they will take us out and shoot us. They will take me out and

110

shoot me too, and what happened under the apple trees will not even be a memory.

She tried to calm herself as she walked up from the river to the house, carrying the fish with one hand in a basket-bag. She carried her shoes and the rod in the other. But she could not even feel calm as she stood still by the door outside the house and listened. There was nothing to hear except the sound of her own heart and the noise of the mill-water rushing away in the silence.

After listening for a moment or two she opened the kitchen door and went in. The lamp was burning on the table and the old woman was laying knives and forks on the cloth. The girl did not speak, but her eyes flickered a little, for the first time, as she came into the light of the lamp. The doctor from the town, whom she knew better than the doctor from the hospital, was drying his arms on a towel. His face looked grey and tired, and he did not speak. She went past him and slid the fish into the sink.

Before she could turn on the tap to wash the fish the doctor from the hospital came downstairs and into the kitchen. He walked straight over to the sink where the girl stood. He was carrying something in a towel. The towel looked like a red and white flag.

'Good fish,' he said.

She looked up and was too startled to answer. He too looked grey and tired. His collar was undone and the black tie had been loosened and pulled down. He put the bundle in a chair.

Her terror became wild and fresh as she saw his hands stretch out towards the tap. It spurted with a great ice-cold jet across her mind as the tap itself was turned and loosened the water. She saw the hands and then the arms, up to elbows, wet and bright with moist splashes of blood, and then the tap itself bloody as the hands were taken away and finally the water itself turning from purity to broken scarlet as the hands were held there. She watched it all for about half a minute without moving, her eyes never flickering, until the blood and her terror were one as completely as the water and her terror had been.

She put her hands on the edge of the sink at last and clung to it as if she were faintly clinging to the edge of the world.

111

In the room behind her she vaguely heard the old woman pushing back the bolt of the door. There was no other sound except the sound of running water, and nothing to be seen now, in her eyes, except the blood of the fish and the blood of Franklin mingling and swirling away in the sink together.

CHAPTER 11

FRANKLIN reached up with his fingers to the edge of consciousness holding on to it by the tips of them. It was his first coherent movement, fully realized. Far back, a lifetime away, perhaps in another life, he was aware that consciousness had reached down to him. It had come in the form of a bowl, cool and hard and held by someone without a word against his throat. He had been very sick into it several times.

His movement now was different. It was positive. He reached up with one hand, holding on to the ledge between darkness and light, waited for a moment before reaching up with the other. Then after a moment or two the horizon of light lowered and became steady. He was looking over the top.

The reality of everything was now heightened by the fact that everything was cut in half. He was lying flat on his back, so stiff that it seemed he might be strapped down, and he could see only the upper half of a chair, a chest of drawers, a window, the wounded upper half of the crucified Christ on the wall, and finally the upper half of the old woman, black and white and immobile, against the blue upper half of summer sky.

He pulled himself fully into consciousness and then became aware, at once, that he had never moved. He lay very still. To be still but also to be aware, to be aware but also to be alive, seemed suddenly miraculous.

He lay looking for some time at the sky. It was vastly blue and very distant. It fixed for him, for the first time, his sense of place. With such blueness, without cloud, he knew that he could never be in England. Through this realization, and through the clear hot blueness of the day, he finally became fully awake.

He became immediately aware of the tightness of his stomach. He needed the bed-bottle. In hospital, he understood, such desires were as natural as requests for tooth-brushes. Now he was faced with the necessity of translating it into another language. He lay thinking for some moments how the French were a people of good sense in fundamental things, but how

113

also, in his French, there was no word for what he wanted to do. Then he knew, too, that it did not matter. He knew that nothing mattered: except perhaps the steadiness and beauty of the blue daylight beyond the window. As long as this light did not recede he knew that his life had been recaptured.

'Madame,' he said. He did not move as he spoke.

The old woman moved at once, as if she knew quite well he was conscious, and even as if she knew what he wanted.

'M'sieu,' she said. He watched her come fully, entire, over the edge of his vision. She stood by the bed with the sick-bowl in her hands.

'You want to be sick now? Again?' she said.

'No,' he said.

'You want something?'

'Yes.'

'What is it? You don't want to eat, do you?'

'No,' he said, 'I don't want to eat.' He searched his mind for the word, but could not find it. He knew one word, but it was, he felt, slightly lacking, even in French, in delicacy. He decided to try bottle.

'The bottle?' she said. Her face lifted itself slightly, unconcerned, earthy, too immensely old he thought to worry about the delicacy of life any longer. She moved away, and then, almost at once, came back. It appeared that the bottle had been standing ready.

The bottle was a dark claret bottle without a label and she came back with it on what was to him the left side of the bed. She held it out without concern. He did not even attempt to take it from her but lay with his right arm uplifted and dead still under the sheet, poised as his mind was poised in the oddest and most awful moment of his life. He was poised bodily as if he were going to overbalance and fall over sideways, like an aircraft without a wing. He knew in that moment that he had no left arm.

The old woman must have understood the moment. She stood quite still, holding the bottle but not speaking, waiting for the shock to pass. He did not move, partly through the shock but partly because of an absurd fear, acutely real, of falling out of bed.

114

'You will feel better when you have used it,' she said at last.

With some difficulty he raised his right arm above the coverlet. He still felt strapped down. He knew that the other arm was not there, but there was no sensation of emptiness, only of distrust. All of his body was stiff with caution. The fingers of his right hand outstretched themselves, stiffened and would move no further. The old woman was forced to put the bottle into it. He remembered then that he did not know what day it was, and wanted to ask her. 'Merci, madame. Merci beaucoup,' he said, but she had moved away.

She gave him two minutes, standing all the time by the window. He spent one of these minutes reaching over his right arm to the left side of himself. Where the left arm should have been there was a circular corset of bandage that wrapped over his chest; hence his feeling of being strapped down. It all seemed very clean and finished and neat. Feeling the shape of the bandage he thought, 'I have to know some time', and let his right hand slip down towards his waist. From somewhere about the height of his ribs there was nothing left. They had taken off the arm above the elbow.

'M'sieu has finished?'

She was standing by the bed. He smiled and drew the bottle out with ironic triumph, like a secret drinker. She smiled, too.

'What day is it?' he said. She took the bottle, meditatively. She might have been thinking, it seemed, that he had done very well. He felt it too.

'Wednesday,' she said. 'It was Monday when they operated.'

'Everything is all right?'

'With you? Yes,' she said.

'No,' he said. 'Not only with me. But with the rest. With everything.'

She shrugged her shoulders and looked at the bottle. 'It is all right. If anything in France is all right.'

'I see,' he said.

'They say there have been riots up in the north. That will mean something.'

She moved away to the foot of the bed, talking a little more, in a low voice, half to herself. He saw her screw up her eyes, into crumpled pouches, greyish yellow against the light. You

115

could not tell what suffering had made up her life, or if only time and sun had wrinkled the skin of her face below the stringy hair.

'I am old enough to remember the war of 1870,' she said. She opened the window and emptied the bottle over the sill.

He waited. The bottle seemed to empty very slowly. He heard the splash below.

'As a little girl, in the Paris district, I saw plenty of arms cut off then,' she said. 'Plenty.'

He felt like a small boy; the distance gaping between them was part of history, half the earth. She held the bottle over the sill some time after it had emptied, and did not move. It occurred to him then that she, being so old, might have become happily confused in time, and that she did not even know which war it was. But he was disillusioned.

'I saw plenty in the Great War too,' she said. 'That was butchery.'

What is she trying to tell me? he thought. He watched her give the bottle a final shake, and then she came over again. slowly, to the bed.

'With a sword,' she said, 'that's how they cut them off. I will put the bottle on the table now. So that it will be there when you want it again.'

'I could drink,' he said.

'There is wine and water in the carafe,' she said. 'Can you drink it if I pour it out?' She picked up the carafe and took off its muslin cover. The wine was red, watered down until it was slightly paler than *vin rosé*. The rosy brightness looked tranquillizing and very cool. 'In the Great War they carted them about like animals. Dear God,' she said. 'Dear God.'

She poured out a little of the wine, the movement casual and meditative, as with the bottle.

'Did you ever hear of the mutiny?'

'Of the French?'

'Of the French,' she said, 'in the Great War. How they rioted at the Gare du Nord and would not go. You have heard of it? And other things?'

'Vaguely,' he said. He raised himself up, with some difficulty. on his right elbow. She stood holding the wine.

116

'It would be vaguely,' she said. 'It was never in the papers.'

'No,' he said. 'It never is in the papers.' This war was after all the same as others.

She held the glass on his lips and he guided it with his own hand. Movement had drawn the entire strength from his fingers, leaving them like flaky shells of dry flesh. He felt they would crumble to pieces. The wine was cold and a little tart on his lips, and as he swallowed it he discovered how sour his mouth had been.

'That was when France was beaten,' she said. 'Not now. In this war. But then. We were never the same after that.'

The light from the window beat on his eyes. He lowered them and drank again. His strength had practically gone. The last crust of feeling peeled away from his fingers.

'Thank you very much,' he said. 'Thank you.'

'We were no good in this one,' she said, 'because we were butchered in the last. Too many of us were butchered.'

Holding the carafe and the glass, not quite emptied, she stood looking at him and yet past him, inconceivably sad and at the same time not flickering the immeasurably stoical colourless eyes. She shook her head several times and then slowly poured the wine back from the glass into the carafe. 'Yes,' she said. 'Yes. You are very lucky.'

I don't quite see it, he thought. If the Jerries come now I shan't be very lucky. His thoughts were incongruous, but not bitter. The bouncing, slamming beat of blood in his head had gone. But from now on, he thought, I have to get my trousers on with one hand. Why am I lucky?

She set down the carafe on the table, slowly, so that he saw in the movement, like a revelation, bitter and reproachful, all the trial and weariness of her life. She seemed in that moment very, very old. He could not bear the age and anguish of her eyes staring past him, and he knew in another moment why he was lucky. It was because, if the Jerries came, it was not he but they who would suffer. They would take him away and put him safely, somewhere, in a hospital. They would take the rest away, the father, Pierre, the old woman, and the two doctors, and shoot them. They might even, because they liked thoroughness, shoot the horse, too. And they would shoot Françoise.

117

He remembered her suddenly with alarm. Oh God! he thought, this is a mess. This is the bloodiest mess I ever got myself or anyone else into. Where is she? He looked up to see the old woman walking back across the room, her face not less anguished than the wooden face, dirty with time and blood, of the Christ on the wall. 'Where is Françoise?' he said. For about ten seconds she moved on without speaking. She crossed into the window square of blue sunlight, ready to sit down. Jesus, he thought, Jesus, something has happened. They've done something to her. He felt something greater than his own strength flare up through his body and blow away with its frightened beat all his weakness. Christ Almighty, he thought, if they've done anything to her! 'Where is she, madame?' he said. 'Where is she?'

Her answer came back as she sat down, slowly, her body terribly reluctant to bend. It shocked him by its infinite calmness. She seemed to be much more occupied with bending her stays to the shape of the chair.

'She is digging worms for fishing,' she said.

He had no answer. Well, God, he thought. The French are wonderful. Amazed, he stared at the ceiling. Fishing? He seemed to see her sitting on the stones below the mill race, with calm and lovely assurance, watching the float still in the dark pool. The image of her strengthened, the sunlight poured across it, and the tenderness he felt for her made it finally real. This tenderness, growing and softening, lifting his amazement into wonder, was so fine and sharp that he could not suppress a comparison. You'd catch Diana doing that. Yes, you'd catch her. Twice, he thought. Diana digging worms and her mother, in the bedroom, emptying the bed-bottle from the window.

His thoughts, almost for the first time unobscured by pain and free to go, went back to England. They took him out of the bedroom on an excursion many times more swift than the movement of the old woman, getting up from the creaking chair and going out at the same time. He thought of Diana. Her other name was Forester. In the days before the revolutionary breaking of an airscrew above the Alps she had been his girl. She seemed, as he looked back, an unreal person, as all experience before that moment seemed also unreal. His life with her had

118

been the life of a thousand pilots. Because it hung on a thread, which you were not sure if the night would break, it was brave to swing it violently. Drinking a lot, dancing, being rather brutally foolish in hotel bars, you persuaded yourself that this happy riot successfully held back all your ideas of apprehension and pain. Like a child, you did not like sleeping in the darkness alone, and after an operation or two over Germany you were glad to sleep with the light burning. It was less terrifying that way. And since you constantly needed light to counteract the darkness you found someone like Diana. It was not right to call her popsie. Clean and bright and smooth, with her bleached blonde hair and reddened fingers and her clear breasts that seemed purposely uplifted, she was much more like a light than a girl. And looking back now he felt that she might have been extinguished just as simply, and without pain.

She will not want me with one arm, he thought. Of the injustice of this, since it was pure speculation, he did not think. He knew only that the life behind him had gone. He thought of various screaming nights in the local towns, crashing traffic lights, with girls screaming in the back of the car, everyone having a wizard time. Wizard: the word had grown crusts on it. What fun! A few more operations, perhaps, and he would have won the DFC. That, too, would have been a wizard thing. She would have liked me with the medal, he thought, more than without the medal; but not without the arm.

Of England, his other thoughts were simple. He wanted a cup of tea. Since it must now be mid-afternoon he found himself alone in the room, listening for the encouraging, clean, beautiful sound of rattled tea-cups. But as he lay there he could hear nothing but the deep and audible silence of the full summer day, so strong and drowsy that it seemed to press both his mind and body deeply back into the bed. Diana and tea and England: all of them like small and faintly unreal clouds, far distant and at the point of evaporation, on the horizon of the present world. A long time before they come any nearer, he thought. Ah well!

Then he shut his eyes, and the moment of first depression came. It's no use, he thought. The arm has gone and I feel as sick as hell about it, bloody sick. I can get most things back, but not the arm. They can't stick that on again. When the depression lifted slightly, swam before his eyes like a moving and darker shadow, and then halted a little distance away, he thought there was something curious about it, and opened his eyes.

The girl was standing by the bed. She did not evoke in him a single thought. He felt only, with his whole body, the bright and serious calmness of her young face. It seemed in fact younger than ever, its youth having a fresh and lovely brilliance, and her eyes, as always, the bright and almost shocking assurance that he had noticed on the first morning. He had nothing to say, and she did not speak either. She gave one short smile and then bent down, reaching towards the bed, putting her face against him. The sunburn of her dark face was very warm, first against his face and then his hand. She let her face remain very lightly against him, and he put his hand on her neck as he kissed her. In the obsession of the moment it was only dimly, and only with small bitterness, that he remembered he would never embrace her again with both hands.

'Everything is all right?' she said.

'Everything.' He smiled. His great surprise about her seemed to uplift him.

'Is there anything you want?'

'No,' he said, 'nothing at all.'

Smoothing with his right hand the whole length of her bare, brown arm he said: 'You're very brown. You've been in the sun.' She smiled. No, there was nothing he wanted: except this, the moment of being fully aware, the brownness of her arms, the secure, beautiful relief of living. She smiled again and pressed her face against him. No, there was nothing he wanted.

'How is the situation?' he said. 'The war?'

'Don't worry about it,' she said.

'Bad?'

'It's always bad,' she said. 'But don't worry about it.'

'Have they given up looking for me?'

'They never give up looking for anyone,' she said.

How soon can I get well? he thought. I ought to be walking. How long does an arm take? An arm you haven't got? He tried to remember somebody to whom something like this had happened. Buddy Saunders, a rear gunner, had a foot shot off by tracer. They kept him on his back three months. Too long. He remembered others. Robertson, a second dicky, with a flak-hole in this thigh big enough to take a cricket-ball. They had stuffed the hole with foreign tissue or something, sealed it and then let it ferment. This lasted two months. During this time the hole gave out, with a stench of rotten fish, all the putrefied elements: the bone, the shrapnel, the threads of cloth and a gallon or so of unholy rottenness. It was four months before Robertson could walk.

But they were legs, he thought. This is an arm. I don't even have to swing it because it isn't there to swing. Therefore I could do it in a few days. He held with his only hand the girl's warm upper arm, involuntarily tightening his hand. In fact, I have to. I'm pretty fit really. It will take more than this to knock me back. I have to do it. I must.

Lying there, touching her arm, feeling the good warm flesh, so tender and smooth, living with sun, he felt new life flow into him. Because of this vibration of new feeling, free and without pain, he felt that there was nothing he could not do if he wanted to do it enough.

He became aware, at the same time, of someone in the room. He looked beyond the girl's black hair and saw the old woman move, quiet as ever, across the sunlight. The girl raised her head. She spread her hands across the counterpane, smoothing it in a gesture of smiling embarrassment. The old woman simply and, he thought, with some irony, said 'Pardon', and came on towards the bed.

He saw that she was carrying a cup and saucer. He tried to think of the French for 'sitting up and taking notice', or some such phrase, having an idea that he would like to show them that he was a man of humour, rapidly getting well. But he could not translate it. He only smiled instead. Both the girl and the old woman smiled in reply, and as he worked himself slightly upright on the pillows, the old woman bent down with the cup.

As she lowered it he saw at last what it was. It was a cup of tea: French tea – pale, creamy, and hot. As it came towards him he made the involuntary attempt to grasp it with both hands. Nothing happened, and he could not bear it any longer.

He suddenly broke down and began to cry.

CHAPTER 12

HE lay there for several days before he realized that August had gone. The constant sunlight, untouched by anything that in England would have been called cloud, had made him think that summer was eternal. On the fourth day after the operation the doctor came in from the town. His hands were very cool on the hot stump of arm above the wad of bandages. The doctor did not undo the bandages, and did not even talk of the arm. Objectively, Franklin looked at himself. Much blood had soaked through the lower end of the stump, coagulating black, so that it looked as if the arm had been charred away. The doctor talked of fishing. From him Franklin learned that Françoise took the boat upstream every evening. 'She seems to be trying every pool for about four miles upstream,' he said. It struck Franklin, long used to girls who desired evenings with more excitement, that it was an odd occupation for a girl.

On the fifth day he got out of bed. He was determined to begin walking as soon as possible. Lying in bed, making plans, considering the problems of how to button his trousers, fix his stud, and tie his necktie with one hand, was rather like the theoretical part of flight. The anticipation of putting it into practice was marked by a feeling of terror in case you should fail. He got out of bed fully expecting to fall down. His feet were very cool on the bare wooden floor, and the feeling was delicious after the clammy heat of the bed. He did not fall down, but walked steadily but slowly to the foot of the bed. He counted the paces: there were twelve. He took ten more to the window and hung on to the sash. As he looked out on the plain and the solid slab of brilliant sky beyond it there was nothing to tell him that August had become September except that the last of the fields of corn were empty now.

After standing a few moments he walked diagonally across the room to the other window. There were sixteen paces. This window looked over the orchard and up the river. He stood there for several moments and wondered about O'Connor and

122

Sandy and the two boys. Things seemed so much less complicated now that he was alone. He took another fifteen paces back to the bed. Twelve plus ten plus sixteen plus fifteen: the triangle was beyond his dreams. Much less complicated. He felt very glad. If he could work on the theory of doubling the length of the first walk and then the third, and then the fourth and so on, he could walk a mile in a week. In theory, he could leave the place in fifteen days.

Even that was long. He got back into bed. He felt something of the feeling of relief, mingled with subdued pride, that he had had after taking his first solo. There did not seem to be anything, in theory, to stop him from multiplying his progress. The feeling of lopsidedness worried him a little, but it was, after all, not unlike flying with one engine. He would get used to it. He was at any rate not going to be depressed about it. He was delighted to discover in himself, instead, an unexpected exhilaration at the idea of being able to walk successfully at all.

What he needed most of all was a map. He had not seen any of his belongings since before the operation. If O'Connor and Sandy had not taken all the maps it was just possible that he could, by questioning the old woman, discover where he was. In that way he could spend the week planning the route to the Pyrenees. All this was theoretical. But he had shown himself, by walking around the room, to be fairly tough, and it did not seem that anything could stop him now.

He shut his eyes for a few moments, pleased with himself. All the silence of the afternoon was compressed into the sound of the mill-race, like the echo of a roar beyond the partly opened window. After a time this sound seemed to increase and come nearer. It broke at last into separate sounds: the sounds of feet on the stairs.

Someone knocked on the door. Neither the old woman nor Françoise ever knocked, and he said cautiously, 'Come in.'

The door opened and Franklin was rather surprised to see the girl's father. He had not spoken to him more than half a dozen times since the morning when he and the crew had first come to the house. He had seemed to him then like a man of reticence and responsibility. The fact that he had not seen him very often since now struck Franklin as having great significance. He knew that he owed more to him than the girl.

'You are not asleep?' The man held the door with one hand and then closed it gently.

'No,' Franklin said. 'No. I have not been to sleep. Please come in.'

'I do not want to disturb you.'

'It is a pleasure,' Franklin said.

The man was in his shirt-sleeves. The shirt was grey, like an army shirt, and was tucked into black trousers. He looked as if he had suddenly come in from the fields. His eyes were slightly out of focus, even troubled, as if the change from sun-glare to shade had been too abrupt for them. They struck Franklin, for the first time, as being of the same black brightness as the girl's.

'I am sorry to come at this hour,' he said again. 'How is the arm?'

'Please,' Franklin said, 'it is very well.' He suddenly felt worried. It was all very apologetic. 'I am very glad of it. I would like to thank you. You have been kind beyond words.'

'I'm afraid you won't thank me for what I have come to say now,' he said.

'Something is wrong?'

The man stood by the bed. The thin fissured cheeks looked narrower than ever. Curious, thought Franklin, that I don't even know his name. The sharp Adam's apple in the man's thin brown throat jerked up and down.

'You remember,' he said, 'how I spoke to you of labour troubles?'

That was the first morning. 'Yes,' Franklin said, 'I remember.'

'It gets worse,' he said. 'Yesterday they broke out again in the town. Unfortunately two Germans were shot.'

'Unfortunately?'

'Unfortunately in the sense that the innocent are bound to suffer.' He did not smile.

It means hostages, Franklin thought. He waited.

'I'm afraid the situation is bad,' the father said. 'They have put a curfew on the whole district. They have already taken hostages. Now they are taking a census of houses.'

124

'You think they are coming here?' Franklin said.

'Unfortunately we know they are coming here.'

Any moment now, Franklin thought. He looked at the father. whose nervousness, now that he had spoken, was more subdued. The situation was now, to Franklin, very clear. He knew there was nothing to be done except to get him away. 'I am ready to do whatever you want me to do,' he said.

'We shall have to move you,' the man said. 'I'm sorry. Pierre and I will carry you.'

'There is no need,' he said. 'I can walk.'

'No,' the father said. 'No. It will be better if we carry you. I will get Pierre.' He moved towards the door.

'No,' Franklin said, 'I can walk. Get Pierre and I will walk.' He began to get out of bed.

The last thing he remembered seeing was the door swinging into the room. It seemed to swing very violently, as if it had sprung off its hinges when wrenched open by the man's hand. He was perfectly certain that it swung across the room and struck him, like a black wall, in the face. Nothing else, he thought in that moment of sharp confusion, could have so surprisingly and completely knocked him down.

When he came round again he was looking up at the sky. He looked forward to see the tall shape of the girl's father before him, and upward to see the blank and thick-lipped face of Pierre above his own. Together they were carrying him down, across the little jetty, to the river.

He knew afterwards, for all the sharpness of his impressions of the moment, that they could have thrown him in the river and he would not have cared. They were carrying him on two planks of wood lashed together by rope to form a stretcher. He could feel the rope against his neck as he moved. He could feel that someone had partly dressed him, putting on his trousers. They had covered him over also with a grey blanket on which his good arm lay bloodless in the hot sun. All his strength lay behind him, in the bedroom.

They set him down on the jetty for a moment and then slid him, very gently and at a slight angle, down to the boat below. The stones of the jetty, as his good hand touched them in passing, were burning in the sun. He heard the sound of a dog,

125

panting and whimpering quietly, and then the voice of the girl, quieting it in reply. As he felt himself going down lower than the level of the jetty he looked up to see the face of Pierre. It seemed to project like the end of a lump of cracked brown wood from the side of the stones. The man was lying on his stomach, grasping the sides of the boat with two brown hands, so that it did not rock. He lay there for some minutes while Françoise and her father slid the planks along the seats of the boat, fixing them centrally, towards the stern end. Then Franklin felt the boat rock very slightly and saw the girl's father standing on the jetty. He saw also the dog sitting in the well of the boat, and then, above him, the girl bending down. He felt momentarily grateful for the shadow she made, a cool break in the glaring space of sun. 'I am going to cover you over,' she said. 'It won't be for long.'

The tarpaulin came over him, hiding her face, the sun and the figures on the jetty. He breathed the smell of tar, warm and secure. The tarpaulin, soaked through by sun, was warm on the underside. He moved it slightly with his good hand. Through the break of light he saw the jetty moving away. When the hot grey-white stone at last slid away and was replaced by reeds he watched the small waves made by the motion of boat and oars gently strike the reeds and shiver them side to side. Soon the reeds grew thicker but farther away, and the motion of the water, in a series of sunlit waves, steadier and deeper. Then he heard in the silence of the afternoon nothing but the gentle sound of water, the regular and gentle beat of oars, and now and then, from somewhere near his feet, the gentler breathing of the dog.

The girl rowed steadily, and after a time he let the tarpaulin down. It was then quite dark; he became insulated from the sun. A slight sense of oppression was counteracted by amazement. To be strapped to the plank and rowed away in the boat, under a tarpaulin, in the peaceful heat of afternoon, seemed whenever he was not too stupefied to think of it a fantastic thing.

The boat moved on, at the same pace, for what seemed to him about fifteen minutes. During all this time the girl did not say a word. Once more he lifted up the edge of the tarpaulin.

Across the water, now, on the river-bank, were lines of willow trees and between them and the boat thick stretches of water-lily leaves, flowerless and curled up in the heat of the sun. About five minutes afterwards he felt the boat slow down.

'You are all right?' Her voice, though in a whisper, quite startled him. It came from very close to his head. All the time he had had an idea that she was much farther away.

'I am all right,' he said. He lifted the tarpaulin higher, until he could see her brown hand on an oar. 'Where are we?'

'We have been going upstream. Not quite far enough yet. I thought you'd like a little air.'

'How long will it be?'

'I don't know. We heard that they were at the next farm along the river. It shouldn't be long. They will signal from the house when they are ready.'

He wanted the tarpaulin off his face, so that he could look at her, but it seemed to be tied down. He could only lift his right hand free and touch hers as it rested on the oar. He felt her skin warm in the sun, and then, running his hand up the arm, the short soft hairs above the wrist. Then he let his hand run down to hers again and this time she took hold of it and held it for about a minute, firm and tender.

In a moment or two she rowed on. He kept the tarpaulin down. The delayed effect of being moved now came over him. He felt very tired and shut his eyes, feeling in the complete darkness the old throb of his arm renewing itself and beating up through the blood of his head.

He was disturbed out of this by the slowing down of the boat. It seemed as if the girl had given up rowing very suddenly. He felt her pulling round on one oar, the boat turning in a half-circle across the stream. Then she gave up rowing entirely and he felt the boat drifting without a sound.

'Don't move,' she said.

He lay very tense and still. 'What is it?'

'They have put the guard back on the bridge,' she said.

Jesus, he thought. 'Can he see us?'

'He is about a hundred yards away,' she said. 'He is looking at us now.'

He did not speak. The movement of the boat, ominously

127

quiet, had almost spent itself. He could hear nothing but the panting of the dog. The girl talked in a whisper.

'There used to be a guard here,' she said. 'He never did much.'

'Yes,' he said. 'But what do we do?'

'I brought the fishing things.'

Too amazed to speak, he lay motionless, feeling against his back the very slight shock of the boat striking the bank at last. He did not dare move, but even through the tarpaulin he could feel the difference between the hot sunlight of the open river and the shade. The crazy tension of the moment filled him with alarm. It was like being shut up in a cupboard for fun, and then finding suddenly that it was locked from outside.

'Tell me what goes on,' he said. 'What are you doing now?'

'The guard is looking at us,' she said. 'I am putting the fishing-rod together. Do you fish in England?'

'Myself?' he said. 'No. I never found the time.'

'I am fixing the line to the rod now,' she said. He waited and she did not speak for a moment or two. At last she said, 'It is all fixed up now except for the bait.'

'What bait do you have?' he said.

'I have no bait.'

This is mad, he thought. 'Do you know the English word crazy?' he said. He tried to be lighthearted, but his arm was hurting like hell.

'No,' she said. 'What does it mean?'

'It means it is mad to fish without anything on the hook.'

'But I am going to get bait,' she said. 'I am going now.'

He lay rigid under the tarpaulin. One moment of suspicion from the sentry, he thought, and everybody will be shot. Oh Christ! he thought in panic. 'Where are you going?'

'There is an elderberry tree up the bank,' she said.

'I didn't know that fish ate elderberries,' he said.

'You are not a fisherman.'

I'm trapped, he thought. I'm trapped in a cupboard! For God's sake! 'What will happen if he decides to investigate?' he said.

He heard her move in the boat, and then felt the boat itself move, as if she was tightening it up by rope to the bank. 'You have the dog,' she said. 'The dog would never let him get into

128

the boat, even if he decided to get his feet wet.' He heard her moving again. Not to know what she was doing was very like being blind.

'What are you doing now?' he said.

'Taking off my shoes.'

A second later he heard her feet in the water. There was no sound from the dog. The sound of the girl walking in the water, taking less than half a dozen paces, suddenly stopped. She was climbing the bank. 'Will you be long?' he said. 'Don't be long,' as if he were a child going to be left alone in a strange place, but she did not answer again.

He resisted a terrible impulse to lift the tarpaulin. Beneath, it was quite dark, and the sensation of being trapped became sharper. It filled him with almost senseless stupidity. The only senses left to him seemed to be hearing, though he could not even hear the dog, and a more than normally sharp sense of pain. All his tension seemed to concentrate itself on the raw edges of his severed arm. He felt he did not breathe at all.

He lay then for what he knew must have been fifteen minutes before he heard her voice. He was staggered to hear it coming from some way off, up the bank. He could hear it because it was talking to someone at a distance. He resisted again the awful impulse to lift the tarpaulin simply because, this time, he knew that it could only help him to confirm a more awful thought. There was only one person to whom she could be talking at a distance, and he knew it was the German on the bridge.

About the same time he became aware, too, of an extraordinary tension in the dog. Since there was nothing to hear, he was not sure how he became aware of it. He only knew, with absolute certainty, that the dog was sitting there somewhere in the boat in a state of intense alarm. He lifted the tarpaulin slightly and put out his right hand. The absurd question of whether to speak to the dog in French or English was never solved. A second later the dog broke free of all tension and began barking violently.

Franklin felt the sweat start out of him in a cold stream. The dog, in his excitement, began to jump up and down. The movement, though slight, rocked the boat in a way that made it seem, to Franklin, as if he were being swung into the air in a builders'

129

cradle. The dog seemed to dance on the edge of the boat. The old absurd question of whether to command it in French or English was, for the second time, never settled. The dog gave a great leap off the side of the boat, rocking it still more, and jumped into the water. He heard it swimming with great excitement upstream.

He lay there and did not move. He decided that someone had come along the bank, become suspicious, and had frightened the dog into hostility. His hand lay outside the tarpaulin and he dared not draw it back. As the boat rocked to stillness he listened for some movement on the bank, but he could hear nothing but the girl's voice, higher pitched now, and the sudden joyous yapping of the dog. He heard, too, a new sound: the clattering of wings, the sound of a bird, in terror, half flying, half swimming, flapping and screeching as it skimmed the water. Finally the scream of the bird died away, leaving the taut silence over the water to be shivered only by the sound of the dog shaking his wet body somewhere on the bank upstream.

It seemed about half an hour before the girl came back. He became aware of her pulling gently at the rope by which the boat was tied. He felt the boat slide in towards the bank, himself helpless and wondering what the devil was the matter again until he heard her voice. 'It's all right, now,' she said. 'All right. All right.'

She climbed into the boat. He was stiff with lying in the same position, his nerves on edge, and now partly tired, partly enraged by his own helplessness.

'Why have you been so long?' he said. 'What happened?'

'I went up to the bridge.'

'To the bridge?' He could not believe her. 'To the sentry? For God's sake!' he said. 'Why?'

'I wanted to see if he could see the boat very clearly.'

She was quite calm; he felt empty and humiliated.

'And can he?'

'No,' she said.

She lifted the tarpaulin for the first time off his face. The shadow of the willow was unbroken on his face, but the sunlight, deflected from the water, still dazzled his eyes. He looked up at her. She was tying back her hair.

130

'Better?'

'Much better,' he said. But in spite of a vast thankfulness, he felt there was something wrong. Then he screwed his head round and said, 'I don't like your face upside down,' and she smiled, moving so that he could see her full face, above him.

'Better?'

'Much better,' he said.

She put her hand on his forehead, warm and wet with sweat. He said something about the dog, and she told him how she had left him near the bridge. 'He will bark if the sentry moves,' she said. 'Just as he did with the duck. Were you frightened?'

'I was frightened,' he said. Like hell, he thought.

Suddenly it all seemed impossibly fantastic: he lying stiff as a corpse in the boat, the girl talking to the sentry, the dog chasing the duck. For a moment he could not believe in it. He felt that the aircraft could never have crashed, he could never have met the girl, he could never have lost his arm.

She squeezed out her wet handkerchief and put it on his face. It lay folded across his forehead, wet on his temples, a cold and slightly shocking stab of reality.

'Is your arm comfortable?' she said.

Which part of it? he was going to say, and then changed his mind. It seemed like the expression of something awfully petty. He was glad he did not say it. He said instead: 'I am tired of lying down. That's all.' The arm, in fact, ached as if it were all there. Its tired pain had spread out and had assumed the shape, for the first time, of the lost limb. It gnawed in turn at his mind.

'There is something to eat,' she said. She unfolded the handkerchief and moulded it, like a cold plaster, on his face. 'I brought apples and some bread.'

'I would rather drink. If there is anything,' he said. The golden afternoon over the river was wonderfully quiet. No wind came across the water, as it would do in England, to beat off the sun. Even the deep shade was warm and undisturbed.

She said, 'There is milk to drink,' and he realized then that she had come prepared to stay for a long time. He wondered, as she uncorked the wine-bottle of milk, what was going on back in the house. Whatever it was would affect them both.

She took the handkerchief away from his head and, putting her hand under his neck, lifted him up. The idea of his walking through France, one-handed as it were, suddenly seemed painfully ridiculous. He partly sat up and the only problem in his life became whether he should use his one arm to prop himself up or to hold the bottle. He finally propped himself up and she held the bottle to his mouth. In the moment of throwing back his head to drink his gaze swung out of the shade into the sunlight of the river, and he saw the German, his bayonet like a pin against the blue sky, standing on the bridge.

Then again, after he had drunk the milk, which was just warm, he wondered about the house. He had forgotten, too, to ask her about the elderberries. 'Will you fish?' he said.

'Towards evening. Yes.'

Evening? He did not say anything. Something told him that things were going to be very serious before night. And suddenly he stopped worrying about himself, his arm, his escape, and the pin-like bayonet pricking the sky above the bridge. He could think only about the house and the three people there. If they took anybody out of it, he thought, it could not possibly be the woman, crusted over with brittle scabs of one war experience after another. There could be no satisfaction in shooting the very old. It could mean only the father and Pierre, and it could only be, he reasoned, because of him.

Thinking this, he was sick with humiliation. The girl sat eating an apple, watching the bridge, her teeth bright as the apple flesh against her dark brown face.

'You think it will be all right,' he said, 'at the house?'

'Yes.' She spoke with readiness, simply, swallowing a piece of apple. He was aware of some enormous conviction in her. 'Yes, I have faith it will be all right. I have prayed very hard it will be.'

He did not speak. It was hardly the time, he thought, to argue about the efficacy of prayer. She, at any rate, was concerned with the apple.

'I have told you that before,' she said, 'haven't I?'

'Yes,' he said. 'In the church.'

'You have faith yourself?' she said.

'Sometimes. Not always.'

132

'You should have faith,' she said. 'When I fish I have great faith and the fish answer my prayers.'

'The fish answer your prayers?' He smiled at her as she took another bite into the apple.

'Yes,' she said. Her eyes were wide and black, and he looked down into their shining and lovely belief. 'Yes. The fish are God's, and so God answers the prayer through the fish. That's simple enough,' she said, turning the apple over.

'Yes,' he said, knowing there was no answer in the world to that. 'That's simple enough.'

She took her last bite of the apple, put the bottle of milk into the bottom of the boat, and then with both hands free held him against her. It was very hard to speak about love, he thought, in another language. He did not even know if it was right to talk to her about love. He wanted the love for her to remain restrained and yet expanding; to be physical, because he felt it in his body as sharp as the pain of his arm, but to be living and growing out of whatever happened. For the first time since the war the inside of himself grew suddenly quiet. What she said about faith smoothed away all complications. The turmoil set up by flying, perhaps by too much flying, was something whirled madly in a flare. Now he felt it settling, calming, growing clear and pure. He lay with his good arm against one of hers. It was brown and gave off all the smooth clear warmth of the summer. He ran his hand down the arm to the finger-tips and then back and ran it down again. What he felt for her was just so simple, now, and uncomplicated. With flying you became complicated without thinking of it, fear complicated with action, action with relief, relief with pain, pain with the inner silence that no one ever penetrated. At first you did not sleep at night. Your eyes were held open, pinned back by the strain of darkness, the pupils hammered by the bright memory of savage stars. All the brilliant recurrent violence of the trip was re-experienced, like a film run backwards. If time lessened the effect of this it seemed only to increase the inability to talk of it to another soul.

Yet if she ever asks me about flying, he thought, I know that I can tell her. He kissed her lightly on the face. She moved her face and kissed him back, as she had done in the orchard, warm

133

and seriously tender. As she did so the slightest breeze stirred across the river and melted in, cool and ruffling, under the shadow of the tree. It parted for a moment the light leaves of the willow, so that the sun flashed down, quick and sharp, in a speck of metallic light.

It was as if the bayonet on the bridge had flashed down on them across the water. But he shut his eyes and did not care.

CHAPTER 13

LOOKING up from the boat he saw Pierre lying flat on the jetty in the same attitude as he had left him in the afternoon, and above him the old woman standing very still in the twilight, and he knew because there was no one with them that something was very wrong. He was still roped to the plank, but now, because it was almost dark, no longer under the tarpaulin. The girl rowed in close to the jetty. As the boat hit the wooden piles and jarred back, Pierre reached out, grasped it, and held it still. The girl helped him off the plank, and he managed to stand upright. His fear was that he would fall down, and he determined not to fall down. He was tired and stiff with lying down, and his arm seemed to ache down to the finger-tips that no longer existed. But he was aware that something else had happened beside which all this and himself were little things. This feeling strengthened his determination not to fall down. Very carefully he put one foot on a cross-piece of the jetty, and then Pierre held his right hand and pulled him up. His anxiety not to fall down became an angry fear. 'I'm all right,' he said. 'Let me walk. Let me walk. Let me walk.'

As they let him walk to the house, Pierre and the girl each side of him, the twilight vibrating each time his feet struck the ground, he clenched his teeth in the renewed effort not to fall down. The house seemed many miles away. It receded and came back and would not remain still. Finally he reached out and tried, with an immense effort, to grasp it in his one hand. To his astonishment he discovered he was holding the door-post. He stood still for a moment, breathing very hard, and then, grasping the smooth friendly wood, swung himself heavily into the kitchen.

A moment later he fell down. He got to his feet with terrified haste, like a boxer who wants to show that he is still fighting.

He was aware after that of sitting in a chair. He was trembling and exhausted, and was drinking a small glass of cognac. The bottle of cognac was on the table and the lamp was burning above it, the flame low beneath the opaque white chimney. Between himself and the light, and sometimes beyond it, he saw the girl and Pierre and the old woman moving. Their faces vibrated as if someone were shaking the light, and it seemed as if they were all talking together.

He discovered after a time that they were not talking together. It was Pierre and the old woman talking, telling the girl what had happened. The girl, for a long time, was silent. He took another drink of the cognac. As the heat of it bit his mouth he felt less tired, and the faces, as he looked at them, no longer vibrated. The face of the girl at least had become dead still, white as the glass of the lamp, the dark eyes steady in the upward glare.

He gathered at last where the father had gone. The voluble excited voices were like fussy flames. He saw the old woman lift her hands in a gesture partly of despair, partly of futility. She had in her hands a big carving knife which she swung down on the table. To his surprise Franklin saw her begin to slice onions.

'There was no need to go! No need! They were here five minutes. They didn't even look at the house. They didn't even come in.'

She slashed the onions into white raw shreds. The strong odour of onion was naked against the warm smell of the cognac.

'It was only when Chausson came over from the farm with the news of the doctor,' Pierre said.

'The doctor?' the girl said.

'That was afterwards, afterwards,' the old woman said. 'We were going to give you the signal. It was about half-past five. And then Chausson came over to say they had taken the doctor.'

The girl still did not move. Franklin watched her standing in the lamplight, white as the glare.

'And how many more?'

'Chausson says fifty. Fifty! Chausson says one German was killed. Only one.'

'It was all right until Chausson came over,' Pierre said. 'But then nothing would stop him. He had to go and find out what had happened.'

'I say there was no need! No need!' the old woman said.

'You know he wouldn't rest,' Pierre said. 'How could he rest?'

'Rest!' she said. 'Rest! Do any of us rest?'

The knife came down again on the onions, slicing the white flesh under the white lamplight.

'He should be back, I tell you!' the old woman said. 'He should be back!'

'I am not worried,' the girl said. 'I am relieved they did not take him. I am not worried.'

'Chausson was going to drive in with the cart,' Pierre said. 'That takes an hour. Then there's an hour to get back. If you count two hours then it's only just time.'

'Ah! You talk! You talk!' the old woman said.

Franklin put the empty cognac glass on the table. The conversation had reached a point of fretful futility. He felt his own thoughts, by contrast, clearing and coming back. He reflected that if they shot the doctor there would be no one to look at his arm. It was a selfish thought, and he was glad when the girl, seeing the empty glass, moved round the table to fill it up.

He saw her reach for the bottle and pour out a little more cognac. Suddenly all the confusion of the day receded and the raw fact of what had happened remained clear and bare before his face. If they shot the doctor it could only be because of him.

'How do you feel?' the girl said.

Far away on the other side of the big kitchen the old woman was beginning to fry the onions. He felt slightly sick.

'I'm all right,' he said. 'But the doctor? The doctor? Is it because of me they have taken him?'

'I don't think so.'

'Why? How do you know?' he said.

'He is a prominent man. As a doctor everyone knows him. It is better to make an example of someone well known. It affects more people.'

'Are you afraid for your father?' he said.

No. He will come back.'

'I am sorry about it,' he said.

'Don't be sorry.'

137

'If you think it safer for me to go back into the mill I will go,' he said. 'I shall be all right.'

'No,' she said. 'You need food now. We will talk about moving afterwards.'

She began to lay knives and forks on the bare wooden table, and then glasses and bread and the wooden pots for salt and pepper. He lay back in the chair, exhausted and hungry to a point of sickness, and watched her. Once she turned and smiled and there was no sign in her face that her calmness was anything but true. It was very true and real, and to him, as he sat there listening beyond the silence of the room in case the silence of the night outside should be broken now, blessedly comforting. He sat there for about ten minutes watching her while the old woman cooked the food and Pierre sat silent by the table, running the edge of a finger-nail round the rim of another. As Franklin sat watching him he realized, for the first time, that he would never cut the nails of his own right hand again; the realization amused rather than bitter as he remembered how, when a child, the right hand had always been the more difficult problem of the two.

Five minutes later, when the old woman brought the supper to the table, a dish of fried green beans and potatoes with the onions now brown among them, Franklin drew his chair up to the table, the girl opposite him, with Pierre on his left and the old woman on his right hand side. It was his first meal with them since the first morning. He picked up his fork and held it in his right hand. Eating would never be the same again. He wondered how the devil, when the occasion arose, he would cut his meat. But the occasion did not arise now, since there was no meat to cut. As the old woman filled his plate with beans and potatoes, in which there was also a little chopped tomato, he saw before him long years of eating with one hand, perhaps even with a spoon, like a baby.

All through the meal the three people did not look at him much, as if they were very aware of all this and did not want to embarrass him. Then he realized that it was not wholly because of this, but because they were listening. He saw their eyes occasionally uplifted and stilled as when people let their eyes follow the track of a fragmentary sound. Yet even when they

138

did not seem to be listening they did not look at him. Then he became aware of how he was dressed: his trousers hastily put on in the moment of getting him out of the house, his torn service shirt loosely bulging over the great wad of bandage across his chest and arm. This suddenly embarrassed him. 'I would like my coat,' he said. 'I am cold.'

'Have mine,' Pierre said. He stood up and took it off and put it across Franklin's shoulders before he could protest.

'Thank you,' Franklin said. 'Thank you.' He felt humble and more embarrassed still.

'Now you look like Pierre,' the girl said. She looked up from her food, the black eyes amused and light in the low lamplight. 'A bit like Pierre.'

'God help the boy,' the old woman said. She ate her food with a spoon, sucking it in, her mouth low over the plate. 'God help him if he looks even a bit like Pierre.'

'I am honoured to look like Pierre,' Franklin said. 'It's better than looking like nothing.'

'You will look like nothing if you don't rest,' the girl said.

'You should be in bed,' the old woman said. 'With that arm you should be tied to the bed. If you were a son of mine you'd go as soon as you'd cleared your plate. And I would tie you to the bed.'

He smiled. The old woman sucked in her food, washing every other mouthful down with a little of the red wine that had been watered down. Then for some time neither she nor the girl nor Pierre spoke again, and he knew by the track of their eyes that they were listening once more for the possible sound of someone coming outside. Sometimes the eyes of the girl paused as they swung slowly upward in this track of listening, and he would meet them with his own, across the light of the lamp, and hold them, full of wonder. Then she would smile a little and look upward beyond the lamp, and he in turn would look down at his food and with his fork begin chasing the scraps of fine vegetable about the plate, wondering sometimes if food would ever again be worth the trouble of eating.

Suddenly he saw again the extreme fantastic stupidity of the situation. To sit there in the house, eating, with a curfew on the district and the Germans not out of the house more than an hour or two, and he himself ready to be caught like an idiot, too weak to run, and without a revolver to fire a shot. He now determined at least that he should have the gun.

'My revolver,' he said to the girl. 'I think it would be better if I had it now.'

'There will be no occasion to shoot,' the girl said. 'They won't come again.'

'It is just for moral protection,' he said.

'A revolver is no good for anything else,' Pierre said.

'Exactly.'

'A shot-gun is much better. I have a shot-gun. Don't worry about the revolver. It is purely a weapon for close quarters.'

'It is also a weapon for one hand,' Franklin said. 'Remember that.'

'It is also a weapon useful for hitting haystacks,' Pierre said. 'Have you ever fired one?'

'At practice.'

'Ah! At practice, at practice!' The words mocked a little. 'I know. Yes. At practice. But practice and the reality are not quite the same. I went all through the last war, nearly five years, and never did I see a man hit by a revolver. I saw men hit by practically every other weapon one can name. Including the catapult.'

'I believe you,' Franklin said.

'The revolver is purely a fancy weapon,' Pierre said. 'If you want to blow a man's guts out hit him with a shot-gun.'

'Nevertheless, I should feel better with it,' Franklin said.

'How, better?'

Franklin did not answer. He did not know at all how much better he would feel. The girl, during this conversation, had gone out of the room, and now, as he sat there, wondering, she came back. She had the revolver in her hands. She laid it quietly on the bare wooden table by his plate. It shone, newly cleaned, in the lamplight, and all four of them gazed at it as it lay there.

Franklin did not know how much better he felt for seeing it there. Looking at it, he remembered a gunner named Watson, once of his squadron, but now dead. Watson, a man of forty who had come to England from Arkansas because he believed

140

in personal warfare, had offered to teach him to shoot. Watson was an excellent shot, and kept ten revolvers, some very large, some quite small with handles of mother-of-pearl, locked in his bedroom at the Mess. Watson's belief in the power of the revolver was so great that on operational trips he took four of these revolvers with him. In the event of being shot down Watson was well equipped to go on killing people right and left. This idea, together with the fanatical belief in revolvers generally, had not saved Watson from being blown to hell in the ordinary way.

'I have cleaned it every day,' the girl said, looking at him.

Franklin looked at the revolver and saw it suddenly as a pathetic and useless thing. He saw his own belief in it as pathetic. He had become so used to handling a weapon as big as a house, and carrying enough power to wipe out a small town, that he had forgotten there are other sorts of power. He looked at the three people sitting in the lamplight waiting for a sound. He saw them, the three generations of one nation, as part of a defenceless people, as part of the little people possessing an immeasurable power that could not be broken. He saw them suddenly as little people who had lain on the ground and had their faces trampled on but whose power was still unbroken. He knew it clearly now as a more wonderful, more enduring and more inspiring power than he had ever believed possible: the power of their own hearts.

He pushed the revolver across the table to the girl, who smiled at him. He knew that he would never doubt them again. The power that is good enough for them, he thought, ought to be good enough for me.

'You had better keep it, after all,' he said. 'Until I am stronger.'

'I will clean it every day,' she said, smiling again.

'You have kept it beautifully,' he said. 'Very beautifully.'

'It should be beautiful, too.' The old woman lifted her head, looking up with slight irony from her plate. 'The way she cleans it every morning you might think it was the silver for the Holy Altar.'

He did not speak. Smiling a little, the girl still looked at him. He knew by that look, so steady and tender, why his revolver

141

was to her like the silver of the Holy Altar and why he would never take it from her again.

The smile on her face vanished suddenly as he heard the barking of the dog outside. He saw her leap up, snatch the revolver, and put it in the drawer of the dresser by the wall. There was an astonishing light of decision on her face, heightened perhaps by alarm or fear. He had not time to think of it before she said, 'You had better go upstairs,' and he found himself shuffling unsteadily across the kitchen, his body stiff from lying in the boat, the girl going before him to open the door.

He was walking slowly upstairs almost before he realized it. 'Don't come down till I call,' she said, and the light from the kitchen door suddenly went out, leaving the effect of the lamp-glare beating in his eyes.

He pulled himself slowly upstairs by one hand, and then, in the bedroom, lay down on the bed. The curtains of the window were not drawn and through the glass he could see, as his eyes got used to the darkness, more and more of the summer stars. He lay looking at them and listening for a sound from below. It was very quiet except for the deep soft roar of water in the mill-race and there was no longer any sound from the dog.

He lay there in the dark bedroom and waited. After about ten minutes he heard the sound of a door opening below, and then of someone coming upstairs. After a minute the door of his room opened and the girl said quietly: 'Everything is all right. Are you there?' And he said, 'Yes. I am here. Come in.'

He saw her cross the square of starlight below the foot of the bed, and then a moment later she was standing by him.

'It was my father,' she said, 'come back.'

'Is it all right?' he said.

'Yes.'

'I am glad. What happened?'

'They have taken a hundred people,' she said. 'They took some this morning and shot them this afternoon.'

Christ! he thought. He felt very sick and angry.

'Your father is all right?'

'Yes. He is tired. He is very tired. But all right.'

His anger and relief about the whole thing suddenly dissolved

142

into pity and then from pity into tenderness for her. He reached up with his good arm and touched her.

'Come close,' he said. 'I can't reach you.'

'I am very close,' she said.

'Lie on the bed with me.' He found her arm and pulled her gently down.

'No. I should go,' she said.

'Please,' he said. 'For a moment.'

'I should go.'

'Please,' he said. 'Only for a moment. And then I will come down, too.'

Without speaking again she came to the bed and lay on it beside him. The strain of the day ebbed away from him in one final wave and left him quite calm. She lay on her back and he knew that she was very tired. His regard for this filled him with great gentleness. He put his hand on one of her breasts and smoothed it across the thin summer dress and then held it still. He could feel below the breast her heart beating with quiet regularity into the palm of his hand. She did not move except to turn her face, to kiss him of her own accord, her lips increasing very slightly their warm pressure as he pulled her body across to him. He remembered then how once, in the room above the mill, he had pained her because he had said, 'This is serious', and yet she had not been sure. He asked her in a whisper if she remembered it, and she said, 'I remember it all. From the first moment I saw you that morning.' She buried her head in the pillow, very close to his face. 'And are you sure now? I want you to be sure about me. Because what I feel is sure.'

'I am very sure.' She pressed her body so close to him that for one second he felt pain flare from the edges of his amputated arm. 'I am more sure than I ever was of anything in the world.'

He carried the unassailable completeness of this moment with him as he followed her downstairs. He walked a little unsteadily, the blood beating in his head, and at the foot of the stairs, before she opened the door and let in the light, he held her for one moment more, partly for love of her, partly to steady himself before going in.

When he finally entered the kitchen he saw the girl's father at the table, in the lamplight. He was lying rather than sitting

143

in a chair. His coat was unbuttoned, showing beneath it the white shirt and black tie he had put on, as if it were Sunday, for the visit to town. His right hand was fully outstretched and held in it, at an angle, a small glass of cognac like the one Franklin had been drinking. His body had an extraordinary flattened and battered appearance, as if someone had smashed him with violence against a wall.

Franklin went over and stood in front of him. 'M'sieu,' he said, 'I am very glad you are back.'

The eyes looked slowly up at him. In the lamplight they were quite white, as if shock had drained them of power.

'If I had a thousand shot-guns I would shoot every one of their guts out,' Pierre said. He was still sitting at the table, where Franklin had left him. The old woman stood beyond, looking down.

'No, no,' the father said. 'That does no good.'

'Good?' Pierre said. 'Good? Who in the name of Christ Almighty wants to do good?'

'Quiet!' the old woman said. 'You shouldn't talk like that.'

'Then how should one talk?'

'Talk how you like. But not with the name of Christ. I don't like to hear the name of Christ like that.'

'You should have been in the trenches in the last war!' he said. 'You would have heard the name of Christ very often then. You would have heard the suffering call Him down.'

'I have seen enough of war,' she said. 'I haven't yet seen enough of Christ. That's all.'

Pierre stood up, looking very wild. 'When they shoot fifty people in an afternoon I begin to doubt if there is a Christ!' he said. 'I tell you I would shoot out the guts of any bastard of them!'

Franklin stood still, looking at the father. The cognac glass was tilted so that the small drop of cognac had reached the edge.

'I hope it was not because of me that you went?' he said. 'I have been too much trouble now.'

'No,' the father said. 'No. I am only sorry there was trouble for you.'

'It was no trouble,' Franklin said. There was slight life now in the flat white eyes. 'Is the situation bad?'

144

'It is the worst yet.'

'I am sorry.'

Franklin looked up from the father to the three people standing now on the edge of the ring of lamplight, looking down at the flattened figure in the chair. It struck him that the girl was still the calmest of them all.

'And the doctor?' he said. 'I hope the doctor is safe?'

The white exhausted eyes did not raise themselves this time. They looked down, almost closed, to where the cognac was trembling on the edge of the falling glass.

'They have shot the doctor,' he said. 'They have shot the doctor.'

EVERY other morning, after the doctor had been shot, Françoise and the old woman dressed his arm. The two doctors had left behind them a small attaché case of dressings; and there was also the first-aid box from the plane. At first he had a great fear of complications, but nothing happened except that by the end of each day the arm ached with steady drawing pain, as if it were trying to grow again. At first he did not want to look at it and lay with his face half-turned on the pillow, staring at the wall. Then on the fourth morning he turned his face and made himself look at the short stump of flesh and was surprised to find that it looked extraordinarily like a pale brown sausage, with the skin lightly drawn into inflamed creases at one end. After the dressing, which took about an hour, the old woman brought a bowl of hot water, a mirror, and his shaving things. While the old woman tidied the bedroom the girl sat on the edge of the bed and held the mirror against his knees. He took great pride in shaving himself with O'Connor's razor, with one hand. She sat smiling at him while he shaved, and after he had finished shaving she held the bowl on the bed and he washed his face and his one hand with warm water. He felt always, every morning, a new joy at being able to do these things for himself, and saw this joy reflected in her face as she sat watching him on the bed.

When this was finished and he was alone again he got out of bed. They had given him back his socks, his shoes, his service shirt and trousers, and his collar and tie. Every morning he went through the same process of putting them on. He determined, however great the effort, to do everything for himself. From the first the trousers and shirt and socks were easy; it was some time before he mastered the collar and tie. Finally he held one end of the collar in his mouth while he fixed the stud in the other. Then he pulled the collar with his teeth, and, perhaps at the third or fourth attempt, fixed it on the stud. Then he drew the tie slowly through the collar and put the left-hand end in

146

the top drawer of the chest-of-drawers, shutting it in. Finally
he held it tight and made the knot, pulling it slowly up while
the end was in the drawer. After this he walked about the room.
He kept at first to his original idea of doubling, each day, the
distance of the previous day, but after the fifth day he lost count
and simply walked round the room and across it and back
again twenty or thirty times. When he was tired he sat down
by the window and looked out across the plain, still burning in
the mid-September sun. The cornfields were like bare slabs of
white rock in the heat, the distances shimmering above them
and above the river, and all along the stream nothing moved
except the strip of dry green reeds flapping slowly in the air
between the water and the rainless brown path. When he had
rested he got up and walked round the room again, forcing himself to walk round it five or six more times than previously. Towards midday it would be very hot, and after the second walk
was finished he undressed again and got into bed. At noon the
old woman came upstairs with the midday meal on a tray:
bread and soup, with vegetables and sometimes an egg and
generally an apple or two and always a little wine. The wine,
drunk in the heat of the day, always made him sleepy, and after
eating he would go to sleep for an hour and then in the middle
afternoon get up again and go through all the process of dressing a second time. This time, having dressed, he tried to walk
round the room several more times than in the morning, and,
for variety, the opposite way. Then, as before, when he was
tired, he sat down by the window and rested. And it was then,
in the late afternoon, when the hot stillness had stifled the last
movement out of the plain and the voices of the house were
silent, that something about the smell of heat and the angle of
golden light made him think of England. He felt very alone
then, and in the sharp misery of a brief homesickness would
walk round the room, rather savagely now, for the third time.
By the time this third walk was over he was utterly tired of the
heat and the day, the bedroom and the view of the plain, above
all of himself and the arm.

Every evening the girl came upstairs to sit with him and talk,
staying until the light across the plain was smoky mauve with
the promise of another day of heat, and on the tenth day she

147

came up, about six o'clock, and brought the second doctor. He looked to Franklin, seeing him for the first time since the confused hours before the operation, taller and thinner than his brother who had been shot. He had a certain sad formality of manner as he asked Franklin to take off his shirt. Franklin looked swiftly at the girl as if scared that she would try to help him, and then unknotted his tie and pulled the shirt over his head. When his head was free he saw that the girl had gone.

The doctor looked at the arm with what seemed to Franklin a kind of detached melancholy, not touching it.

'You are very lucky,' he said.

'You think it's all right?'

'You are a very healthy person,' the doctor said. 'You heal up like a young tree.' He stopped looking at the arm and looked at Franklin's face. 'How do you feel – yourself?' he said.

'I feel well. I get tired, that's all.' He looked at the grey, quiet face. He remembered, out of the split sections of a confused dream that would never be whole again, some similar moment, just before the operation, when he had looked up and seen the face, cool and tense but not then sad, in the light above him. He knew that he would never know anything of how difficult the operation had been, and that it would be better not to know. He felt only that it was a wonderful thing. 'I would like to thank you,' he said. 'I would like to thank you very much.'

'You have yourself to thank, too,' the doctor said. He began to re-bandage the arm.

'I am sorry, too, about your brother,' Franklin said. 'I had some fear it was because of me.'

'No,' the doctor said. 'No, it was not because of you. It was because he was a citizen everybody knew. It is better to shoot men of prominence. It was also because he had no discretion. He said what he felt. And what he felt was very strong. He was a man of great courage.'

Franklin looked at him. He was extraordinarily like the brother, except for the beard. 'You were both men of great courage,' he said. For some reason it was easier to say in French. The word, in English, had a slightly artificial sound.

'Thank you,' the doctor said. He wound the last of the

148

bandage over the arm, and fastened it. 'Shall I help you on with your shirt?'

'I like to do it myself,' Franklin said.

He picked up the shirt and wriggled his arm through it, making an opening through which he pushed his head. In ten days he had become very deft at this, and the shirt came easily over his head, his right arm slipping through the sleeve at the same time.

'You have progressed,' the doctor said. He smiled.

'That is something I want to talk to you about,' Franklin said. 'Is there any reason why I shouldn't go from here?'

'There is the reason of the extra restrictions. They are still in force. There are barriers at all the roads and it is necessary to have a permit to travel.'

'Could one get through?' Franklin said.

'A man with one arm is always conspicuous,' the doctor said.

'But it is not impossible to get through?'

'Not impossible.'

'Is there any danger of complication with the arm now?' Franklin said.

'No. Except that you probably could not travel and heal at the same time. You are not strong enough for that.'

'I feel quite strong,' Franklin said.

'In the bedroom, yes,' the doctor said. 'But why do you want to go?'

'Because of the people here.' He wanted to go and yet he knew that the time of going, without the girl, could only be one of pain. The pain of leaving her would multiply and fester, until the loss of her would be more acute and terrible than the loss of the arm. Yet he felt also the pain of the doctor's death in the house, and, the fear and the bitterness spread by it, even though it was no longer discussed, into the lives of the people about him. Back in England, in the station, where bombers constantly did not return and the faces in the Mess were so often changing because of death, death itself was not discussed. Sometimes it seemed as if it did not matter. Death became a form of absence; it was the quiet removal of a face from the dinner-table and soon, however much you missed it, another younger, more eager and perhaps more likeable face replaced it, hiding its memory.

But the shooting of men, as ransom, by a wall, was very different. It left him with a memory of impotent savagery. Because
of it he understood the violent feelings of Pierre better than the
feelings of anyone else, and he knew that he could not bear the
chance of it happening again.

'I want to go solely because every moment I spend here is a
complication for them,' he said.

The doctor stood looking at Franklin tucking his shirt into
the top of his trousers with his one hand. His expression of re-
flective sadness had in it a sharp touch of stoicism.

'You do not seem to be aware that they know what they are
doing,' he said.

Was there an answer to that? Franklin fumbled blindly with
his shirt. There was no answer. He was a fool who had not even
the sense to hide behind his former humiliation. As if they did
not know – as if they had not considered and dismissed, long
ago, the consequences of this thing.

'They will keep you here until they have made the arrangements and it seems safe for you to go.'

There was still no answer. He felt the smallness of himself
shrivel into a kernel of impotent bitterness.

'It is perhaps the only right and honourable thing France
has done,' the doctor said. 'It is all we have been able to do. The
rest of us is of no consequence. We have stopped counting.'

'I would not say that.'

'I say it,' the doctor said. 'I am a Frenchman and I say it.'

He walked across the room and stood by the window, slowly
rolling the sleeves of his shirt down and even more slowly but-
toning them at the wrist. He had previously taken off his jacket
and hung it on the back of a chair. Now, carefully and rather
reflectively, he put it on. Suddenly his hands dropped, the coat
hung open and he spoke again.

'You are the only ones who count,' he said. 'You.'

'The English?'

'No, not necessarily the English. Simply you. The young.'

'You think we shall be any better than the old?' Franklin
said.

'It does not seem to me you could possibly be worse.'

He stood for another moment without moving and then

smiled and began to button up his coat. Suddenly he held out his hand.

'Good-bye.'

He spoke in English. The familiarity of the word to Franklin was very touching. He took the hand and shook it very firmly. 'Good-bye,' he said, in English, too.

'Good-bye,' the doctor said. 'I am only sorry it was I who had to take off the arm.'

'I am glad,' Franklin said. 'I would have given my right arm for all you have done for me.'

The doctor did not speak, and Franklin saw the tears spread to his eyes and glisten there without falling, like dew. It was very painful to speak, and it was some moments before Franklin asked him if he would come again.

'Probably not,' he said. 'The curfew is difficult and the arm is wonderful. It does not need me now.'

'Not even for the fishing?' Franklin said. 'I would be glad to see you again.'

The doctor smiled. 'I am going to do a little fishing now,' he said. 'Françoise is going to row me up the river.'

'She is a wonderful girl for rowing up the river,' Franklin said.

'She rows up every morning,' the doctor said. 'Yesterday she rowed beyond the bridge. She is getting to know the sentry there.'

'It is very mysterious,' Franklin said. He was about to make some joke about Françoise and the sentry, but checked himself in time.

'I don't think so.'

'No?'

'No,' the doctor said. 'She is a girl who has reasons for the things she does.' He looked at Franklin with eyes not entirely sad now, but still shining with unfallen tears, and smiled for the last time. 'Yes, she is a girl who has reasons.'

The doctor walked straight to the door and opened it and went out without another word, the abruptness more like shyness than the result of any conscious resolution, and Franklin walked slowly over to the window. He stood there for some minutes looking down at the plain and the river below. He felt

151

glad about the arm. He was getting stronger every day now, and he determined to increase the exercises, doubling them if necessary, day by day. Down below, the river was dead smooth and thinly skimmed with a transparent skin of dusty scum after the heat of the day. He watched a straw or two, fresh and yellow, perhaps from some late harvest field upstream, float slowly down on the steady current, sailing smoothly southwards. He watched them for some moments until at last he saw the surface of the stream broken by the waves made by the boat coming upstream. He saw the waves ripple and beat against the reeds, flapping them as if a wind had sprung up, before the boat appeared between the trees. Then he saw the boat, wide and flat and very heavy looking, but travelling surprisingly fast, going past the house upstream, with the girl using both oars and the doctor sitting rather upright in the stern, holding the heavy wooden tiller with one hand.

Franklin watched the boat slip past. He saw the fishing rods lying in the bottom of it, and the heavy tarpaulin, rolled up now, under which he had hidden. The girl was rowing strongly. She was dressed in the short green skirt and the thin white blouse in which he had seen her before. The motion of rowing drew her skirt above her bare brown knees, and the blouse tight across the smooth breasts. She rowed with calm, long strokes, sitting very upright, her face held well up, so that she seemed to be looking just above the horizontal line, past the doctor's head, past the top branches of the hanging willows, towards the hills in the north. As she rowed past, in sight for about thirty seconds before the boat disappeared beyond the orchard, he wondered why she was staring so intently, and what she was thinking, and he wondered also, remembering the doctor's words, why she was rowing so strongly and seriously, as if she were just beginning a long journey.

CHAPTER 15

ON the tenth day after the operation Franklin walked out of the house for the first time. In the dusk of evening it was safe to come down and walk, for about ten minutes, up and down the roadway between the mill and the house, and as far up the slope as the first apple trees. The girl walked with him and took his right arm. The sensation of walking on dry earth was so different from walking in the bedroom that his body seemed to vibrate at every step. His empty sleeve, tucked into his jacket pocket, felt strange, too. But the strangest moment was when he stooped down in the orchard to pick up an apple and, without thinking of the balance of his arm, almost fell down. It gave him an odd sensation of being struck a violent blow on his left side, so that his body swivelled round.

After that he walked out every night. It was now late September, and each time the dusk seemed to come a little earlier and he was able to walk a little farther. There was no break in the weather, and in the orchard, after the hot days, the dusk was smoky orange through the trees, and he could feel the sweat on the apples as he picked them up out of the grass, greasy and scented and sweet with full ripeness. There were many trees of pears, too, big and golden now, bending the long pear branches down so that they swung like ropes of solid yellow bells, and invisible in the grass so that he and the girl trampled them underfoot. He would pick them up and eat them idly as he walked, thinking of orchards in Worcestershire where the pears had been ripe, too, in the late September weather, and he had eaten them often with their summery, juicy sweetness running down his chin. Now, though the taste of pears was the same, and all the odour of late summer just the same. England seemed far away. All his life there had gone, with the complication of flying, all the life governed by the great dark hangars, the black Wellingtons, the wide grey strips of tarmac, and the friendly grass beyond them smoothed down like combed silk in the winds that blew in across the drome from the sea. It was cut off from him by the nightmare of the operation, so that he saw it through mists of remembered sickness. It was a life sometimes without faces. He could not remember what people looked like. Sometimes even when he thought of Taylor and Goddy and O'Connor and Sandy he could not remember their faces, and then suddenly, in an unexpected moment, he could remember Sandy's bald ginger head and the effect would startle him into the pain of a simple fact: that something must happen soon and that soon, however one part of him hated it, however complicated and painful it seemed, he would have to go.

On the seventeenth night after the operation he walked up through the orchard to the farthest corner of it, where it joined the vineyard on the slope above the river. It was a distance of about two hundred and eighty yards. Now he could walk it quite well. He could even walk it above normal pace, up the slope, without being tired. He had got used, too, to the feeling of being unbalanced, and now he walked with a short and rather jerky swing of his right arm, like a crab, as if for support he had to clutch and hold the air. His left arm had begun to pain him much more in the night now, and he did not sleep much, his eyes pinned back by the sharp stars as he looked at the sky. But it was a good pain; he could feel it grasping the broken sinews of the arm and pulling the tissues with a clean deep ache together; it was a living pain, itching and with its dull violence keeping him awake.

He did not realize how fast he walked until he reached the top of the orchard and leaned against the fence there. The girl leaned there, too, smiling and panting a little at the same time.

'You make me run,' she said.

'Run?' He was astonished at his own progress. 'Did I walk fast?'

'Very fast.' She smiled again. 'It comes of practising a great deal. We hear you walking in the bedroom.'

'Oh no! I'm sorry,' he said.

'There is no need to be sorry. We hear you walking up and down, up and down. It's a good sound. Now you can really walk. Quite fast.'

She stopped smiling and looked at him, leaning back on the fence, her arms crooked back, horizontally. In the dusk she

154

seemed very serious, her eyes very black and still but looking slightly oblique, a little past him.

'Soon you will need to walk,' she said.

'Soon?'

He spoke without thinking. He knew quite well now what she meant. He felt the dusk about him still and deep, and he breathed in the heavy smell of it, cool but heavily fragrant still with sun and leaves and the winey juice of fruit fallen and crushed in the grass. He knew quite well, with a feeling of apprehension in which there was misery and excitement, that something had happened.

'My father has gone to arrange the pass for you,' she said.

'To-day?'

'He will be back to-night,' she said.

Oh God! he thought. He felt the ripeness of the world split by the pain of his own reluctance. He did not want to go, he thought, he did not want to go. After all this, after the planning and the waiting and all his intense scheme of recuperation he did not want it. He felt the misery of departure come out of the future and felt the foretaste of it, sick and bitter in his mind. He did not want the agony and the loneliness and the complications of being without her.

'When?' he said. 'When must I go?'

He took hold of her with his right arm, holding her at the waist, pulling her body forward until the shape of it was clear and firm against him.

'To-morrow,' she said. 'Perhaps to-morrow.'

It was very sudden. 'To-morrow?' he said.

'Or the next day,' she said. 'My father will know.' She lifted her face and looked at him, very serious and tender. 'You will be glad to get back in England.'

He did not know whether it was a question from her or not; he only knew that he would not be glad. He did not know what to say to her now, and she said:

'What will you do when you are in England again?'

'Fly,' he said. He spoke without thinking. The decision to fly, determined by the fears that he would never do so again, must have lain already made in his mind. He seemed to pick it out unconsciously. And having expressed it, he knew that some-

155

how, some day, he had to fly again, that it was an essential part of his life, without which living was not complete.

'But the arm?' she said.

'Men have ridden bicycles with one arm,' he said. 'If there is something you want to do very much you will do it.'

'Will you fly the bombers again?' she said.

'I hope so.'

'Over here?' She lifted her head a fraction higher, and he saw the faintest gleam of light flash in the dark pupils. He understood what it meant and could not bear it and held her suddenly very close to him. He understood now what it would mean to fly over France again: how the infinite darkness or the moonlight with its Alpine distances of crumpled cloth would have for him the complication of additional fears. He saw the irony of flying over France, twice a night, perhaps twice a week, for all the months and perhaps all the years of the rest of the war, and how in the moonlight he would look down and see the glassy line of the rivers, thinking always of this river, and how she herself would look up at every sound of aircraft in the night, wondering if it might be himself flying above her. If we send five thousand bombers across France, every night of the year, he thought, nothing could change her wonder. If I go to-morrow, he thought, nothing can alter that one fact. Once I am gone we are a million miles apart. The war splits us apart with infinity.

There was only one thing to do. 'Listen,' he said. 'Listen. Please do something for me.'

'I will do anything for you,' she said. As she spoke he felt the inside of himself crying, dry and bitter. 'I will do anything.'

'Then do this,' he said. 'Before I go tell me the name of the river, the name of the town, and your father's name. So that I shall know and can come back. Will you do that for me? Please.'

'Yes. I will.'

She spoke very quietly, but the words had for him all the depth and solidity of the earth. They had an everlasting permanence that nothing could shake. He could carry them beyond this moment, and beyond any moment of doubt that the future might hold, and take comfort from them.

'And will you tell me where you live?' she said. 'So that when the war is over I can write to you.'

'Yes,' he said.

Suddenly she held him with great desperation, crying bitterly to him. 'Don't fly again. Don't fly. I don't want you to fly again.'

'It's all right,' he said. 'I shall be all right.'

Jesus, she knows, he thought. He stood stupidly staring across the darkening orchard, through the narrow avenues of trees. The pain of all the things which had troubled him as a pilot and of which he had never spoken to a soul now seemed to stand simply before him. All of his flying life had been in a sense screened round by fear. It had been carefully screened from his mother, from Diana, from his friends; it was screened from them by his behaviour, his language, by all the expressions on his face. It was screened even more securely from himself by his own emotions. Yet underneath it all, underneath the pretence which many continuous operations sometimes made very brittle, he had a curious and infinite belief in his own immortality. Other pilots could go and not come back, but never himself. It had not ever seemed possible for him to die. Now, because of his arm, because of the night of confused and bare terror in the bedroom, when pain had ripped the superficial skin from every emotion, it was possible to think of death. Yet he knew, all the same, yet without any reason that he could name, that he still would not die. He had simply become, through pain and the loss of his arm, a more conscious person. Because of the girl part of himself had come from behind the screen. But behind it all, still, very deep and infinitely secure, lay that absurd and untouchable belief in his own immortality.

She roused him from these few seconds of thinking by saying suddenly: 'We shouldn't talk of things that may not happen. It is time to be sensible. My father will be back with the pass for you.'

'Yes, it's time to be sensible,' he said.

It was awkward to hold her with his one arm, and now he turned her body slightly so that his arm was across her breast. He began to kiss her, and while he was kissing her he touched

157

first one breast and then the other, holding them with tenderness. It seemed to him that this was, perhaps, not the first but the last moment beween them. He pulled the blouse gently away from her shoulders. She moved herself so that first one arm and then the other came clear, and until he could feel all the upper part of her shoulders naked and smooth in his hand. Then she turned a little and pressed herself very closely, half sideways, against him, so that her bare shoulder pressed against the stub of his severed arm, until the pain of it shot up through his body and broke at his lips in a little gasp, making him break away.

'This is not sensible,' she said.

'You said you would do anything for me,' he said. Down beyond the dark avenues of the orchard there was no longer any light from the sun. His tenderness for her as he touched her breasts was as infinite as the darkness stretching out beyond the plain.

'Yes, I will do anything,' she said.

Françoise's father went into the room behind the kitchen and lay down on the sofa in the darkness. He lay there flat and motionless, staring upwards. He had eaten nothing since early morning, but he did not feel at all hungry now. His stomach felt as if it had become pushed up into his chest and slowly now the sour weariness of it was oozing up into his throat and mouth. Now and then he tried to swallow the sickness back again, curling his tongue over his dry lips, but each time his throat seemed to close, forming a trap that held the sickness up. He lay there for about ten minutes, pressing his hands on his stomach, too tired to shut his eyes, until he heard the voices of Franklin and the girl.

He lay there for about another five minutes, not moving, until Franklin opened the door and came in.

'I am lying down,' he said. 'Please forgive me.'

The door remained open an inch or two as Franklin crossed the room, following the sound of the voice. The light pouring through it was thrown in a long yellow stick across the round mahogany table on to the wall and the sofa beyond, and he walked round the table until he could see the light crossing the hands that lay clasped on the stomach. For a few moments longer he could not see the face.

'They said you wanted to talk to me,' Franklin said.

'Yes, I have something for you.' The hands moved a little higher, towards the chest. 'I have the papers.'

'I am most grateful,' Franklin said. 'It has been a great trouble for you.'

'A little trouble. One expects that.'

Franklin, seeing better now in the darkness, looked at the face. The lines in the cheeks, normally deep, were now like dark cracks in the faintly visible flesh. The eyes were not yet visible at all.

'You are very tired,' Franklin said. 'I am sorry.'

'Don't be sorry. It is not altogether that.'

'Should we discuss it in the morning?' Franklin said.

'No.' he said. 'It is better now.'

Franklin saw the hands move and unclasp themselves. He saw the white gleam of a square of paper.

'I have the papers here. I thought it better to explain it to you.'

'Yes,' Franklin said. Beyond the kindness of the voice he detected an odd note of reservation, almost despair. It seemed very strange to him also to be talking in the dark.

'The papers will cover all normal emergencies,' the father said. 'The question of your arm is covered. You are the victim of industrial accident. It is quite simple. You are travelling to Marseilles for treatment in hospital there. The necessary papers are there, signed by our friend the doctor.'

'I see,' Franklin said.

'To-morrow night Pierre will hand you over to friends of ours. I am not certain where they will take you. They have their arrangements. It should not be complicated.'

'Yes,' Franklin said.

'In two days you should be in Marseilles.'

Franklin did not say anything. He could see the eyes more clearly now. The door had swung open a little, throwing a broader bar of light. In this the eyes had a curiously dead appearance, the lids stiffly curled back, the dark pupils fixed, staring upward.

159

'Now, as to money.'

'I have money,' Franklin said.

'Good. Then clothes. We have clothes for you.'

'Thank you.'

'Is there anything else you need? It will be better not to take your maps. If anything should happen it might be very awkward.'

'I see. I need the revolver,' Franklin said.

'You could take it, but it is not essential.'

'I had better take it.'

'Very well.'

Franklin wondered where the revolver was, but he did not say anything. He did not want to express, once again, his distrust about it.

'I have it,' the father said. 'I will bring it up to you. It would be better if you had everything ready to-night.'

He held up the papers to Franklin.

'In a little while I will bring up the clothes and the revolver,' he said.

'Thank you.' Franklin bent down to take the papers. 'There are some things for which there are not thanks enough,' he said. He took one of the hands and held it in the darkness. Its dry coldness and the limpness of the fingers shocked him. 'I am truly and infinitely grateful.'

'There are some things for which no thanks are necessary,' the father said. 'It is our privilege to have done anything for you.'

'Thank you all the same,' Franklin said. 'I shall never forget.'

'We too shall never forget.'

The hand slipped away from Franklin's, hanging for a moment in the air, as if too tired to drop.

'You are very tired,' Franklin said. 'I am sorry.'

'Not altogether tired.' The voice was the voice of someone who has been shocked into impotence; the words were mere husks of speech, without any spirit at all. 'To-day I have been to see the family of the doctor.'

Franklin could not speak. Each time he thought of the doctor, of the grey kindly face without illusions, he felt helplessly furious. The bastards, he thought. The bastards. What have they done now? He did not know what to say.

He said at last, the anger warm in his voice: 'It is a sad and terrible thing.' He tried to put into the words some of the viciousness he felt.

'Yes. Unhappily it is not all.'

The defeat in the voice was very clear now; it had the same dead prostration as the body lying there in the dark.

'There have not been more shootings?' Franklin said.

'No. No more shootings. More suffering, that's all.'

Franklin did not speak.

'To-day I went to see the doctor's sister,' he said. 'I have known them all since I was a boy. They used to come here and row boats on the river with us. Every summer. The two doctors and the sister. She was so nice. So charming.' The voice, though very slow, gathered up a little strength. 'I was very fond of her. There was a time when I thought she might marry me. Many years ago. But you know how it happens.'

'I know,' Franklin said.

'Possibly it was better to be fond of her as a friend.' He went on talking with a little more strength, slightly faster, telling Franklin of summers before the war, when the two doctors and the sister would come to the mill, and perhaps the doctor's son and Françoise and Françoise's brother, and how in the evenings after the heat of the day they would take boats and row far up the river, fishing and picnicking and perhaps swimming in the cooler backwaters, under the willow trees. As he talked he mentioned, for the first time, Françoise's mother, who had died five or six years before the war, and Franklin saw the situation as it must have been, with the wife dead and the doctor's sister coming on Sunday and the father turning over in his mind the idea of marrying again, and perhaps neither rejecting it nor accepting it, but letting it slide on, partly troubled, partly with pleasure, Sunday after Sunday, without decision, until the war or some other circumstance decided it all instead.

'She was younger than both the brothers. Younger than myself. Perhaps that was it. Perhaps she felt that it was not right to marry an older man.' Franklin saw the truth now; how the decision had been for the woman to make and how, for some

161

reason, she had never made it. The explanation came in a moment. 'I think she was too devoted to the brothers. You know how there are women who are like that. In a way they get married to their brothers and do not want another man.'

'Yes,' Franklin said. 'I know.'

'I do not know quite why I am telling you this.'

'You were going to tell me what had happened.'

'Yes,' he said. 'Yes. That was it.' He stopped talking for about a minute, the face quite still in the darkness. In the silence Franklin could hear the rush of the mill-race outside. ' I used to take her something nice when I went into the town,' he went on. 'A little butter or something. Perhaps a chicken. To-day I went to see her, and I had a small chicken. But she was not there. They had taken her away.'

'Away?' Franklin said. The bastards, he thought, the bastards! but it was not that. The voice said very quietly:

'Ever since they shot the doctor she has not been the same. She has been going out of her mind.'

Franklin stood looking indecisively at the bar of light cutting into two black halves the motionless body on the couch. He knew now the meaning of its prostration. He did not say anything. The voice coming up from the couch seemed very distant and small and lonely.

'I feel as if I am quite lost,' it said.

Franklin stood for a moment or two not saying anything and not knowing what to say. It seemed better to go, he thought at last, and he moved away from the couch towards the middle of the room. He saw the face slightly turn as he did so, the light falling more fully across it, so that the eyes became clear and awake for the first time.

'Tell them I am not coming in to supper. I would rather lie here for a while. I shall feel better.'

'Would you like a drink?' Franklin said.

'No. You are very kind. No thank you.'

Franklin moved across the room and opened the door. As he did so he looked back. In the broad strong bar of light the white face turned to watch him, its tears shining and slowly falling, without a sound, as if the eyes had come alive at last and the voice were dead.

In the kitchen he ate supper with Françoise, the old woman, and Pierre, the bread dry in his throat, so that he found it hard to swallow. Every now and then he looked up and across the table, past the lamp, at the girl. Her eyes were very clear but full of a sort of indecisive wonder, and he was slightly oppressed by a feeling that everything was not right. From the girl he would look to the old woman, slopping her bread in her soup and then sucking it in wetly with her old heavy lips, and she, too, in turn would look up and regard him with oblique steadiness for a few seconds, as if she knew all that had been going on. He did not say anything about the father, but all through the meal he wanted to say something about himself: to express simply, but very deeply, his gratitude about what had happened, but whenever he tried to speak he looked up and saw the eyes of the three people listening, as it were for a sound from the other room, just as once before he had seen them listening for a sound outside.

When supper was over the girl came with him to the foot of the stairs to say good night. As he held her there, touching her tenderly with his hand again, it seemed like the hardest moment of his life: the moment when all that he felt for her, new and intimate, had to be frustrated. He knew now that leaving her would be the hardest thing he had ever known. He kissed her once or twice in the darkness, the kiss full of long and painful warmth, his sense of frustration growing as the agony for her grew, until he knew that she, too, could feel it and could bear it no longer.

'I should go now,' she said.

'All right.' He knew, under his frustration, that there was no sense in stopping her. 'Did you mind what happened to-night?'

'No. I wanted it to happen.'

'I am going to-morrow,' he said. 'You know that?'

'Yes. I am glad it happened.'

'There is only to-night then,' he said. 'Would you come to see me again?'

'If you go now I will try to come to see you. It may not be easy.' She stood away from him. He heard the old woman washing the dishes in the kitchen, but no other sound. 'Do you want me – however late it is?'

'However late,' he said.

In another moment she went away without speaking, and he went slowly upstairs and into his room and lay on the bed. He did not undress, but lay quite motionless, looking through the window at the summer stars. He had come to the moment he dreaded. He felt like a man who has gone into strict training for the simple purpose, finally, of jumping off a building. I should have torn the bandages off my arm every day, he thought. It would have kept me here. It would have been less painful, too.

Lying there, thinking, he slowly took off his collar and tie, and then his shoes. The night was warm and the stairs were very soft, and he watched a planet going down across the plain, west-ward, like a trembling orange flower. He watched it for a long time before he heard the sound of feet on the stairs. He raised himself on his elbow and waited. The footsteps came up to his door and after a moment the door opened.

'Are you asleep?'

It was the father. 'No. I am not asleep,' Franklin said. His heart was beating heavily.

'I have brought the clothes and the revolver,' the father said. 'I will put them on the chair. Don't get up.'

'Thank you,' Franklin said.

'The revolver is in the pocket of the jacket,' the voice seemed firmer and calmer now. 'And the cartridges. You will find them in the morning.'

'Thank you,' Franklin said. He lay propped on his elbow and watched the dark figure move across the starry window, putting the pile of clothes on the chair. He waited for it to move back again, and then said good night.

'Good night,' the father said.

He shut the door very quietly, and Franklin lay back in the bed and waited.

He lay there for another hour, waiting for the girl. Once or twice he raised himself up on his elbow again, listening, but there was never any sound except the noise of the mill-race, so steady and continuous that he heard it only when he listened consciously. At all other times it was part of the silence, warm and drowsy everywhere in the house and all across the plain. Finally he shut his eyes and lay half asleep, not listening, his thoughts streaming away in ribbons of bright confused pictures, until the ribbons snapped and he was fully awake again.

It was very late then, and he got off the bed at last and began to undress. He hung his jacket on the back of the chair by the window and then picked up, in a moment of curiosity, the jacket the father had brought. Lifting it up, he was surprised by its lightness. He took it over to the bed and spread it out, feeling in the pockets. The ammunition was in the left-hand pocket, but there was no revolver. He turned the coat over to feel in the inside pocket, but there was nothing there. He went over to the window and picked up the trousers, but they were very light, too. He dropped them on the floor and ran his hand across the chair seat in the darkness. He knew suddenly that the revolver had never been there at all.

He stood for a few moments longer by the window, wondering what to do. Then he opened the door of the bedroom and, in his stockinged feet, went downstairs.

When he got to the kitchen the lamp was still burning on the table, but the room was empty. He stood for a moment and looked about him. A single plate and knife and fork had been left on the table, and with them a glass, a loaf of bread and a bottle of wine. He stood for about half a minute longer and then went across the kitchen and opened the door of the other room.

As he opened the door he saw the broad bright bar of light fall across the room. It fell across the table and the sofa and the wall beyond. Franklin walked round the table and then, in the full lamplight, saw the father lying on the sofa. His face was turned away from the light and was partially buried in a cushion, as if he had fallen asleep in the attitude of a child crying itself to sleep in the pillow. Franklin stood for a moment and looked down, wondering if to disturb him. Then he bent down and touched the cushion with his hand.

In that moment he saw that the cushion, the revolver and the head were one: a mass of brilliant and bloody confusion falling out of his own shadow into the bar of light.

CHAPTER 16

FIVE days later Franklin stood alone in the room above the mill, by the small window where he had once clung sickly to watch Goddy and Taylor disappear beyond the vines. He stood watching the rain beating on the road below and on the little funeral party, made up of one coach and a hearse, followed by the dog, just leaving the house. He watched the rain beating on the black roof of the coaches and on the priest's hat and on the bare heads of Pierre and the father's brother and on the black dresses of the old woman and Françoise. It fell slantwise, driven in on a westerly wind. The wind was squally and seemed at last to screw up the funeral party like a scrap or two of black paper and blow it up the wet road behind the house, until it disappeared. The dog followed behind, shaking itself in the rain.

When it had gone he stood watching the rain. He was a man who had trained himself to jump off a precipice; now the precipice had gone. His gun, which had destroyed it, had gone too. He did not know what had happened to it, and at first the idea of an English revolver in a French court had scared him very much. He had reflected, too, on the uselessness and stupid irony of that gun: how he had taken it on nearly forty trips, over Germany and France and Italy, and how he had never fired it, and how, at last, it had blown a good, decent, broken Frenchman out of the world. He was bitterly glad he would never see it again. He remembered the only time he had ever fired it. It was on the short range at the station, on a dull March day. He fired six shots and cut two small ineffectual-looking holes on the target, one at four o'clock and one at seven. He was rather ashamed and determined to do better at the second shoot, but it came on heavily to rain and the shoot was cancelled, and he stood with the rest of the two flights of his squadron under a corrugated iron shed and watched the rain, driven also on a westerly wind, blowing cold and fast against the little black and white targets at the end of the range. It was then that Watson, the American, had offered to teach him to shoot. He was sorry afterwards he had not learned, but now he was glad. He had revised his opinion about the effectiveness of the revolver as a weapon. It had the power to shake a world.

It had shaken the world of the old woman, Pierre and Françoise to pieces. He stood thoughtfully watching the rain driving across the plain below. It reminded him, every moment, more and more of England. After weeks of sun, of the long, bald days of glittering heat, the rain seemed almost unendurably soft and friendly. And he knew as he watched it blowing steadily down, washing the dust from the summer grass, from the apple leaves and the late fruit still on the boughs, washing the summer scum from the river and the reeds, what it meant to the English as a people. The rain woke in him, as nothing else had woken in him, all his feeling for England. It woke in him the misery of an exile and the longing to be home. It was a longing deeper, at that moment, than his feelings for the girl; deeper than the mere desire for escape; deeper than the war, the things the war had done, and the desire for the war to be over. As he stood there all the memory of rain in England washed down through his blood and steadily increased the ache of homesickness until he was suddenly and utterly tired of the mill, the house, the river, and the flat French plain, tired of the smell of France, of speaking and thinking another language and, above all, of the complications. He felt all the Englishness of himself washed bare to the surface, clean and clear and simple as the rain.

He opened the window an inch or two and looked out, hearing the rain. The sound of it, like the smell and motion of the wind, was very cool. He put his hand on the window-ledge and the rain blew down on it, wetting his fingers. The land was grey across the plain, so that in the farthest distance the fields became nothing but indefinable lines of vapour, like low cloud.

He stood there looking at the landscape, all neutral under the rain, and thought of his position. In the empty mill, under the low cloud, watching the sky filled with rain, he felt very alone. It suddenly seemed to him that he had never known the family. They were part of the illusions of a summer dream. The rain had washed them away, with the wet black horses, the shining black hearse, and the black wet priest, up the muddy road, as it would wash away, soon, the leaves of summer. They seemed less and less real as he thought of them. Even the sight of the revolver, which seemed to have blown out of the cushion a mass of tangled scarlet stuffing, seemed unreal also; and with it went the unreality of the screams of the old woman, yelling to God to bring back her son, and the calm white face of the girl.

After the father had shot himself they had hidden him again in the mill. The unreality of four days slipped away, too. The rain neutralized with its cool sound and its grey beauty the horror of the blood in the lamplight, the misery of not being able to sleep at night, the worry about the revolver, his agony for the girl. It washed away the blood that he felt was on his mind. It cooled and calmed him until finally he stood there considering what seemed to him the most natural idea in the world – of how he would get away, alone, that day.

He shut the window and stood with his back to it, thinking calmly. All his belongings were on the floor, tied in readiness in a paper bundle. He was wearing his service shirt and tie, and the black coat and grey trousers given him by the family. He took off the collar and tie and put them in his jacket pocket, and then, in place of them, knotted his handkerchief round his neck. In his pocket he still had the papers given him by the father. Now all he needed was a little food, which he could get in the house and, he thought, a little luck before nightfall. With a little luck, under cover of rain, he could make ten miles before darkness. He would walk south-westward and trust to luck. So far his luck had been good; very good, perhaps too good. It had seemed to run like the weather: in a long bright spell, all in his favour. Even the arm in a way had been lucky. Now that the weather had broken he had a superstitious feeling that his luck might break, too. He stood with his small bundle of things under his arm. I have to go some time, he thought. The rain beat against the window and the roof, and there was no other sound. He felt suddenly that he could not bear the pain of farewell. It would be better to go now, alone, while the reality of the faces in the house were dissolved. He took a last look round the room where he had first slept with O'Connor and Sandy and

168

the two boys. Not since that time had there been a moment when the faces seemed to have less power to affect him than now.

He opened the door and began to go very quietly down the wooden stairs. All he needed was a little food. He would leave a letter for Françoise on the kitchen table. Oh hell! he thought, I can't do it. God, I can't do it! He tried hopelessly to translate for himself the things he must say to her, and realized that there were no words, either in her language or his, for all the love and anxiety and confusion he felt. He stopped on the stairs and knew suddenly that he did not want to go, and yet that he had to go. If he couldn't write the words, how could he say them? There were no words for the pain of separation.

He stood still on the stairs, arguing with himself. The stairs came down in two flights, with a landing breaking them at the first storey. He stood on the landing and stared at the small window in the wall, not really looking out of it but only at it, seeing only the flat squares of glass, without distance, blobbed with rain.

He stood there for about a minute before the glass lost its flatness, and he could see through it and through the grey pattern of rain to where, below, the road ran by the house in a strip of stone and mud. Even when he saw the road he could not believe, for another minute or so, that what he saw on it was real. Down in the road was a man Franklin had never seen before. He was looking at the house in the rain.

Franklin lay flat on the landing with his face against the corner of the window. The man was wearing a dark grey overcoat and a bowler hat. For some time he stood quite still. Then he turned on his heel and looked back up the road, towards the river. He was sucking a cigarette. He had a grey moustache which habitual cigarette-smoking had stained a dirty amber underneath. He took the cigarette out of his mouth, held it as if to throw it away, and then changed his mind and pinched it out with his fingers, putting it in his overcoat pocket. Then he turned and looked up the road again, as if afraid of being watched, or as if, perhaps, expecting the funeral to come back. From the window on the stairs Franklin could see the whole front of the house and the road as far down as the river. The

169

distance between himself and the man was about forty feet. If I had the revolver and I were a good shot and I were lucky, he thought, I could shoot him. I could aim at the hat. He did not know at all why the idea of shooting occurred to him. It seemed very natural. Unfortunately I haven't got the revolver, he thought, and I wasn't a good shot, so what the hell. Still the idea of shooting the man seemed natural. It even seemed desirable. Then Franklin had another thought. If he comes into the mill and finds me here I'm sunk. I shall have to kill him. He accepted the thought quite calmly. The man moved across the road and peered into the window of the house. He had his hands in the pockets of his overcoat. It seems odd he comes on the day of the funeral, Franklin thought, when there's no one here. Whoever he is I shall have to kill him. I can't afford not to. Four people know I'm here, and five is one too many. He watched the man move along the front of the house, towards the door. At the door he stopped for a moment, looked back to the river, and then took a hand from his pocket and tried the latch of the door. The door was locked: as I might have known it would be, Franklin thought.

The man hesitated again, as if in no hurry before moving, and Franklin, tense on the stairs, one knee bent in readiness to spring up, waited to see what would happen. The funeral had been gone about half an hour. It was still raining quite fast, but the man did not move, as if he knew quite well how much time he had. Then suddenly he raised his face and looked up. He seemed, in that moment, to look straight at Franklin. Franklin did not move. All right, he thought, you bastard, come up. Whoever you are, come up. For fully a minute the man down below looked up at the window. Franklin saw the rain shining like dew on his bowler hat and driving past his upturned face. Make up your mind, he thought.

Finally, the man seemed to make up his mind. He turned slowly and walked down towards the river. Franklin watched him go down and stand on the edge of the jetty. He seemed to stand there in thought, as if fascinated by the stream going past in the rain. Then Franklin realized that he was looking not at the stream but at the boat. He looked at it with the same un-hurried contemplation as when looking at the house and the

170

window. Once or twice he looked up and down the stream. At last he squatted down on the jetty and cautiously put one hand on the edge of it and leapt down into the boat. Franklin saw the boat rock slightly with the impact, and then the short body of the man stoop down so that only the bowler hat could be seen. It remained like that for a moment or two before coming upright again. Even then there was no hurry. The man remained in the boat, quite still, in contemplation of something, for another two or three minutes, until at last he turned, put both hands on the jetty, and pulled himself up.

Franklin, as he watched him walk slowly back to the house, knew that his chance of escape had gone. But for some reason it did not seem to matter. He watched the man stand before the house again. The rain still did not trouble him. Franklin, waiting for him to move, looked at his boots. They were black and shiny, but the mud of the road had speckled them with yellow. Then he saw the man go for the second time to the kitchen window and look in. He saw him shade his eyes with one hand and then, as if he still could not see inside, rub the rainy glass with the palm of his hand. This time he remained for some minutes with his face pressed sideways against the glass. Above him, from the iron guttering of the roof, a dribble of rain became caught in the wind and ran down like a spiral of water, breaking on the bowler hat. Startled by it, the man looked sharply up and took off his hat to shake the water from the brim, and in that moment Franklin saw him full-faced, the head bald as a dome of lard and the small black eyes, unshaded by the hat, blinking with annoyance at the rain.

The man shook his hat and put it on again and stood for a minute longer. Then he took out his watch. He looked at it, put it back into his waistcoat and did up the buttons of his coat. He seemed to have made up his mind not to wait any longer. He walked slowly up the road, not hurrying at all, as if he knew quite well what time he had, and Franklin watched him go, changing his position over to the other side of the window, so that he could watch him better, keeping him in sight until he reached the path above the river. Up there he stopped again and turned and looked back. Standing on the path, he took out of his pocket the half-cigarette he had put there. He lit it in the cup of his hands, and Franklin saw the smoke caught in the wind like a vaporized puff of the grey rain. And he realized, as he saw it, and as he watched the man disappear finally beyond the river, that the rain had lost its friendliness and that there was nothing to do but wait again.

He waited at the window about an hour, but the man did not come back. The rain slackened a little and finally, when the funeral party came back, the sky was breaking up and the rain was like blown mist that settled like a grey bloom on the coach. He lay at the window and watched four people get out of the coach: the old woman, Pierre, Françoise, and the dead man's brother. The dog was wet with rain. The brother took the arm of the old woman and led her into the house. After a few moments the coach drew away and the priest came riding down the hill on his bicycle. His hat was hung on the handle-bars.

Franklin lay and waited. The door of the house was shut. Pools of rain lay in the road and were ruffled by the wind. They shone white from the reflection of the breaking sky.

After about ten minutes the door opened and Françoise came out. As soon as he saw her he went back upstairs and waited for her in the top room. She came up at once and he held her by the wall, with one hand, not speaking.

'Were you all right?' she said. 'Did anything happen?'

He knew that he must tell her. 'Yes,' he said. 'Something happened.'

Dressed in black, the collar high up to her throat, she looked calmer than ever.

'What?' she said. 'What happened?'

'Someone was here,' he said. 'A man.'

'A German?'

'No,' he said, 'I don't think so.' He began to tell her about it. She was very calm and waited for him to finish.

'He was quite bald,' he said. 'Would you know him?'

'Yes,' she said, 'I would know him.'

'Who was he?'

'He was from the village.'

'No good?'

172

'He is one of those people who can never keep their mouths shut.'

'Then he's no good?'

'No,' she said, 'he's no good. No good to us at all.'

She stood by the wall, looking past him, thinking. He felt how much he loved her in the black dress. Her eyes seemed to swim into the distance, in long thought, and finally came suddenly back.

'Would you be ready to do something?'

'For you?'

'For yourself,' she said.

He nodded.

'Would you be ready to go?' she said.

'When?'

'To-night.'

He did not answer.

'The man who came here is no good,' she said. 'He was here for no good. We know him. He has an idea of something, and if he has an idea he will talk about it. You know how ideas grow.'

'Yes,' he said.

'Would you go?' she said.

He knew that there was no choice, but the thought of going was very hard again, and he hated it now.

'I will come with you,' she said.

'Good Christ!' he said. 'What?'

'I will come with you,' she said. She looked up at him. Her eyes were very still.

'What are you talking about?' he said.

'I will come with you,' she said. 'I have always planned to come with you.'

'But for Christ's sake!' he said.

'Don't let *grand'mère* hear you say "for Christ's sake". She knows I am coming.'

'But not now,' he said. 'How can you? Your father's dead. How can you? Not now.'

'I can come. The dead are dead. Besides, you could never go alone.'

'Why not?'

173

'With the arm. They would pick you up in a minute.'

'Then they would pick you up if you came with me. That would be two of us. That would be worse.'

'They won't pick you up the way I shall take you,' she said.

'No?' He looked at her closely. She was utterly and imperviously calm, and he knew that she had long ago made up her mind. 'How will you take me?'

She took his right arm and held it, putting her hand flat against the palm of his.

'How strong are you? Could you row?'

'Row?'

'A little way. Sometimes.' She said: 'I could row most of the way, but it would help if you rowed a little. It would keep your mind occupied.'

He opened his mouth to say something, but he was too astounded to form the words. He knew now why she had so often rowed up the river.

'It is the only way to go,' she said.

'How far is it to the Unoccupied zone?' he said. It seemed better to be practical.

'We would row for two nights. Perhaps three nights. Perhaps a week. The river goes on a long way to the south.'

'And how far would you come?'

'All the way,' she said.

'All the way?'

'Yes,' she said. 'As far as you go. All the way.'

'To the frontier?'

'To the frontier. Yes,' she said.

He thought of the hell of leaving her at the frontier. Rather than go through that he knew that he did not want her to come.

'It will be very hard at the frontier,' he said, 'leaving you.'

'You won't leave me at the frontier,' she said.

She stood with her hand flat against the wall, decisive and upright and very certain.

'But you can't come on,' he said.

'Yes,' she said. 'I can come on. I can come to England.'

She stood by the wall, quite still, smiling at him because the surprise was so clear and abrupt in his face. He could not speak. He could only look at her standing there with sublime certainty,

174

knowing that there was now no arguing against her. He felt that she was holding something in her hands that was very precious, like a new doll, and he knew that it would be cruel to knock it out.

He took her hand and drew it towards his face and held it there. He kissed it once or twice and waited for her to speak.

'You see, it's no use being silly now,' she said.

'Am I being silly?'

'No,' she said, 'but we have waited a long while, and now the time has come.'

'All right,' he said. He knew that deep inside himself he was very happy that she was coming. His only doubt was about England. It was something they would have to decide later. 'When do we go?'

'To-night,' she said. 'Just before dark. The priest and my uncle will go in about an hour. It will be dark early after the rain.'

As he held her his doubts were renewed.

'I can go alone if you think it would be better,' he said.

She did not speak.

'Are you sure?' he said.

She still did not speak. Her eyes were calm and very steady, and her lips were tightly fixed in a half-smile, and he knew that nothing he could say or do could change her determination now.

CHAPTER 17

HE stood in the kitchen for the last time, holding the brown
paper parcel that contained his razor, soap, and change of
clothes. He watched the old woman wrap up two sticks of bread
and a piece of soft white cheese in a table-napkin and finally
pack it all, with a few ripe green grapes, about a dozen apples,
and the two cold hind legs of a rabbit, into a black cloth bag.
The girl had a brown attaché case containing her clothes and a
bottle of wine wrapped in a towel.

It was almost dark outside. The time had come to say good-
bye, and now Franklin did not know what to say. He felt that
it would be nice to give something to the old woman, as a farewell gift, but there was nothing to give. He stood for a moment
by the kitchen table, watching her pack the food, and then he
held out his hand. The old woman took it in both of hers and
pressed it, shaking it silently up and down. Her hands were cold
and rough, and she, too, had nothing to say. She could only
shake his one hand tremblingly up and down until at last he
turned suddenly and went out of the house and down to the
jetty, with Pierre.

He stood under the wall of the mill with Pierre and waited
for the girl to finish saying good-bye. Pierre carried the attaché
case. It was not raining now, but the cloud was low and the
wind broke sharply across the river, in dark irregular waves.

'You have everything?' Pierre said.

'I think so,' Franklin said. His stomach was light and warm
as if he were going on an operational trip. 'I would like to thank
you.'

'Don't thank me.' Pierre looked up and down the road in the
twilight. 'Would you like this?'

He pulled the revolver out of his jacket pocket.

'No,' Franklin said.

'I have cleaned it.'

'I don't want it,' Franklin said. 'How did you get it?'

'I said it was mine,' Pierre said.

'That was dangerous,' Franklin said. 'The revolver is an English make.'

'It made no difference. Armaments are international.'

'The French should know,' Franklin said.

'We know,' Pierre said. 'Don't you want it? It is a very good revolver.'

'No,' Franklin said. 'You keep it. As a present from me. As a little thanks for all you have done.'

Pierre put the revolver in his left hand and held out his right. 'No thanks are necessary. It's I should thank you. It has been an experience to know you.'

'It has been a great experience for me, too,' Franklin said. 'One day I will come back and we will fish together.'

'One day,' Pierre said.

They shook hands and after a few moments the girl came out of the house. She was wearing a dark blue coat over the white blouse and the green skirt. The old woman was not with her. Pierre and Franklin came out from under the wall of the mill and joined her. They walked down to the river together.

'Get under the tarpaulin,' the girl said.

Franklin got into the boat and Pierre came in after him, holding up the tarpaulin so that Franklin could get under it. The tarpaulin had on it small pools of rain which ran off as Pierre lifted it. Franklin lay with his knees bent in the stern of the boat. Pierre put the attaché case and the bag of food underneath the tarpaulin. He got out of the boat and did not speak again.

'Are you all right?' the girl said. Franklin felt the boat rocking slightly as she came into it.

'Yes,' he said.

'It's not for long,' she said. 'There are two bridges and then you can come out.'

'I am all right,' he said.

He heard the iron ring on the jetty ring against the stone as Pierre slid the rope through it and let it fall. It was the only sound in the twilight, except the uninterrupted roar of the mill-stream and the sound of the wind on the river, until at last he heard the girl pushing one oar against the stone and pulling the boat round with the other.

177

'You are quite sure about my brother's wife?' Pierre said. The voice was low for the last time from the jetty.

'Quite sure.'

'Number 67. Once you get there you don't need to worry.'

'I shall remember,' the girl said.

The boat pulled round against the wind, and then at right angles to it, and Franklin felt the girl begin to pull with both oars, making very little sound, the boat moving in steady even sweeps, rocking very slightly on the wind-broken water. And then as it moved forward he heard a new sound. It came from the river-bank, and was like the sound of someone crying. It increased to a high-whimpering, and finally became the wild howling of the dog.

For a minute the girl stopped rowing and he felt the wind rock the boat in midstream. He heard the dog struggling in the reeds, threshing the water, and then the voice of Pierre in a desperate whisper telling it again and again to be quiet. He heard the dog crying again, struggling wildly on the water's edge, and finally the sound of Pierre beating it into silence, hitting its flanks with a mournful hollow sound of his flat hand.

The girl began to row again, and there was no sound from the dog except a constant, small, thin crying. As it began to die away the sound of the mill-stream smothered it. Finally that sound, too, died away until there was no sound except the quiet noise of oars and the ruffle of rainless wind blowing across open water.

Franklin lay still and did not speak. He did not know what to expect, but as the boat went smoothly on he remembered how evening after evening the girl had rowed it upstream, whenever she could, so that whoever guarded the bridges would get used to the sight of a girl going to fish in the twilight. He did not know what to expect at the bridges that night: some shooting, perhaps, at least a challenge, perhaps even death, but he lay there under the tarpaulin and nothing happened. Once he lifted the corner of the tarpaulin and looked out. He could see the grey evening sky, not quite dark, swimming past above the wet leaves of the willows. He did not see the bridge. But in time he knew that they must have travelled far enough to be beyond it. He waited a little longer, keeping the edge of the tarpaulin raised, and then saw the shadow of the second bridge go past. The bridge was low and there was a second or two of darkness that held them down. Then it broke, and it was as if they had come out of a tunnel into the light beyond.

Five minutes later the girl stopped rowing. 'All right now,' she said. Franklin moved the tarpaulin aside and sat up. It was still not dark, and he could see the girl's face as she rested on the oars. She was panting a little and looked rather tense. 'Are you all right?' he said.

'It was the dog,' she said. 'The dog frightened me. I tied him up and he broke loose because he knew I was going.'

He did not say anything. He knew that it meant very much to her. He covered the tarpaulin over the bag of food and the attaché case.

'Are you ready to go on?' she said.

'Yes,' he said. 'I can row, too, now.'

'I am all right.'

'I am going to row, too,' he said.

He stepped over the tarpaulin and moved up towards the bows of the boat, sitting behind her. She changed the oar for him and he took it in his right hand. It felt good to be holding the smooth end of the oar. It gave him a feeling of responsibility.

'Ready when you are,' he said. He felt that he could row strongly, for a long time.

'There is no hurry,' she said. 'Rest a moment. We can row all night.'

She rested a moment or two longer. He looked at the stream. It seemed about seventy or eighty feet wide and was running strongly down, with thick colour, after the day of rain. The current was quite strong, and it did not seem to him like the same stream. He asked her about it, and she said:

'No. This is the real river. The mill is on the backwater.'

'Does it go far like this?' he said. 'So wide?'

'It goes down to the Unoccupied line,' she said. 'And then on to the south. For a time it *is* the Occupied line.'

'Can we get past there?' he said.

'We can get past,' she said. 'Are you ready to row now?'

He did not speak at once. He saw her neck very brown in the

179

twilight below her black hair, and he leaned forward for one moment and put his face against it. All that he wanted to say to her in thanks and love and admiration came together in a moment of tenderness that he could not express. He let go the oar and put his hand on her bare neck and pressed his face against her.

'This won't get us to England,' she said.

'It will,' he said, 'in time.'

'Not loving.'

'In good time it will.'

'Do you want me to come to England?'

'I want you to do whatever you feel is best. Do you want to come so much?'

'I want to come,' she said. 'Will they like me?'

'Will who like you?'

'Your family,' she said. 'Your mother.'

'There will be a private war if they don't,' he said.

'Do the English hate the French?' she said.

'We will talk about that later. Are you ready now?'

'I'm ready.'

'Bless you,' he said.

They began to row together a moment later. At first, each time he pulled, he felt the need for his other hand. He felt himself grope for it in the darkness. His hands had always been rather large, and he did not feel now any awkwardness in holding the oar with one hand. He felt only an odd sense of loss. His amputated arm was a ghost that seemed to be trying to become part of the rhythm of rowing. After a time this feeling grew stronger. He gradually felt that the arm was there, and that it went forward with the other arm, in unison, sharing the strength of each stroke.

They rowed for the first time for about an hour without stopping. After the first quarter of an hour he was very tired, but he did not say anything. He sucked in his lower lip and bit it hard under his teeth, and sometimes shut his eyes. The illusion about his arm grew stronger in the darkness. He was frightened that if he stopped rowing the illusion would stop, leaving him empty again, without the comforting sense of strength it gave. All the time the current in midstream was very strong; more water was coming down after the rain, and sometimes, on the wide bends of the stream, the wind was strong and quite cold, coming in long explosive gusts that broke on the willows like high waves. As he rowed his tiredness and his determination not to be tired became one. He did not think of anything, but he felt the soreness of his one hand increase until he could feel nothing with his mind except the painful slit made by the oar on the palm of his hand.

All the time he watched the girl, seeing her white blouse in the darkness. He was determined not to give up until she gave up. But after a time he became very tired and did not know quite what he was doing, and was surprised to see the branches of trees spreading rapidly in towards the boat from the shore. He was still rowing automatically, clinging to the illusion about his other arm, some moments after the girl had given up.

'We'll rest a bit,' she said. 'Are you very tired?'

'No,' he said. 'Not very tired.'

'I'll get the food,' she said.

'I'm not hungry,' he said. 'I'm thirsty. That's all.'

They were close into the left bank now, under a stretch of willows, out of the current and the wind. He leaned out of the boat and put his hand in the water. It was very cold and the soreness sprang out of the flesh like the pain of hot wire. But after a moment he felt the soothing of the water, and he let the hand remain in it until the girl had found the food and the wine.

'Will you eat something?' she said.

She sat facing him now.

'I would like some wine, that's all,' he said.

She handed him the bottle. 'You drink,' she said. 'I'm hungry.'

He took the bottle and pulled the cork with his teeth, and then drank some of the wine. It was dry and cold, and after a moment he felt better. He held the bottle between his knees and let the wind blow coolly on his wet, sore hand.

'Are you very tired?' she said again.

'No.'

'If you are very tired we won't go on.'

'I will go on as long as you go on,' he said.

'We should go a little farther to-night,' she said. 'We can rest all day to-morrow and then row again.'

'All right. Let's go on,' he said.

They rested about half an hour. The girl ate some of the apples with bread while Franklin drank more of the wine. Finally, while the girl was packing up the remainder of the food he dipped his handkerchief in the water and wrapped it round his hand. He held it against the oar and kept it there by pressure when he began to row again.

They rowed on for a long time after that, keeping closer into the bank, out of the wind, because it was darker now. Once the river turned in a great bend, eastward, and for a time the wind came full downstream, stronger than the current, and helped to blow them along. At intervals the illusion about his severed arm came back to Franklin, but never for long, and he felt himself instead using the old trick of sitting relaxed, as he had done when flying, foreshortening his mind and never thinking of the moment ahead. He did this until the movement of rowing was not conscious, and even the fiery slit across his palm could not be felt any more.

They came into the bank again after nearly three hours of rowing. Branches of trees spreading out low over the water brushed his face as the boat went in underneath them, and swung in close to the bank. He was too tired to move for a moment or two, and sat with his head on his knees, the blood hammering in his ears while the girl pulled the boat tight against the reeds. As he sat there, all the time meaning to move and help her and all the time not moving, she finished tying up the boat to the tree.

'Shall we sleep in the boat or on the bank?' she said. 'I think on the bank is better.'

He was quite startled by her voice.

'Oh! On the bank,' he said.

He managed to get stiffly to his feet and help her with the tarpaulin.

There was an odd and disjointed unreality about the moment of throwing the tarpaulin on the bank and jumping to follow it and slipping in the reeds and feeling the sharp weeds cut the naked sores of his hand when the handkerchief had fallen away. But after a moment or two he felt better, and together they spread the tarpaulin on the grass. They folded the tarpaulin in

182

half, and then lay down together on one half of it, pulling the other over them, with the girl's coat on top. Franklin put his arm under her head and she lay against his shoulder, using it for a pillow. His eyes were hard and tense with tiredness, without flexibility, and he could not shut them for a long time after he lay down.

'Have we come far enough?' he said.

'Far enough, I think,' she said.

Her voice had all the calm quietness he had always known it to have: the calmness that seemed not quite real, as if nothing surprised her, as if everything had been planned for her beforehand and shaped, in its happening, by her faith.

She did not speak again, and he lay there for a long time awake and terribly tired, listening to the wind across the water. All the time she lay there calmly against his arm, not moving, as if she were already asleep. Finally he fell asleep, too, and then woke again much later, his body stiff and his arm bloodless where the girl had lain against him. It was still very dark, and now the girl had turned over and was lying with her face the other way.

He lay for a long time listening to her crying in the darkness. She was crying deeply and heavily, with terrible relief, as if all her wonderful calmness had broken at last. He did not say anything to her and did not try to stop her, but only held her in the darkness, tenderly.

CHAPTER 18

FOR a long time in the morning Franklin lay on the river-bank and watched herons circling above the water downstream. They flapped hugely in monotonous circles above the willows, yellow now in the grey light. The wind seemed grey, too, as it whipped fast across the deserted river, brushing across it sudden paths of dark waves that were clean and calm again a moment later. In these sudden squalls the wind seemed to rain from the western bank in yellow squalls of dying willow leaves that gathered in shoals and floated northward in the dirty water. Everywhere he could see, for a mile or two up and down stream, the river was empty, and the war seemed very far away.

He was very hungry all that morning, in the cool fresh west wind, and he was not tired. The stump of his arm did not ache and the palm of the other hand was not very sore from rowing. After he and the girl had eaten breakfast, finishing up the apples and the first loaf of bread, he wanted to be going. But the girl shook her head.

'Why not?' he said. 'There's nothing very suspicious about a boat. We could row all morning and sleep this afternoon. And then row to-night. There's nobody about.'

'There is a town round the bend of the stream,' she said.

'What town?'

'Wherever there is a town there are Germans,' she said.

'What about food?' he said. 'Don't you have to get more food?'

'Yes,' she said. 'I will get that.'

'Where?' he said. 'In the town?'

'Yes,' she said. 'I will walk in and buy more bread and fruit this morning.'

'Not without me.'

'It is very easy,' she said.

'No,' he said, 'not without me.'

He was conscious of a slight impatience. He remembered the first march, in the moonlight, with O'Connor and the rest of the

184

crew, and how this same feeling of impatience had fretted him all that night. He looked back on all the weeks in the bedroom, at the mill, as part of a sharp and curious nightmare. Now, on the river, in the grey light after the rain, the situation seemed very real. It also seemed to him very simple. All his life had become clear again. All that they had to do now was to travel; to travel fast, and to travel out of the Occupied zone. Above all, they had to travel together.

'You go nowhere without me,' he said. He felt very determined about this.

'We must have more food,' she said.

'All right,' he said. 'We will go and buy it together.'

'That's impossible.'

'But what are you talking about?' he said. 'If one can go then both of us can go. We went to the town together before. You were not afraid then. You said so. You needn't be afraid now.'

'I'm not afraid.'

'Then what is it?' he said. He went on talking rather rapidly, half knowing all the time it was not she who was afraid, but himself. He was afraid of the uncertainty, of the loneliness, afraid above all of losing her. He went on talking quickly, driven by this fear, until suddenly he saw that she was crying again.

'Oh, God,' he said.

She was sitting on her heels on the river bank, her hands flat against her sides. She was crying with her head down, and it seemed to him as if someone were beating her slowly down to the ground.

'Please don't,' he said. 'Please.'

She did not say anything. He felt very dry and miserable, and took hold of her hands.

'You don't have to cry because of me,' he said. 'You don't have to cry again.'

'Again?' She lifted her face now.

'I heard you crying in the night,' he said. 'That was easy. Why are you crying now?'

'You're very impatient,' she said.

'I did not mean to be impatient.'

185

'Getting out of the Occupied zone into the Unoccupied isn't always easy,' she said. 'It may take a long time.'

'How long?'

'I don't know. A day or two. Perhaps a week or two. After that it will be easier. It is like crossing a frontier.'

God! I'm a fool, he thought. He did not say anything, but remained holding one of her hands, thinking of himself only as a blind, impatient, and utterly selfish fool, the victim once again of his own mistrust. He knew that his impatience rose from anxiety, but he felt rising in him, too, his awakening consciousness about the war. He wanted to get back, to fly again, to bring to the war and his part in it the clearer anger of a new experience. He did not want to find himself left out. All the things that had happened to him in France, and the things that he had seen happen to other people, had now to be expressed, and he felt that they could only be expressed in terms of flying: not in the old way, for flying's sake, but in a new way, positively, harshly, with the bright anger of new purposes. He had never flown with personal hatred, but he had known men who had, and he remembered among them Jameson, a very young boy good at football who lost his parents in a blitz: who for a whole year tried to shape his sorrow and fury so that he could fly better, more often and with more deadly intention. In the agony of this eagerness Jameson pranged kite after kite, getting nothing from it but dusty bitterness. As this went on, and Jameson drank with determination to counteract it, Franklin felt less and less pity for him, not understanding the huge agony of anger felt by Jameson, an emotion that seemed to be overplayed against the ordinary hearty life about him. It would have seemed better sometimes if Jameson had taken his sorrow less violently, alone. But Franklin now understood what Jameson felt. Something very like it in himself, an agony and a sorrow ripped raw by the deaths of the doctor and the girl's father, his friends, had similarly to be avenged. And now the word itself, which in more ordinary days would have seemed violent and grandiose, seemed just and right. It was something which belonged, as Jameson's emotion had belonged, to larger things than personal hatred. It belonged to all little people, to all little, honest, decent, kindly people everywhere. It was a fine

186

purpose, and it seemed too bad that Jameson, as so often happened, had been blown to bloody and dirty pieces before he could accomplish it.

Because he could not explain this to the girl he put his one hand on her neck, quietly kissing her face. 'Please don't cry,' he said. 'We will do whatever you think is best.' He knew it was better that way.

'Don't be impatient,' she said.

'I won't be.'

'If you like we will row a little farther and then it will only be a short way into the town.'

'We will do whatever you think,' he said.

'You should have more faith,' she said. Her eyes were calm and clear now, the pupils very bright after the tears. 'If you have faith anything will happen. Look what has happened to you now. You have been very ill, but after all you didn't die.'

'Die?' he said. It was the first time they had discussed it. 'Did I nearly die?'

'There was a night after we had been gathering grapes,' she said.

'Grapes?' he said. 'I don't remember.'

'No,' she said. 'You were very ill all through the grape-harvest. Very ill. But I had faith about you. It began by being a small faith, and then it got bigger with every bunch of grapes until it was really quite a big faith. The biggest I ever had.'

'There must be much wine from the grapes of such faith,' he said.

She smiled and he tried to think back to the time when he had nearly died. He did not remember the grape-harvest; he did not remember any particular night of terror. It seemed clear that there were many things that would never come back.

'I think we should get the food now,' the girl said. 'It will be safe to row. And I can get in early at the queue at the bread shop.'

She undid the catches of the attaché case and lifted up the lid. 'Do you want to shave now?'

'No,' he said. 'I will shave when you have gone. It will pass the time.'

187

'I'll wash my face,' she said.

She took a towel out of the attaché case and went down to the river. He saw her wet the end of the towel and dab it over her face. She had left the lid of the attaché case open, and he saw in it her nightdress and comb, another pair of shoes, some stockings, and a hat. He saw, too, where she had stencilled her name on the inner side of the lid, and he knew that she must have put it there as a young girl. The black stencilling was uneven, and after her name and the name of the mill, and the name of the town, and the department, she had stencilled FRANCE, THE WORLD, and then after that THE UNIVERSE, SPACE. He was still looking at it when she came back from the river, drying her face with the towel.

'Now you know,' she said.

'I'm sorry,' he said. 'I didn't mean to look.'

'It doesn't matter,' she said. 'I did it when I was a little girl. My mother gave me the case.'

'It is a very nice case,' he said.

'Yes,' she said. 'You can put your things into it, too, if you want to. It will be better than the paper parcel.'

'All right,' he said.

From the brown paper parcel she took his few belongings and packed them beside her own in the case. He watched her close the lid, with its black-stencilled THE WORLD, UNIVERSE, SPACE, and, remembering how he had many times written the same things in his books as a child, felt a moment of new and great intimacy between them.

'Now you know I won't leave you,' she said.

'Now I know,' he said.

'Do you mind because I am coming to England?'

'No,' he said. 'I want you to come. More than anything I want you to come.'

'Will they like me in England?'

'They will like you very much.'

'Is it true that the English don't like the French?'

'It is true of some of the English and some of the French. For instance, O'Connor.'

'Who is O'Connor?'

'He was the older one of the crew,' he said. 'He thinks there is nothing on earth like England, and that there should be nothing on earth but Englishmen.'

'I wonder if he got free?' she said.

Franklin wondered, too. He picked up the attaché case and gave it to the girl to hold while he rolled up the tarpaulin. Good old O'Connor, he thought. Nothing would hold him down. He was the invincible, impossible Union-Jack-in-the-box popping up anywhere, for ever. To think of him was like the pain of remembering England.

He hitched the tarpaulin under his arm and walked down to the river. The sky, so like an English sky in October, was still unbroken. Little paths of waves were scuttling darkly across the stream. Up and down, as far as he could see, the river was empty.

The girl sat in the boat, holding both oars.

'I can row,' he said.

'No,' she said, 'I will row. It will rest your hand.'

He got into the boat with deep humiliation, not speaking. It had never once occurred to him that she might notice his hand.

They rowed upstream to within two miles of the town, and pulled the boat into the bank, under a clump of alders. He stayed there and shaved himself and ate a few grapes while the girl went into the town. He did not know quite what to expect that morning. He still did not share the sublime enormity of her faith, and once the terror of losing her hit him like one of the dark waves of cold wind that shivered the grey light on the river. But after about an hour and a half she came back, bringing three loaves, some more apples, and a lump of brown meat paste, and he could have cried at the sight of her carrying these very simple things. He noticed that the bread was greyer and heavier-looking than the bread they had been eating, and the girl apologized for the meat paste. It was the best she could get. she said, but you could eat it if you were hungry.

'Was it difficult?' he said.

'No,' she said. 'It's a poor town. Consequently there aren't many Germans. And there is no bridge.'

They stayed there all that day and then, in the twilight, with the wind cold and rainless and still fairly high and flapping like a wet flag on the heavy sides of the boat, they began to row again. They rowed as they had done the previous night, each taking an oar, but this time the girl knotted his handkerchief across the palm of his hand, so that now it was cool and easy for him to row. They rowed in the late twilight past the town and from the far bank he could see the black outline of warehouses and a church against the cold western light, and then, lower down, by the water's edge, the shape of a boat or two rocking up and down in the wind. They rowed quietly past the town and beyond the last of the lightless houses until there was nothing about them again but flat open country with low lines of willows and, finally, nothing but the night shaped into its degrees of solid darkness. He could hear the rainless wind all that night sweeping through the trees of the river-side and bringing the low and whistling sound across the water like a gathering wave. They rested twice, rocking in mid-stream, eating a little bread and drinking some of the wine. He was never really tired, and after the second rest, either because of a bend in the stream or because the wind had turned, they seemed to be able to pull the boat along in longer and smoother strokes. He felt the wind in his face for all the rest of the night, blowing cool in his hair that was slightly wet with the sweat of exertion, and cold and solid, like a mouthful of cool food, whenever he opened his mouth for breath. And as he rowed, looking at the girl in front of him, he felt that they were closer than two people had ever been, and that they were close because of a series of little things: because of the little difference of the morning, because she had bandaged his hand, because of their few belongings together in the attaché case. They were close because, as he had felt once or twice before, they were both very young, living their lives on the sharp, thin edge of the world.

They rowed for about four hours, pulling into the bank in the very early morning, while it was still dark. They lay on the bank as they had done the night before, under her coat and the tarpaulin, but this time she did not cry, and he knew that there was no regret or difference or distrust to keep them apart. He lay very close to her, his own shape clear against her, quite tired now but not exhausted.

The wind was dying when he woke and the sun was white on the water. He could see the red tops of houses above yellow autumn trees diagonally across the river, about a mile upstream, and beyond them in the distance a grey line of hills. The girl was awake, too, and was standing behind a clump of alders, watching something across the water. He got up and stood by the alders with her and saw what it was.

It was a boat. It was rowed by a man with a grey check suit and a big puffy grey cap, and he was keeping close to the bank on the north side. He was rowing steadily, with caution, and as he rowed he kept looking over his shoulder. Franklin was aware after a few moments that he knew they were there.

'If he comes don't say anything,' the girl said. 'Don't talk.'

Franklin was watching the man. He was now about fifty yards away. He was a man of about forty-five, rather swarthy, with a black moustache. The back of his pale grey cap cut a clear half-circle across his black hair.

'He's coming in,' Franklin said. 'He's probably reported us already.'

'Don't talk,' the girl said. 'Whatever you do, don't talk.'

He stood on the bank and watched the man pulling the boat round. As the boat made its angle towards the shore he raised the oars and rested on them. The boat came in close and the man looked over his shoulder and gave a final pull or two, bringing the boat broadside on to the shore.

'Going very far?' the man said.

'No,' the girl said.

'You want to get over to the other side?'

'No,' the girl said.

'If you do I can help.'

'We are all right,' the girl said. 'We are taking a holiday.'

'A funny place to take a holiday,' the man said. He pulled the boat several yards nearer the shore. He looked at their own boat, keeping about an oar's length away. 'The Vichy border.'

The girl did not say anything.

'I am your friend,' the man said. He looked up and down the river, and then at the girl. 'I am your friend. It's all right.'

'How do I know that?'

'I shouldn't have bothered to come if I were not your friend.'

191

The girl did not answer. The man looked at Franklin. 'Wouldn't that be so, m'sieu?'

'He doesn't talk,' the girl said.

'How? – he doesn't talk?'

'He is the victim of an industrial accident,' the girl said. 'He lost his arm, and the shock of losing the arm deprived him of speech.'

The man looked at Franklin, and Franklin looked back. It seemed clear to Franklin that he did not believe a word.

'You are going over to the south,' the man said.

It was a statement. As if quite aware of it the girl said: 'Yes.'

'You propose to go in the boat?'

'There is no reason why we shouldn't,' the girl said.

'Except that you cannot carry the boat on your backs,' the man said. 'You will not need the boat once you are across there.' He pointed across the river.

'Once we are across?'

'You speak as if it were impossible to get across. It is not impossible.' He looked up and down the river again, and then across it. On the far bank Franklin could see the white smoke of a train. 'Given the facilities it is not impossible.'

'What do the facilities cost?' the girl said.

'Oh, little or nothing! Little or nothing!'

She stood very calm, slightly ironical.

'Which do you mean? Nothing or little?'

'Two hundred francs,' the man said. 'For the two of you. I will do it cheap because you are very young.'

'We are very young, but we are not very idiotic,' the girl said.

'You are very idiotic if you think of staying here long. They search the bank every forty-eight hours. And over there every twenty-four hours.' He looked up and down the river again. 'They have machine-guns farther up, covering the river.'

'We haven't got the two hundred francs,' the girl said.

'All right,' he said. 'I will take the boat.'

The girl did not answer. The man made a pretence of enormous surprise, taking off his hat and swinging it about.

'You wouldn't get more than three hundred francs for the boat anywhere,' the man said. 'For the boat I will get you out and throw in the papers and enough food for the journey.'

'We have the food and we have the papers.'

The man put on his cap; it was like a gesture of pity for them.

'Papers? What kind of papers? There are papers and papers.'

'These papers are all right,' the girl said.

'You think they are all right.' He made a pretence of looking very tired. 'What way are you travelling when you get over the other side?'

'Train.'

'There you are,' he said. 'You have papers. You think they are good papers. You get on the train and the gendarmes arrest you. That's the sort of papers you've got.'

Franklin looked at the girl. She did not move. It seemed to him that she was not sure. Looking at the man in the boat, he was far from sure himself. He was only sure that he did not want to be arrested by gendarmes.

'Why travel by train?' the man said.

'We want the quickest way.'

'What is a day or two?' the man said. 'You go a quick way and don't get there. You go a slow way and you arrive.' He looked up and down the river again, and then pulled the boat a stroke nearer shore. 'If you come up to my house I have a proposition.'

The girl hesitated.

'It won't cost you anything.'

'What about our boat?'

'I will send my boy to look after the boat. He is a good boy.' He pointed up the river. 'I have an estaminet. It is about five minutes.'

The girl hesitated, and then made up her mind. 'All right,' she said.

'You can have some breakfast there.' The man pulled the boat close in shore until it grounded on the tiny gravel beach under the alders. Franklin picked up the attaché case.

'How does he know we are going?' the man said.

'He is not deaf,' the girl said. 'It is only his speech. He can hear.'

She picked up the bag of food. It seemed to Franklin that she distrusted the whole business, and yet was not sure. As he took up the attaché case and followed her into the boat he felt extra-ordinarily stupid and defenceless.

'I have an estaminet and you can have hot coffee. Real coffee.' The man kept repeating this as he rowed them up the river. The sun was warm now, and over on the far bank, beyond the autumn trees, the puffs of train smoke were again white in the clear air.

They rowed about half a mile upstream, keeping close to the bank all the time. When finally the boat grounded Franklin saw a road about a hundred yards back through broken woodland, and along it a line of telegraph wires. He followed the man and the girl up through the trees. The man kept turning round and saying, 'Don't worry. Don't worry. The boy is a very good boy. He will look after the boat. Don't worry.'

'We are not worried,' the girl said.

Like hell, Franklin thought. Suddenly he saw the estaminet ahead of them. It was a one-storeyed house on the roadside. Once it had been painted blue. But the sun had burnt off the cheap blue plaster in large flakes, and now the plaster lay on the earth, washed by the recent rain and padded down by hens that pecked under the fruit trees. A few small round iron tables stood under the trees and under the eaves of the house brown bunches of beans were harvesting in the sun.

The man walked up the cracked concrete path under the fruit trees. Franklin could smell the sour odour of hens, of dust washed by rain and now warmed again by sun.

'It is all right. It is all right,' the man said. He held open the door of the house.

The door opened straight into a small room in which there were two tables and a counter and half a dozen chairs. 'Sit down, sit down,' the man said. 'It is all right. I will tell the boy.' He went out through the back door of the room.

The girl sat staring at Franklin, eyes calm and brilliant. 'There is nothing to be afraid of,' she said.

He kept silent.

'That's right,' she said. 'I said it to annoy you. I wanted to see if you would speak. It will be better if you don't speak at all.'

He grinned, aware of the tenseness, the silence, and the beauty

194

of the moment. He wondered if she was afraid. She did not look afraid. She laid her hands on the table and he smoothed her arms tenderly with his hand. She looked at him very tenderly in reply, and he felt that all their complications were refined in the clear simple moment.

Presently the man came back. He went to the door and opened it and looked out. 'The boy is going now,' he said. He came to the table and sat down.

'You can have hot water to shave with,' he said to Franklin.

Franklin shook his head.

'It doesn't matter,' the girl said.

'It's no trouble,' the man said. 'The water is heating for the coffee. You have plenty of time. You won't go to-day, anyway.'

'Not to-day?'

'It is essential to work with the system,' the man said. 'The Germans do everything at fixed times. Every forty-eight hours it is dangerous. You have plenty of time.'

'When could we go?'

'To-morrow night.' He took off his cap and laid it on the table. 'You can trust me. I am your friend.'

'No one said you weren't.'

'No. But it is natural to be suspicious,' he said. 'Especially on an empty stomach. Where are you making for?'

'Marseilles,' she said. 'He has to go to hospital there.'

'It is a curious way of going to hospital,' he said. 'In a boat.'

'It is the way we like,' she said.

'Just so, just so,' he said. 'Exactly.'

The door opened a moment later, and a young woman of twenty-four or -five came in, carrying a tray. On the tray a big coffee-pot stood among cups and saucers, and Franklin could smell the deep strong aroma of the fresh coffee.

The young woman put the tray on the table but did not speak. With the coffee there was bread, in slices cut from the stick, and butter.

'Real butter,' the man said. 'And real coffee. All right?' He smiled.

The young woman went out.

'Help yourself,' the man said. 'Real coffee.'

195

Françoise began to pour out the coffee. It smelled very good and there was white sugar in a bowl; very white against the clear black coffee.

'I tell you what I will do,' the man said. 'I have to make a living somehow.'

Françoise put hot milk in the coffee and gave one cup to Franklin. He took a slice of bread and spread butter on it. The bread jumped about on his plate because he had no other hand with which to hold it.

'As a favour I will buy the boat for three hundred francs.'

'And out of that you charge two hundred francs for taking us over?'

'I have to make a living somehow,' the man said.

'No.'

'You need the money. You said so.'

'Not as badly as that.'

Franklin drank his coffee. It was strong and hot and very good. He looked at the girl : she was holding her cup with both hands, blowing on the coffee and watching with clear, bright eyes the little waves of steam rise into the sun.

'What is your idea of the value of the boat?' the man said. 'I want to be fair.'

'You know what it's worth,' she said.

'How should I know? I don't know. I'm just trying to make a living with the estaminet.'

'A thousand francs.'

The man made an enormous gesture with his arms. It seemed to embrace every impossibility in the world, leaving him very tired.

'We shall never get on like this.'

'It is a very good boat,' the girl said.

Franklin tried to butter himself another piece of bread. The bread bounced on his plate, and at last the girl took it and slowly and calmly spread the butter on it herself. He felt helpless and small as he watched her.

The man seemed to go off into a dream. The girl, after she had buttered the bread, picked up her coffee and again blew the steam gently into the sun.

'All right,' the man said. 'I tell you what I will do. I do it because you are young and because the young man has had a misfortune.' He looked very tired. 'I want to be fair.'

Slowly, without looking up, the girl sipped her coffee.

'You give me the boat and one hundred francs —'

'We have no money,' the girl said.

'Holy Mary, Mother of God!' the man said. He picked up his cap. 'Just pay for the coffee and we will call it off.'

'What were you going to say?' the girl said. 'Without the hundred francs.'

'All right.' The man laid his cap on the table. He was still very tired. 'I will do this. I will make an exchange. You give me the boat and I will give you the means of transport on the other side.'

'What transport?'

'Bicycles.'

The girl did not answer. Drinking her coffee very slowly, looking over the brim of the cup into the sun, she seemed to consider it. Franklin, watching her, wondered if he could cycle with one hand, and then decided it was better to cycle than to be thrown by the gendarmes off the train.

'It will take longer to cycle,' the man said, 'but you will get there.'

The girl was still considering it, slowly drinking her coffee.

'If you come back this way I will buy the bicycles back,' the man said.

'What about food?'

'I will give you food for one day,' the man said.

'What about the oars?'

'Oars?'

'There are two oars and a very good tarpaulin in the boat,' the girl said. 'What about them?'

The man got up from the table and walked about the room, swinging his cap up and down as though at last he had lost all hope in the girl. After a few moments he came back, very weary, and sat down.

'Listen to me,' he said. 'You need a room to-day and to-night. You can't sleep out there. For the tarpaulin and the oars I will give you all the food you need to-day and somewhere to sleep to-night. That's fair.'

197

'And you take us over to-morrow night?'

'I take you over to-morrow.'

'All right,' the girl said.

She reached across the table and buttered another piece of bread for Franklin, and then took his cup and poured into it more milk and coffee.

'How many rooms will it be?' the man said. 'One or two? I don't ask questions.'

The girl sat smiling into the sun, blowing the steam of her coffee into the air in a little trembling cloud.

'It will be a bargain for you if we have one,' she said.

CHAPTER 19

THEY rested all that day and all the next, talking in low whispers in the end room of the estaminet. On the wall of the house was a fig tree and its big green leaves flapped continually against the window in the breeze that came off the river. And as the sun got round in the afternoons the large broken leaf shadows trembled expansively on the grey distempered walls above the bed. The sunlight was soft and golden, and a feeling of autumn blew into the open windows with the wind.

'To-morrow we shall be free,' Franklin said. He was very confident and very happy.

'Free?'

'At least no Germans.'

'Don't talk yet of being free,' the girl said. 'We have a long way to go.'

At five o'clock on the second morning, while it was still dark, they rowed across the river to the other side. The man from the estaminet put the bicycles in the boat. 'You are getting a bargain with the bicycles,' he said.

'It is about a fifth of the bargain you are getting with the boat,' the girl said.

'You have a wonderful wife,' he said to Franklin. 'Wonderful.' His voice was full of ironical admiration.

Franklin did not speak.

'If she bargains as well at the hospital in Marseilles they will probably give you a new arm and a new tongue.' He sighed in the darkness. 'The bicycles alone would cost you two thousand francs apiece anywhere to-day.'

'I will remember that,' the girl said. 'In case we wish to sell them if we come back.'

He gave up at this and, tired, silent, and in gloom, rowed them across the river. It was still quite dark, the sky cloudless, with many stars, and there would be no light for more than an hour. Half-way across the dark water the man rested on his oars and told them, for the last time, where they must go. 'There is a little gravel path with a fence each side it. Keep to it for about half a mile. It comes out on to the road. Turn left there. If you turn right you'll end up in the yards at the railway station. They have guards there. Keep left whatever you do.'

'We would like to thank you,' the girl said.

'That's all right. I have been your friend,' the man said. 'From the first moment. There was a time when you doubted me, but I was your friend.'

'I apologize for doubting you,' the girl said. 'We thank you very much.'

'I do not hold with Vichy,' the man said angrily. 'Blast them. I have an elder boy and he is a prisoner. He would not have been a prisoner if we had gone on fighting. France is in great trouble. If you want a friend when you come back don't forget me. I know how it is.'

'We won't forget,' the girl said.

'I hope your husband will get well,' the man said. 'Have you got everything? The bread and wine? The sausage? I put in some mustard for the sausage. It is very good mustard.'

'I think we have everything,' the girl said. 'Thank you for everything again.'

'That's all right,' the man said. He lifted the oars and began to row again. 'Don't talk any more now.'

He rowed them across in silence, and on the other side pulled the boat into a narrow strip of muddy shore. Franklin could smell the mud and the cold water, and sometimes, on the wind, the smell of locomotive smoke drifting from the railway yards down the river. He got out of the boat and took one of the bicycles and held it while the man from the estaminet strapped the attaché case on the back. The girl took the other bicycle and hung the bag of food on the handlebars.

The man held out his hand and spoke in a whisper. 'Good-bye,' he said. 'It is a little after five now. You can walk till daylight.'

'Good-bye,' the girl said.

'Good-bye, m'sieu.'

Franklin held out his hand; the man grasped it and shook it.

Franklin could just see the small face, with its black moustache, uplifted in the darkness.

'You don't mind if I say something?' the man said. 'I heard you talking once in the bedroom. It is all right. Nothing to worry about. I just wanted you to know. Good-bye. I hope you have luck.'

Franklin spoke for the first and last time. 'Good-bye,' he said. It did not seem to matter now.

He turned and pushed the bicycle up the bank, following the girl. He grasped the handlebars in the centre. He could see quite well: fringes of trees, the wires of a fence, and once, as he looked back, the reflected stars in the quiet black water; and then, for the last time, the boat itself, moving away.

He saw the double lines of fence and wire at last and pushed the bicycle between them. A breath of wind came up from the river, bringing with it once more the thick and in some way friendly smell of locomotive smoke, and away in the darkness a line of trucks shot against each other, with the slow repeated sound of a gun firing flatly. The path between the fences went on for about half a mile, and the tyres crackled on the cinders. After about ten minutes the girl stopped ahead of Franklin and, without speaking, pointed to the left. He saw the white neck of her blouse showing from beneath her coat, and then she moved on with the bicycle. The cinders ceased to crackle under the tyres, and he knew now that it was the road. After a moment or two he drew level with her. A curious feeling that someone was following him made him turn round, but there was nothing there in the darkness, and when he turned again, his face towards the south-east, the wind blowing slightly at his back, he saw the first line of light in the east, a pale break above the hills, and he knew then that the morning was coming. He knew then that he was free.

The mustard was bright yellow in the brown sausage as they ate it, sitting on the top of a hill, about two hours farther on. Below them spread wide deep country, and there were views of bright bronze, with finer veins of yellow, in the many dark woods between the fields. Franklin sat with sausage and bread in his hand, and felt the sting of mustard on his tongue like the

201

sting of his own exhilaration. He looked at the enormous autumn valley shining in the early morning sun below, that seemed to stretch away, green and bronze and summer-faded, to the edge of the world, and remembered the day when he had looked down, with Sandy and O'Connor and the two young sergeants, on just such wide, deep country. The river was flowing below, white in the morning sun, as it had done then: the same river as far as he could guess, but narrower now, coming up with a long sweep from the south between red and white clusters of houses and stubble fields intersected now with brown bars of autumn ploughing. In two days the river would be nothing but a spring in the southern hills. In less than a week they would be in Marseilles.

And suddenly as he sat there the delight of being free went through him with a stab of wonder. It was fine and beautiful to be in the cool autumn country. It was fine and beautiful to be going south, farther and farther south, out of German range. It was fine and beautiful to be eating the mustard in the late October air. He remembered with kindness the man at the estaminet; how suspicious they had been, how the girl had beaten him down about the boat, and how they had slept late in bed in the morning, lazily watching the broad flapping leaves of the fig tree and then sleepily watching the afternoon sun quivering on the wall, and how the man had called Franklin the husband. All that was fine and beautiful, too.

'What will we do in Marseilles?' he said.

'First we have to get to Marseilles,' she said. 'It's a long way for you. With only the one arm.'

'I can ride all the way with no hands,' he said proudly. 'What will we do there?'

'I don't know. Get a train I expect.'

'Would you marry me in Marseilles?' he said.

She did not answer. He saw the youth in her face still and grave, as if he had shocked her.

'Let's get married,' he said. He felt very sure of himself, impulsive and light-hearted but very sure. 'There may be an English parson there who hasn't gone. We could find him perhaps. There are plenty of English still in Marseilles.'

She still did not say anything.

202

'Please,' he said. 'Let's get married.'

'I don't ask it,' she said.

'You mean you don't want to?' he said. He was still light-hearted, almost light-hearted at the thought of being free. 'We're almost married now. We have our things in the same case and we stayed together at the estaminet.'

'It's not that,' she said. 'I mean I don't ask it of you unless you want to give it more than anything in the world.'

'Oh, Jesus,' he said. He put his face against her shoulder and felt the smallness and selfish light-heartedness of himself die away. 'I do want it. Oh, Jesus, I do want it. I want it so much. Believe me, please.'

She looked at him simply, with bright wonder.

'Then it couldn't be otherwise,' she said.

'It never has been,' he said.

The thought of marrying her somewhere, ultimately, if not in Marseilles then in England, remained with him all that day and all the next, not diminishing, as they bicycled down the river valley in the October sun. Sometimes, too, side by side with the clear simple idea of marriage, there flowed along with him a chain of entangled ideas about the war. He was getting closer and closer to it again, and he wondered now what the state of it was. He tried to remember what had been happening in August, before the crash, but all the events of the year, stale and sterile as they had seemed even then, had already become part of a vacuum, quite meaningless and void. The war that would begin for him soon, when he reached England, would be a new war. It would be stiff, of course, with the old stupidities, but he would be aware of them, and perhaps, in reality, it was only himself that would be new. The person who had flown out over the Alps, grasping at the edges of fatigue, caring more about flying than about people, scared into a dishonest but inevitable show of bravery, very afraid to die because dying seemed a personal thing that had never happened to anyone before – that person was not going back. A man can die only once, he thought. The doctor had died, and the father had died; and back there, in the mill, on the scorching bright afternoons, he knew that only merciful clouds of pain had kept him from knowing the closeness of death himself. He could never go back so lightly to life again; he would never again feel that death was a special personal pain. The doctor and the father had lifted him above that now.

They rode on like this into the third day, sleeping each night in small hotels in villages beside the river that narrowed rapidly until it was not much more than the width of a small road. When the food from the estaminet was finished they bought whatever they could from bread shops in the villages: generally bread, greyer if anything as they went farther south, perhaps a little cheap meat paste, and always apples. In the woods on the roadside the trees of Spanish chestnut were ripe, their big papery fawn leaves floating down in the clear October air to cover the green husks of shining nuts on the black earth. At noon they would push the bicycles into a wood and the girl would husk sweet chestnuts and then peel them for Franklin. They were clean and sweet to eat after the meat paste and mustard, and right and beautiful with the wine.

They bicycled on for most of the third day, seeing the last of the river, a small bright stream flowing past between woodland, about noon. Franklin was not tired, and had become very adept with the bicycle. He rode sometimes with his feet on the handlebars, as he had done when a boy, and was very happy because the girl was scared. The happiness of being together, cycling on through the autumn countryside, unoppressed, and as it seemed to him, entirely and finally free, had never been so beautiful as now.

They came into the outskirts of a small town late that afternoon. The seedy edge of the town, its paths of concrete broken, its small low concrete houses unfinished on half-developed building lots, gave way to streets that seemed to have become grey and harsh from long sun. On the brick walls of empty houses there were many posters of political leaders, Pétain among them, and many chalked slogans about Peace and France and Unity. Some of the slogans had been rubbed out. Sometimes at some of the shops there would be a queue of people, mostly women, and over on the opposite side of the street, a waiter leaning at the door of a café to watch them. Franklin then remembered the waiter in the rue Richer, back in August, who had stood in that same lost attitude, staring into nowhere. He had seen many a small bombed English town in which there was more light and pride in the queues of waiting faces. The odour of bombing, sour but angering, had never seemed so desolate as the dusty smell of this small tired town. It had never smelled so dead.

'I don't like this place,' he said. 'I'm not tired. Let's go on.'

'We have to stay here,' she said. 'I have friends here.'

'What friends? I don't like it.'

'Pierre's sister,' she said. 'Don't you remember? He gave me the address and I promised to call. This is the place.'

He felt impotent and depressed.

'You wouldn't want to disappoint Pierre?' she said. 'Would you?'

'No,' he said.

'They are very nice people and we could stay the night,' she said.

He did not say anything else as they pushed the bicycles through the town, past the waiting queues. Going out of the main street, into smaller side streets empty of traffic, he felt miserable and frustrated. Dust in small ground clouds blew on a rising wind out of the sun. It bore along the pavement dirty scraps of paper that became flattened against walls and the pavement edge. For a time the wind would hold them there and then suddenly the wind would drop and the papers would fall, emptied of life until the wind listlessly caught them up again.

He stood on one side of the street, holding the bicycles, while the girl knocked at a door on the other. He looked up and down the street. Nothing was happening except that a man and a boy were shuffling up the gutter. The boy had no shoes or stockings, and he was very adept at turning the dirty papers over with his feet. Sometimes the man bent down and picked up a paper.

On the opposite side of the street the girl was talking to a woman. The woman leaned on the door-post, thin, dark, lifting her hands with occasional gestures of tired protest. He saw the number on the door and remembered it: sixty-seven. The man and the boy came up the street.

Suddenly they became aware of Franklin, holding the bi-

205

cycles. They stopped searching the papers. Only the boy, as from habit, rustled them with his feet. And as they came nearer Franklin looked at his feet. They were very thin and long, and the toes, dirty and hooked, were curiously rapacious. The boy whirled them and turned the papers each time with a little savage movement, and then clipped them aside. In this way they came slowly up the street. They saw Franklin, and then he knew that it was not himself they were really looking at, but the bicycles. He heard the boy say something to the man. The man wore brown canvas slippers; he was quite young and very smooth on his feet. The boy was wearing a woman's red jumper and dirty grey trousers; the pouched, once-filled bust was loose on the haggard chest. And as they came along, the man sometimes looking back up the empty street, they stared at the bicycles as if they were very hungry and were seeing their first food for a long time. Finally they saw Franklin's arm.

A moment later the girl went into the house. Franklin watched the closed door with a sense of desolation; it was as if he were never going to see her again. In the gutter, about ten feet from him, the man and the boy had stopped. They were looking straight at him and he knew what they were thinking: two bicycles, a man with one arm, and no one in the street. They were very good bicycles. Two persons with four good arms against one person trying to hold two bicycles with one arm: there was nothing to stop it. The wind curled a little dust, with a few dirty papers, out of the sun.

Franklin stood waiting. He was not sure what to do. If he started fighting a gendarme would probably come round the corner and that would be the end. They would probably hit him in any case on the stump of his arm. The bastards could do that, he thought. That's just what they would do.

He decided to spit. He worked the saliva in his mouth, sucking it with his tongue into a solid ball. Spitting spit was part of a universal language. He looked at the man and the boy for about half a minute. They did not move. The spittle was hard in his mouth, and suddenly he shot it out. It whipped off his tongue with a brisk sound of contempt and hit the dust of the gutter in a white ball.

For some moments the man and the boy looked at it and did not move. All right, you bastards, Franklin thought. Come on. The eyes of the boy, very narrow in the head, seemed consumptive. As they flashed sick and wild in the evening sun he said something to the man, and the man moved nearer Franklin. As he moved, the boy walked into the middlle of the street, looking up and down. 'All right!' he said, and the man moved nearer Franklin, putting his right hand in his pocket.

All right, Franklin thought. He felt extraordinarily vicious and calm. He turned his body so that it was behind the bicycles, and the stump of his arm away from the man.

The girl came out of the house a moment later. He saw the boy skittle back across the street and begin to shuffle his feet in the papers. The man had not time to move, and the girl came across the street.

Suddenly she looked frightened. She looked at the man and the boy and said: 'Who are they?'

'It's all right,' he said.

'What do they want? Who are they?'

'Take no notice,' he said.

'This is a bad town,' she said. 'Things are very bad here. We must get out.'

The man and the boy did not move. A little wind, harsh with coarse street dust, blew among the papers.

'What about Pierre's sister?' he said.

'She has left here. She lives in Marseilles now.'

'Then let's get out,' he said.

'This was a bad town to come to,' she said. 'There is a bad class of people here. I'm sorry.'

'Don't stop to apologize,' he said. 'Let's get out.'

The girl took hold of her bicycle and turned it in the street. Franklin grasped the handlebars of his own and turned to look at the man and the boy. They had not finished yet. On their faces was still the waiting hungry look, the eyes cast low against the sun.

Franklin and the girl pushed the bicycles down the street. A curling wind flattened a piece of paper against the spokes of a wheel. It flapped like a flag, and Franklin stooped to take it out. As he stooped and turned he looked back down the street.

The man and the boy were coming. He got on to the bicycle. In front the girl was riding round the corner. He pedalled sharply. Then as he turned the corner himself he once more looked back. The boy was shouting now and running hard the other way.

He pedalled level with the girl. 'Have they gone?' she said.

'They were running the other way.'

'Running?'

He knew that they might be running to cut them off. He felt grim and angry. He felt nauseated by the little town, the filthy dust, the prideless, staring people. They rode on again through half-built lots on the edge of the town, where the concrete had cracked on the pavement and the walls were scrawled and plastered with slogans in dirty chalk, and where men sat on the edge of the gutters, squinting against the evening sun, idle, pathetic, not caring. Every hundred yards or so Franklin looked back. The man and the boy were not coming. He wondered if they could come another way. 'It's a bad town,' the girl kept saying. 'There is no food, and last week they had riots. It's a bad town.'

They passed the gasworks on the far edge of the town. The gasometer was at half level, with the evening sun low behind it and the shadow huge on the dusty road. The wind as it blew across the yards brought a thick odour of coal smoke and gas and steam, but it was a cleaner smell, to Franklin, than the smell of the town, where the sun had burned the life from the dust and defeat had soured the life of the people. That smell was something he breathed in with his mind and could not eject again.

He looked back for the last time. The boy and the man were not coming, and the road was empty. He still felt angry. He felt the insult of the moment in the street flaring up in his mind.

'I am humiliated about what happened,' the girl said.

'Humiliated?'

'I did not want you to see that sort of France. That sort of people.'

He looked at her and saw her face twisted and very thoughtful, sad in the evening sun. He did not know what to say. The last of the houses had gone now and there were fields by the roadside, with clean strips of ploughed land between late root crops and clover, and in one field a woman was untethering a white cow and leading it slowly in for the night.

'You see what I meant,' the girl said. 'We have not finished yet. We have some way to go.'

IT was already November when they came down to Marseilles. The weather was fine and mild and a warm wind blew in from the sea. It seemed to blow from Franklin's mind the last sour breath of the ugly little town.

He wondered all the time if there were an English clergyman in Marseilles. Ever since the moment in the street when the youth and the man had watched him while the girl disappeared he had had a curious premonition about losing her. This feeling increased as time went on. Pierre's sister kept a small green-grocery shop on the north-west side of the city. The shop was very small, with only a single room at the back and two bed-rooms above. Pierre's sister and her husband slept in one room, with Françoise in the other. They arranged a room for Franklin in a small hotel one street away. It was very safe, they said. He did not like the hotel. It was clean and empty and desolate, and brought on him a sense of loneliness and separation. The carpet had been taken up from the floors and the stairs, and the feet of himself and the few visitors going up and down made hard and hollow sounds that echoed. It seemed as if everyone were ready to run away.

Three times a day he and the girl took their meals at a small restaurant farther up the street. Every evening, after saying good night, he went up to his room with a feeling of loneliness and lay down on the bed. He never wanted to sleep very much, and for some time he would lie there, without the light on, and wonder if there were an English parson in Marseilles and how soon they could find him and get married and leave for Spain; or he would lie there, with the light on, and try to read the papers he had bought during the day. They were always French papers, censored by Vichy, and it was impossible to tell from them how the war was going on. The French language, very roundabout and formal and well-dressed, lacking the flexibility of English, seemed more than ever like the wrong language for a newspaper. Its stiffness gave him the impression that the same man wrote all the articles in all the newspapers: an aggrieved, indignant, perplexed person holding out his hands, appealing to be better understood. After a time Franklin got completely bored with the papers and would lie on his back, with the light still on, staring at the ceiling. The nights were very quiet, and in all Marseilles there was hardly any sound of street traffic, and in the hotel any sound but the occasional hollow echoes of feet on the stairs, and all the time, in the next bedroom, the small irregular noise of someone using a typewriter.

At first he did not take much notice of this sound. Then after a few nights he listened for it consciously. He got the impression of a French office clerk, working late in his spare time, earning a little extra money. Every few moments he heard the noise of the typewriter and the tinkling of the bell. Long after the feet on the bare stairs had become quiet the sound would go on. After a night or two the sound became for Franklin more than part of the life of the hotel. It became a personal thing. Sometimes he would go to sleep and wake again. Once as he woke he heard a clock in the town striking one o'clock, and then, in the silence, the sound in the next bedroom still going on. Half asleep, he lay listening to it for a long time, wondering.

In the mornings, when he got up and went out to have breakfast with Françoise at the restaurant up the street, there was no sound from the next room. He got the impression of the clerk getting up early and going off to his work. Franklin woke about nine o'clock and took about half an hour to dress himself. He had now become very adept at knotting his tie by holding the end of it shut in a chest of drawers. He tied the laces of his shoes in the same way, but only in a knot. The knot held until he got to the restaurant, when the girl untied the laces and tied them again in a bow. One morning Franklin came out of his room and at the top of the stairs met a small Frenchman of about fifty. He wore a black trilby hat and a dark grey suit with black stripes; he carried a thin brown walking cane over his arm, and it seemed very possible that he was the clerk who worked in the bedroom. They stood at the top of the stairs, waiting for each other to pass. They both said 'Pardon' at the same time, and the Frenchman made a short bow. He seemed to make it a deference to the amputated arm. Then as he bowed

211

he saw Franklin's shoes, with the laces tied in knots. He bent down and laid his walking-stick on the top of the stairs and began to tie up the shoe-laces. Franklin did not know what to say or do as the little Frenchman carefully tied the laces into small neat bows. The Frenchman kneeled for some moments on the carpetless stairs, running his fingers over Franklin's shoes. Then he smiled and looked up. 'They are very fine shoes,' he said. 'They are very beautiful shoes. It has been some time since I saw shoes like that.' He looked at the shoes very enviously again and then picked up his cane and got up. Dust from the carpetless floor had made a grey patch on the left knee of his trousers. He brushed it off with his handkerchief. 'You will excuse me for passing a remark about the shoes,' he said. 'They have the quality one was formerly used to.'

Franklin said 'Of course', and bowed. He was afraid the Frenchman would notice his English accent.

'You have lost the arm in the war?'

'Yes,' Franklin said.

'It is a very great pity.' He was gravely sympathetic. 'If there is some small thing I can do for you at any time?' He smiled and made a small movement of his hand. Franklin did not speak.

'Such as the necessary papers?'

In the eyes of the little Frenchman there was now quite a different look. It had a quality of crystalline sharpness that dissolved away the charm as he looked up and down the stairs.

'I already have papers,' Franklin said.

'Are they adequate?' the Frenchman said. 'For you, I mean? For your particular case?'

'They have been adequate so far,' Franklin said. He was very guarded. The front door of the hotel was open at the foot of the stairs, and now and then he could see the shadows of people sliding past the entrance in the morning sun. He put his hand on the banisters of the stairs as if to go down.

'I have helped many Englishmen,' the little Frenchman said. The words were not abrupt. He spoke obliquely, as if to no one in particular, looking down also at the shadows passing the door in the sun.

Franklin knew suddenly that it was no use pretending. It

212

seemed altogether surprising that no one had hitherto challenged his identity, unless it was that they were too tired or bored or disillusioned to care. Now he did not care himself. He felt the Englishness of himself passively waiting, phlegmatic, not going out to the moment of crisis, but letting the crisis, if it were a crisis, come to him. Then as he stood there still holding the banisters he remembered something.

He remembered how he had wanted to find an English padre. The little Frenchman put his left hand, then his right, into the inside pocket of his jacket, searching for something.

'If you have no use for papers,' he said, 'perhaps there is something else?'

He took out of his pocket a brown leather address book. He opened it and began to write in it quickly, with pencil. The pencil was silver, and Franklin watched the lead screw forward, a small black spot, before the Frenchman began to write.

'If there is anything you want in Marseilles go to this address. Anything at all.'

He folded the page of the address book very neatly and tore it down the fold. He folded it again between his fingers, and then again, holding it like a flat cigarette.

'If you get into some difficulty. If you want something.' He held out the paper towards Franklin, smiling, and Franklin took it, looking straight down into the crystalline polite eyes. They struck him suddenly as being quite fearless, quite irreproachable, in their steady and brittle clarity. He said slowly:

'There was something I wanted.'

'Yes?'

'Something I don't suppose it is possible to find now. An English padre.'

The Frenchman sucked at his lower lip. It became white and then red as the blood receded under the pressure of his small white teeth.

'No,' he said. 'It is something I don't know. But at the address they will know. They will know or they will find out for you. Go there. They have helped other Englishmen.'

'How do I get there?'

'You go down towards –' He began to give directions, lift-

213

ing his walking-stick, pointing down the stairs. 'You will see the Quai de la Joliette. It is behind there. Don't get lost.'

'Thank you,' Franklin said. 'Thank you very much.'

'You are going now? Don't thank me.'

'I shall go this afternoon.'

'Go as soon as you can. I hope you will have success. Don't get lost.'

He smiled and lifted his walking-stick. The swing of it in the air seemed suddenly to unbalance him, so that he seemed to trip downstairs. As he floated through the hotel doorway into the sunshine, small and dapper and almost unreal in his sharp neatness, Franklin followed him slowly down.

It began to rain slightly in the late afternoon in short spits whipped in by the wind coming from the sea, as Franklin walked down past the cathedral to find the address. It seemed like the first sharp cold rain of early winter. It spat into his face, never continuous, but like short bursts of misdirected cold gun-fire before the wind blew it away. The sky was low with grey cloud, and it seemed as he walked between the old tall houses as if the whole of Marseilles were closing in on him like a trap. Walking there in the rain he felt extraordinarily alone: even as if the girl, to whom he had said nothing about what he was doing, did not exist. It was a kind of loneliness that seemed to exaggerate his personal self: so that he felt that the wind, the cold sea-spit of rain and the streets that he did not know were all against him. He caught once, as he turned into a street that ran down at right angles to the docks, the smell of locomotive smoke, together with the sound from a train shunting wagons somewhere down on the quay. The smell was no longer friendly, and he no longer had the feeling of security brought about by being a stranger in a strange town. He felt the lone-liness and the strangeness become part of a queer hostility. They became one with the rain, spitting out of the sea-wind into his face.

He was within sight of the dock, walking along by the rail-way track, when he decided to turn back. He suddenly did not care about the address, the padre, and whoever it was who helped Englishmen. The hostility of the streets in which the smell of rain and coal-smoke and sea was alternately thick and sharp became merged into a single heavy nausea that was something like a sickness – a sickness to be home, in England, safe, away from it all. He longed bitterly and sickly to be out of France, and walked along for some distance, with his head down against the wind beside a stationary line of trucks, black against the grey sky. The wind bored in compressed gusts that lifted low clouds of sharp coal dust that hit his face. He heard the buffers of trucks far down on the quay as they clocked against each other like a line of repeated gun-shots. He heard from farther away still the boom of a ship, hollow and borne away over the sea by the rainy wind. He kept his head down, utterly sick for England and home, for the fields of Worcestershire and the sight and sound of his own people.

The line of trucks began to move forward, the couplings swinging loose, then tightening, then loosening and tightening again. Something made him look up and down the quay. There was no one in sight. He was aware suddenly of being pulled forward into a movement that he had not made. He looked quickly up and down the quay again, and then, seeing it still empty, ran over to the trucks. They were moving in irregular leaps forward, the couplings tightening and loosening as the engine pulled forward far down the quay. And he knew that as he walked beside them all he had to do was to step on a brake-handle, pull himself up the side of the truck, and get inside. He did not know at all why he should be thinking like this. The unexpectedness of the moment, of a new chance of escape suddenly opening up before him, seemed to fascinate him remorselessly. He remembered afterwards working out, for a second or two, as the trucks began to move slightly faster, how he would put his foot on the brake-handle and how quick he would have to be to lever himself up. He remembered seeing the silken steel edge of the truck-wheel shining below the brake-handle: seeing only the two things together in the entire world, all the rest shut out. His life seemed suddenly to depend on those two pieces of steel. He actually grasped the brake-handle with his one hand and began to run beside the faster-moving truck, not knowing why he was doing it, but seeing only the brilliant steel rim of the wheel running away from him and his hand on the brake-lever to test it finally before he leapt.

215

He felt his body tauten for the leap and then, in the split second before its tension, like the tension of a catapult, shot him upwards, something again made him look up the quay. And in that instant his mind acted, letting the brake-handle go. His fingers did not for a moment release their grasp. Only his body stopped quite dead, in the act of surprise, while his hand remained grasping the lever, as if he actually wanted to hold back the train. In this second he felt the speed of the train wrench at the socket of his arm with awful sickness before he let go.

The shock of this violent pull at his arm seemed to wake him up. He stood for about ten seconds on the quay beside the moving train, quite still and clear in mind and conscious of what he was doing.

The gendarme about a hundred yards down the track also stood quite still, watching him. Franklin had caught sight of him in the moment before he prepared to leap on the truck. Now for a few seconds they stood watching each other. The gendarme had a rifle. It was slung diagonally across his back. His feet were apart and Franklin could see the wind flapping the legs of his trousers.

Franklin began to walk on, in a diagonal line across the quay, away from the train. It seemed better to move forward rather than back. He had the impression that if he once turned back he would begin to run and that, moreover, if he began to run, the gendarme would shoot him. He did not want to be shot. As he came away from the shelter of the trucks he felt the wind flap the empty sleeve of his coat. And now as he looked at the gendarme he had the impression also that he was looking not particularly at Franklin, but at the empty sleeve.

All the time Franklin walked across the quay the gendarme did not move. Between the gendarme and the edge of the quay, up which the railway trucks were now going smoothly forward, there were ten or fifteen yards through which Franklin had to pass. There was still no one else in sight, and now Franklin knew why there was no one else in sight. He knew suddenly that many other people beside himself must have come along that quay in search of a train. If you could hide in a train you could, with a little luck or a little patience or both, hide in a ship. It was clear that the gendarme did not carry a rifle to keep himself warm.

He walked the last fifteen or twenty yards before he reached the gendarme with a stiffness of a marionette. There was something menacingly comic about the stiffness of the gendarme, too. He stood as if waiting also to be pulled into life by invisible strings. But when he finally came to life it was smoothly, with very quiet precision, so that before Franklin was aware of it the gap through which he could pass was closed.

'One moment.' The voice was very abrupt, and the gendarme did not do anything with the rifle. He lifted the first two fingers of his right hand in a small correct gesture that was also hostile. 'Your papers.'

Franklin stopped. He did not say anything. He was trying very hard to think. It seemed to him quite certain that once the papers got out of his hands he would never see them again. Whether they were correct papers or not seemed now to make no difference. He put his hand on his chest, first one side and then the other, as if feeling for the papers, trying at the same time to think what he should do. All the time the gendarme was looking down at his empty sleeve.

Franklin put his hand into the inside of his jacket. It struck him that it might be better to pretend he had no papers at all.

'What were you doing on the truck?'

'The truck?'

'You were going to get into the truck.'

'Truck?'

'All right, all right.' The gendarme made a pretence of playing irritated piano scales with one hand. 'The papers. Come on, come on.'

Franklin put his hand inside his jacket, on the left-hand side. His papers were there. He felt them with the tips of his fingers. He pulled his hand out and tried to feel in his outer jacket pocket. It was quite difficult. The gendarme stood watching, silent, lips pressed together, and in this moment the silence of the whole darkening afternoon seemed to compress itself. It seemed to hold them both together. For a second or two there was nothing at all to be heard. The trucks had come to a standstill down the quay; the rain was small and quiet in a sudden spell of calm. The gendarme silently flipped his fingers like a

217

man asking for a card in a game, and Franklin put his hand in his right-hand pocket. His mind seemed to flounder with extraordinary stupidity while the silence compressed itself still further until it seemed almost as if he could feel it pressing down through his body, holding his frightened feet on the quay.

This impression that his feet were frightened did not seem fantastic. The feeling of the whole body was concentrated there. It was a cold and tingling and very intense sensation. He recognized it as a desire to run.

Still feeling for his papers, not really thinking, he pressed his feet hard on the quay. He suddenly had the most violent difficulty not to run. He had to hold himself down. With his mind he did not want to run. If he ran the gendarme would shoot him. And for a moment it was rather like a dream: he was trying to run and yet could not. In spite of the most violent desire to run his feet did not move.

The gendarme was suddenly very angry. He made a violent shrug with his shoulders that brought the rifle forward, within reach of one hand. It looked for a moment as if he were about to unsling it. At the same time he seemed about to say something. And to Franklin, stupid and helpless, even his pretence of fumbling for his papers not very good, the moment was ominous. It seemed like the moment of arrested silence before the shooting begins.

To his astonishment the sound of shooting came rattling through the silence a moment later from far down the quay. He mistook it for a moment for the noise of shunting railway trucks. Then in the second before he saw the gendarme's head abruptly whipped round he knew that the sound was lower pitched. It had with it a kind of singing whine. Between the sounds also there was a longer interval of silence that could only have been made by the firing of a rifle. In one of these intervals there began the shrill of a whistle, continuous and desperate, as if blown in panic.

The eyes of the gendarme were white with violent surprise. He looked at Franklin extraordinarily like a small child as he put his whistle to his own mouth. He held it for a moment like a piece of silver sugar-rock between his pursed lips, his cheeks inflated in the comic moment before blowing.

In that moment Franklin lifted his good arm. He did not think at all. All the irritant sensation seemed to leap up out of his feet into this arm. Not for any other moment since coming down in the marsh, with the moonlight bursting with bloody and glassy splinters into his face, had he felt anything happen to him with such explosive violence. He hit the whistle with great force with the flattened palm of his hand. As it caught the sound of whistling and choked it he felt the whistle itself hit the bone at the back of the gendarme's mouth. It was as if it were a nail driven deep into a cup of jelly.

He saw the gendarme fall backwards in the second before he himself began running. He saw the blood spurt scarlet against the silver whistle. He remembered shutting his own mouth very hard and throwing up his head and leaping forward. He had about sixty or seventy yards to cover before he reached the building on the corner of the quay. Without thinking he ran in series of short diagonal bursts, from side to side. It seemed very foolish. The sideways swing of his running, together with the lopsidedness from his one arm, gave him a motion extraordinarily crab-like. With his one arm he seemed to claw at the air and pull it frantically towards him.

He expected any moment the sound of shooting. Yet when it came, in short bursts as before, intermittent and erratic, he felt as if it shot his own heart with surprise. He had almost reached the corner. In a moment of astonished terror he felt it was the gendarme shooting at him and then, far down the quay, beyond the railway trucks now moving gently backwards, he heard the whine of the shot, low and then high, in the wind.

He was round the corner a moment later. He was still running very fast. He was aware of nothing except a short open space between himself and another and stationary line of railway trucks. He went straight under the trucks, rolling clear under the far side. He felt the stump of his amputated arm hit the steel cradle on a sleeper as he fell, and the brutal shock of it made him stagger. His balance, with one arm, was for a moment or two so upset that he spun round, catching wildly at the air with his good hand. In this moment he saw his world. It revolved with intense reality: the line of trucks, a warehouse, another space, another warehouse. There was no sign of the

219

gendarme, no sound of shooting. In that second he spun his body straight again and ran madly for the space between the warehouses.

Round the corner of the warehouse he saw the world open up into new avenues of trucks, with stacks of coal, more warehouses and, far away, the motionless loading gear of the dockside black against the windy sky. He rolled under another line of trucks and heard the shooting again, staccato and then whining, over on his left hand. It seemed a little nearer. As he went under a second line of trucks, stooping this time, his mouth eating at the air for breath, he felt suddenly a little sick from the shock of hitting the stump of his arm. He leaned against the buffers of the truck, half hidden, while he looked before him. It was still raining, and now he noticed it for the first time on his face. Then as he wiped his hand across his forehead he knew that it was not rain alone, but rain and sweat, in fine cold drops, together.

He remained there, hidden by the buffers of the truck, for about thirty seconds. It seemed like an enormously long vacuum of time. Nothing seemed to be happening behind him. But before him, now, the firing seemed to be sweeping across the yards. The staccato, singing sound of shots swung clear down the wind. He began to walk cautiously up the side of the trucks, the air sweet and painful as he took it through his open mouth in heavy gasps. Suddenly he was comforted by the gloom of the sky. In half an hour it would be too dark for shooting, and in about an hour too dark for a man to be seen. His breath began to come back as he walked along the trucks, and with it his thoughts and his steadiness. It was only when the firing broke out afresh, suddenly, quite near and almost dead ahead, that he was startled again.

And then, for the first time, he realized what was happening. It struck him suddenly that they were shooting at someone else. He did not quite know why he had missed this simple fact. It made him for a moment more nervous than if they had been shooting at him. The violence of the moment when he had jammed the whistle into the gendarme's mouth had splintered completely the clearness of his perceptions. He suddenly grasped that he was running from one danger into another. Without thinking he turned to go back. I'm in a bloody mess, he thought, a bloody mess, an awful bloody mess. I've got to get back. Somehow, I've got to get out of this, I've got to get back. He looked quickly back between the trucks. In a few seconds of turning his head the firing broke out again, about a hundred and fifty yards ahead. The nearness of it made him turn back his head. In that moment he saw a man running desperately towards him down the long alley between the trucks.

For a second it was almost like watching the reflection of himself. The man wore a blue striped shirt and black trousers and no coat. He threw himself under the trucks about fifty yards from where Franklin stood. It was just as Franklin had thrown himself. In the second before diving under the trucks, too, Franklin saw the head of the man thrown back with abrupt surprise as if someone had hit it. The face was very thin and white. It had the look of a face that had been running in desperation for a long time.

Franklin lay on his belly between the wheels of the trucks. He could look up the tunnel made by the wheels and see, about fifty yards away, the other man lying there, too. His face was pressed down against the chips between the sleepers, his arms folded over his head, to hide and protect it. He lay very still. The shooting did not begin again, but for a few moments, over to the right of the trucks, there were voices. They seemed to be joined by a voice behind him: the voice of the other gendarme shouting, giving new directions. As the two lots of voices converged, growing confused, somewhere about fifty yards away, Franklin pulled himself slowly along on his belly, grasping the edges of successive sleepers with his hand, then moving forward. He could smell the oil of the sleepers and the grease-boxes of the truck wheels, and with it the smell of coal and coal-smoke and the fresh wind. He pulled himself forward slowly, stopping at intervals to listen, hearing the voices converge and move over beyond the trucks. As he moved on he kept his eyes on the other figure lying between the wheels. It had not moved at all. From the broken and flattened attitude of the head, held down on the sleepers by the hands, it might have been crying with exhaustion and fear. It looked as if it had given up. There was no more shooting now, and the voices seemed to be arguing rather than shouting, and were farther away. Franklin pulled himself steadily along the sleepers, tired too, his body chilled where the wind blew in against the sweat of it, until he was about ten yards away. Then he spoke, calling in a whisper.

'All right?' He spoke in French. 'Are you all right?'

There was no answer; the hands did not move from the head.

'I think it's all right now. Did they hit you?'

Lying so flat, between the wheels, Franklin could feel the darkness of the afternoon slowly thickening. If they could wait for a few minutes longer they would never be seen; only a few moments, he thought, only a little longer.

'Did they hit you?'

As he pulled himself a little nearer, waited for a few moments and then crawled forward again, he saw the hands over the head clasped together, but spread out, the ten fingers forming a net, as if to protect it.

'It's all right,' Franklin said. 'They were after me, too. It's all right now.'

He was within touching distance of the man now, the breadth of two sleepers separating them. The man did not move or speak. On the back of one of his hands Franklin could see now where the flesh had been sliced across by something, perhaps a shot, but so close to the bone that there was scarcely any blood. The fact that there was no blood struck him for a moment with terror. He pulled himself another inch or two and touched the hands. They gave a start and fell away from the head almost automatically. Without them the head itself rolled over on the sleepers and the man spoke, with a kind of scared and exhausted anger, for the first time.

'The bastards!' he said. 'The bastards! Who are you?'

The words in English were more startling than the first firing of the shots had been. They struck Franklin with an amazing violence even greater than the moment when he had smashed the whistle into the gendarme's mouth. He spread his hand across the tired face and wiped back the wet hair. The voice hit him with such pain and joy that his own was almost crying in answer.

'O'Connor!' he said. 'For Christ's sake, Connie! Connie! O'Connor! O'Connor!'

222

He was kneeling now, and the face of O'Connor, old and tired, was looking up with slightly open mouth, the lips too startled and weak to come together.

'Skip,' he said. 'Skip. Oh Jesus!'

As Franklin knelt above him, the silence complete again without even the distant shouting of voices, and only the sound of rain beating gently on the tarpaulins covering the trucks, O'Connor looked up and saw the loose sleeve of Franklin's coat. He stared at it for a full minute, not speaking, his thin face white against the oil-dark sleeper in the increasing darkness under the trucks, before he began crying and talking quietly at the same time.

'Jesus, Skip, what have they done? What have they done?' he said, and the words were so old with anguish and defeat that Franklin could only lie down on the wet sleepers himself, by the side of O'Connor, with nothing to say in answer.

CHAPTER 21

SOMETIMES as Franklin looked down at O'Connor, prostrate on the bed in the room of the hotel, the brandy still wet on the grey lips that were too tired to accept it, he could see the lines of a dead face. He recalled the moments when he had crawled under the trucks, pulling himself slowly along the sleepers, towards a man who did not move, and how even after the moment of recognition O'Connor had still lain there, staring upwards, eyes dark with fear and hunger and great weariness as they shone from the thin face, very white in the gloom of the afternoon. He recalled the journey back through the dark streets of Marseilles, and how it had seemed a very long way because O'Connor sometimes could not go on without rest, and how he would rest, suddenly, without warning, against the wall of a house, flattening himself back against it, and how Franklin would wait for him and hear the agony of dry breath sucked through his mouth, in quick crying gasps like broken words, as if he were trying to speak and breathe at the same time.

Now on the bed he was breathing quietly, but the words were still not fully alive in the half-living face. It was the face of a man who had been beaten back wherever he went: the face of a man thrusting his face through the bars of a prison, first in one place and then another, only to have it beaten back, and then only to thrust it out again and have it beaten back again, until there was a last time when he lay down and could not get up and could bear it no longer.

'I tried it all ways, Skip.' The dark mouth hung open, trembled and seemed to try to bite at the words. 'All ways. Swam rivers — Got – got – got —'

'Don't talk,' Franklin said. The small room was full of the sound of O'Connor repeating the one word, dry and helpless, like a child with a fit of coughing. When the agony of it broke at last the short rush of new words was almost too low and tired to hear.

'Got all my money pinched, Skip; took all my money.'

224

He gave the most unaccountable smile of bitterness, screwing up the thin cheeks until they were double-creased with dark fissures on either side of the mouth. The O'Connor that had once thrashed his way buoyantly over every kind of trouble seemed to have died. Franklin held for a moment one of his thin wrists. The flesh above the upraised pebble of bone was ruckled and cold. He let the wrist go and unloosened O'Connor's shirt at the chest, opening the shirt out so that he could feel the chest, cold as the wrists themselves. It was quite hollow under the hair between the outer frames of bone, holding for a second or two the few drops of brandy he poured down on it. As he put the bottle down by the bed and began to rub the brandy into the chest, moving his hand circularwise and slowly across the furrows of bone, O'Connor smiled again and said something about 'Reminds me when I was a kid. Chest rubbed.' Franklin rubbed the chest until his hand was dry, and then poured a little more brandy on it and rubbed again. When it was dry a second time he poured the brandy on the chest again, but this time flattened the palm of his hand in it and rubbed it first on one of O'Connor's wrists and then the other. As he did so he saw another kind of smile come on O'Connor's face. It fixed itself there, very quiet and in a way quite solemn; the smile of relief after pain. Soon he saw it grow under the motion of his hand. He saw it spread upwards through the face, spreading warm film across the eyes, until the smile there seemed liquid, living, and O'Connor let the lids close down as if he wanted to seal them against the overflowing joy.

When he opened them again Franklin had finished rubbing his wrists. He got up and poured a little more brandy into his tooth-glass. He turned to see O'Connor sitting up. His hands were flat on his thin knees, and where the shot had ripped across the bone of one of them there was a mark as if a hot nail had been laid there and hammered in. It did not seem as if the wound had bled at all, as though the fleshless skin of O'Connor's hands was also bloodless, and now, for the first time, O'Connor looked at it, the smile still fixed on his face, very solemn, very quiet, and gravely determined. He took the brandy from Franklin's hand and drank it without speaking and without changing the expression on his face. He looked at his hand for a long time, as though he were fixing the gravity of it on his mind. Franklin, remembering how he had first seen it as he crawled under the trucks, and how, seeing it, had thought O'Connor dead, now saw the significance of this long stare. Another inch or so and O'Connor might have been dead there under the railway trucks, and himself as good as dead, too, lying with him. Even before O'Connor spoke he saw the small bloodless wound as the culmination and the symbol of all that O'Connor had suffered.

'Some bastard will pay for this.'

'Now don't start talking cock.' Franklin put into his voice the old ironic friendliness of their common world.

'Some bloody Frenchie will pay for it, too.' The words were coming quite easily now, released from their stuttering pain. 'The sods have rooked and swindled me all down the country. Everywhere!'

'Now steady.'

'Steady? Oh Skip! Oh Skip!' The bitterness of the thin face suddenly exploded in a way that seemed to Franklin unreal. The hands danced nervously on O'Connor's knees: the big, ageless, comforting hands that had borne him across the river and that could have carried him like a baby, and that were now themselves dancing like the hands of a fretful child. 'They pinched my papers, they pinched my wallet, they would have pinched my clothes if I'd let them. They even pinched the little food I had. The only thing they didn't pinch was my revolver. Thank Christ I kept that. At least I got a chance to shoot one of the bastards in return.'

'You'd better take it steady,' Franklin said.

O'Connor, not speaking, gasping for breath, sucking it down into his mouth in painful gulps again, stared with horrible fascination at Franklin's empty sleeve.

'Oh God!' he said. 'Oh God!'

'Lie down.'

'No,' O'Connor said. 'No. It's only I can't believe the arm. Even when I look at you I can't believe it.'

Franklin said abruptly, 'What happened to the boys?' He did not want to talk about the arm.

'No idea, no idea,' O'Connor said. 'I suppose they made it.

226

Taylor was very smart at the lingo. They'd get through.' He looked up, newly troubled. 'Come to that, how the hell did you get here? With that – that business and all?' He nodded towards the arm.

'The girl got me here,' Franklin said. 'We came down together.'

'Girl?'

'At the mill. You remember.'

'Oh, the girl!' O'Connor said. His eyes were vague as if he were not very interested. Franklin decided not to talk about the father or the doctor. O'Connor screwed up his eyes. Suddenly he was interested. 'What made the girl come with you?'

'We're going to be married,' Franklin said.

'Married?' O'Connor looked vaguely and wildly round the room. 'Am I barmy?'

'No,' Franklin said. He was laughing at the troubled face. 'No. I said married.'

'Well, I give up,' O'Connor said. 'I give up. You marrying a French girl.'

'You can be best man,' Franklin said. 'If not here, then in Spain. If not Spain, then England.'

'England,' O'Connor said. He got up for the first time and took a few steps about the room. Halting, he looked back at Franklin, shaking his head. 'I never thought I'd cry my bloody heart out to be back home,' he said. 'But that's what I've been doing. Honest, Skip! Crying my bloody heart out.'

He came back and sat on the bed. He looked at Franklin with incredible unsteadiness. It occurred to Franklin that he was very like a man who had reached the breaking point after many operations. He sat down on the bed. The time had come to talk of something practical.

'We'd better get you out of here,' he said. 'Pierre's sister keeps a shop round the corner. Get your kit ready and we'll go round now.'

'My kit?' O'Connor said. 'You're making me laugh, Skip. My kit?'

O'Connor laid out on the bed two handkerchiefs, a thin piece of white soap, his revolver, and ten rounds.

'That's all I got,' he said. 'The bloody issue.'

227

'I seem to remember you carried a pantechnicon on ops,' Franklin said.

'I did,' O'Connor said. 'I did. I had it organized.' The comedy of it seemed to strike him momentarily; a small wave of smiles slipped over his face. 'Razor, soap, knife, chocolate, chisel, screwdriver, cards, darts, pliers, torch, revolver. Everything. Everything.'

'What happened?'

'The sods pinched it I tell you, Skip! They pinched it. Wherever I went they pinched it. Look at my bloody face!' He ran his hands angrily over the thin cheeks with their two-day beard. 'Somebody pinched my razor.' The eyes looked wildly up from the dark face.

'I – I – I —' he was stuttering again in his search for words.

'Steady,' Franklin said. It seemed perhaps it would be better to go. Outside, if they could get a little air, perhaps a little food, O'Connor would feel better. He looked at the troubled face of O'Connor, grubby and tragic, the mouth wildly open, and remembered the rain. The rain itself would do him good.

'If that's all your things,' he said, 'we can go.'

'It's all. Thanks to the bloody Frenchies,' O'Connor said. He wrapped the soap in the handkerchiefs and put them into his pocket. His revolver was very bright and clean. He held it in one hand, weighing the ammunition in the other. 'At least I still got that.' He gripped the handle very tightly, so that the bones of his hand were white.

'Keep it out of sight,' Franklin said. The clean blue steel of the revolver annoyed him.

'You bet,' O'Connor said. 'No Frenchie is pinching this. This is the only sensible thing I got.'

'It might not be so sensible either,' Franklin said. 'If they searched you at the frontier and found that it wouldn't be so sensible.'

'It would be a sensible thing to shoot a French bastard with,' O'Connor said. 'Which is what I will do before I'm much older. I got some scores to pay out.'

'Good old Connie,' Franklin said. His annoyance remained, but it seemed better to cover it up. It seemed probable that O'Connor's desire to shoot Frenchmen was only temporary. It seemed better, therefore, not to condemn it now. It could only do O'Connor good to feel aggressive once again. He stood up and said, 'Can you walk?'

O'Connor put the ammunition and the revolver in his pocket. 'I think I can,' he said. He stood up unsteadily, smiled a little and nodded. 'All right,' he said, and suddenly Franklin felt deeply and wonderfully glad of the scruffy, tired, friendly face, the wonder of hearing an English voice, the wonder of a coincidence that was a miracle for them both. It seemed in that moment like the next best thing to regaining his arm. He put his arm on O'Connor's shoulders and pressed his fingers against the bone. 'Come on,' he said.

They walked down the bare stairs of the hotel and out into the street. It was still raining gently in the darkness, in fine cross sweeps sometimes twisted by wind. It felt very good and clean and cool on Franklin's face.

O'Connor turned up the collar of his jacket. Rain and darkness together seemed to restore something of himself.

'I suppose I should congratulate you,' he said.

'Thanks.'

'You're right for each other. I see that now.'

'You be nice to her,' Franklin said. 'I'll brain you if you're not. If it wasn't for her I wouldn't be here.'

'That's enough for me,' O'Connor said. 'Until you turned up my luck was out.'

'So you see you owe it to her, too.'

'That's right,' O'Connor said. 'So I do.'

They walked on up the street in the rain, and at intervals the rain, blowing through the cool night air, had in it a smell of the sea. It scattered for both of them the feeling of being trapped in a foreign city. It made the short experience of walking up the dark street something like the re-living of an old experience. It was as if they were back in England, in Cambridge, walking the dark street in search of a late taxi, after the pubs had closed, before going back to the station. Through the fresh rain came the memory of their old identity. They began to recapture the feeling of interdependence, the confidence that, because they were together, nothing could happen to them now.

In the next street Franklin rang the bell of the greengrocery shop, and in a moment or two, through the glass door, he saw the crack of light from the living-room shine through the dark shop. It was Pierre's sister who answered the door, and in another moment he and O'Connor were following her through into the room beyond. Franklin caught the friendly smell of earth and fruit in the darkness, and then he and O'Connor were standing blinking in the light of the room behind. Franklin looked from Françoise to Pierre's sister, and from the woman to the husband. The woman was small, with very black hair parted in the middle, and wide black eyes with large pupils. The man was small, too, and very stocky, with dark brown skin. He wore an imitation brown leather jacket.

Franklin saw the bright, almost violent surprise on the three faces.

'My friend O'Connor,' he said.

All of them were smiling. O'Connor was smiling, too. He looked at the startled black eyes of the girl, calm and amazed.

'He has had a bad time but he is all right now,' Franklin said. 'He has lost most of his things. His papers and everything. But he is all right now.'

'We will get papers,' the man said. 'In Marseilles you can get most things if you know how.'

'He needs a room, too,' Franklin said.

'We will manage it here,' the woman said. 'Somehow.'

'You see?' Franklin said to O'Connor. He spoke in English now. 'They can arrange everything and it's O.K.'

O'Connor grinned and said 'Merci, merci', several times. Then he said 'Merci beaucoup very much', and everyone laughed. On the round table in the centre of the room there remained a few plates and glasses, dirty from supper. The woman began to pack them away, stopping at intervals with a glass or plate poised in the air to laugh with O'Connor.

'He believes in miracles now,' Franklin said. 'Don't you?' He spoke in English to O'Connor. 'I tell them you believe in miracles. Don't you?'

'By God I do!' O'Connor said. 'Oui! Oui!' he said, grinning again. 'Oui! Beaucoup, beaucoup.'

'You see,' the girl said.

She stood smiling under the bright light, her face brown with

230

sun, her eyes clearer and brighter than Franklin ever remembered them, he looked back at her and felt the clear brightness of her face magnify the happiness in his own.

'You see what I always tell you,' she said. 'You need only have faith. With faith you can do anything.'

'Yes,' he said.

'Faith and a little luck,' the woman said. Smiling, she packed the plates one on top of another.

'Even only with faith,' the girl said.

'I used to talk like that when I was young,' the woman said.

The girl did not speak this time. Her wide eyes were fixed on Franklin. They seemed to hold him, shining under the bright light, with a great unbroken gaze of adoration. 'All you need is faith,' she said.

O'Connor looked from Franklin to the girl.

'What is she saying?' he said.

Franklin smiled.

'Something about me?'

'Yes,' Franklin said. He felt in that moment that the little room with the four people, the bright light and the wonderful unshakable faith of the girl, contained almost all he wanted in the world. 'She says you're a very lucky man.'

O'Connor grinned until his teeth were brilliant above the black and scruffy beard.

'No trouble at all,' he said. The common, solid, imperishable Englishness of the sergeant was slowly coming back, clear as the light in his eyes. 'No trouble at all. Does she understand?'

'She understands,' Franklin said.

All the time he could see O'Connor's hand in his pocket, holding the revolver.

CHAPTER 22

THE wife of the concierge in the rue des Jardins did not know anything about an English padre in Marseilles, but she did not shut the door. Franklin, who had been walking all day and asking the same question, walked across the street, turned and looked back. The door was a heavy double one, in light brown wood, with four deep square panels and a large iron knob in the centre. He saw one hand of the woman grasping the door-post and the other the edge of the door, and the door just open enough to admit her keen pale face above them. She was watching him very closely. He wished he hadn't turned to look back. Then as he went on down the street, remembering the day in the rue Richer when he had tried not to hurry, and trying in the same way not to hurry now, he turned involuntarily and looked back again. The woman was still standing there, very pale in the late afternoon air, her head leaning forward now, sharply and slightly askew, like a hen looking through the slat of a fence. He remembered then that it would be his arm, of course, that fascinated her. A man with one arm asking for an English padre in Marseilles: he remembered how she had stared at his empty sleeve. He remembered, too, seeing the wall telephone in the lobby behind her. Very simple to report him: perhaps one of those too simple things that she would never think of doing. He kept his face rigidly forward and walked steadily on down the street. He had been walking most of the day.

He walked out of the rue des Jardins and into a wider street at the top. It had been a fortnight since he found O'Connor. He started to walk across the tramlines. On the second track a tram was approaching, and he waited for it to pass. A few dry brown leaves bounced up the lines in the wind. He had been trying for a fortnight to find a padre. As he waited he turned out of habit to look back. There was no one following him. There never was. But somehow, after a fortnight of going from place to place in

232

search of the padre, of asking questions of strangers, of waiting for O'Connor's papers, of lying awake at night and listening and wondering if footsteps on the stairs in the hotel were footsteps coming for him, he had got into the habit of thinking there would be. He had also suffered, wherever they went, from the Englishness of O'Connor. He hadn't yet got used to the loud unsuspected voice of O'Connor suddenly speaking in English in a crowded street. O'Connor had regained much of his buoyant confidence and did not care. In Marseilles, too, there was an atmosphere of curious tension, the tension of rottenness, that Franklin did not like. The tram came down the track, quite fast, and swept past him. In the air, after it had gone, a shower of leaf fragments scattered and fell in the wind like the light debris of an explosion. He looked back for the last time and walked over.

He went out of the street with the tramlines into a small street beyond. He had had nothing but a few cups of bad coffee all day and he was hungry. A boy came running across the tramlines and up the street carrying newspapers, shouting something, but Franklin did not catch what it was. He was not really listening. He was thinking of how he wanted to marry Françoise; he wanted desperately to marry her before it was too late. He could think of nothing else as he walked out of one small street into another. How was the war? He had not seen a newspaper for several days. In Marseilles the war seemed to matter less than anywhere else he had ever been. The war was a decayed legend, and it seemed to him that people spoke of it as little as possible. Marseilles smelled of its own decay. He could not tell what rottenness was going on there, and had gradually found that he did not bother. He had become interested only in O'Connor's papers and the idea, by now absurd and slightly stupid, of finding an English clergyman somewhere in the city.

The leaves were not blowing in the small street that went due westward, but short tracks of sunlight were trying to shine down it from the far end. Franklin walked more slowly. Some people were coming towards him, on the same side. The high fronts of the pensions, with their big panelled doors, were gloomy in the flat sun. As Franklin looked up and down the street, ready to cross over, and then back to the people coming towards him, he saw that they were two women. He decided not to cross over and went on towards them instead.

About a hundred yards away he could hear their voices. Suddenly they stopped. And he noticed that there was no more talking until they had gone some distance past him. One of the women was sitting in a light metal invalid chair, with a brown plaid rug over her knees. She was a very big woman, with grey hair and large grey jowls that flopped down on her high lace collar. The woman pushing the invalid chair was very small, and her hair was quite white. It seemed to have been laboriously stuck on her pink head in separate strands of fine white cotton. She had small devoted icy-blue eyes that looked straight ahead. She was so short that she could only just see over the large black fruit hat resting on the back of the chair.

The two women went slowly past him, both silent now. The woman in the bath chair gazed at the pavement. Franklin looked at them and felt for a moment as if he had made a hysterical discovery. The icy-blue eyes of the small woman were frozen in space. He went on for about thirty yards and then stopped. He suddenly knew that no women in the world, except the English, looked quite like that.

He turned and went back. The invalid chair was going at the same pace, very slowly, but the women were not yet talking. The setting sun was clear of cloud now and shone flat on the white cottony head of the little woman pushing the chair.

Franklin let them go on for a short distance and then hurried on a little and finally drew level. They were still not talking, but in the instant before he spoke they jerked their heads towards him, startled, as if they had been tied together with a single piece of string.

'Are you English?' Franklin said. He looked quickly up and down the street. It was quite empty. 'I am English.'

The invalid chair stopped. The icy-blue eyes of the little woman were dancing.

'I am really Scots,' the woman in the chair said. 'My name is Campbell. Miss Baker is English.' Her voice was steady and rather masculine. It clipped the ends off some of her words in an aristocratic fashion half as old as herself. She looked to be about eighty. 'How do you do?' she said. She held out her hand and her voice was formally calm.

Franklin said, 'How do you do?' and held the large cool hand for a moment in his.

'This is my companion, Miss Baker.'

'I lived many years in Leamington,' Miss Baker said. She, too, held out her hand. It was very tiny, and rather to Franklin's surprise, quite warm.

They both noticed his arm. He did not know what to say.

'I am afraid we did not notice you as you passed,' Miss Campbell said. 'We have got out of the habit of speaking to people.'

'I knew you were English,' Franklin said.

'Scots,' Miss Campbell said.

'I am sorry.'

'Even in Marseilles there is a difference.'

'Of course.'

She smiled; it was quite firm and friendly. Her grey hair, curled into full flat rings down on her forehead, was like a doll's. She looked again at his arm.

'How do you come to be in Marseilles?'

'I am looking for an English padre,' Franklin said.

'There isn't one.'

Franklin looked up and down the street. It was empty in the flat sun. He saw Miss Baker turn her tiny hand over and look at her watch.

'What time is it?' Miss Campbell said.

'Nearly four.'

'We have tea at four,' Miss Campbell said. 'How do you come to want an English padre?'

'I want to get married.'

'Not to a French girl?'

'Yes.'

Miss Baker leaned her small body against the handle of the invalid chair.

'Even in this crisis?'

'I'm rather afraid I'm continually in a crisis,' Franklin said. 'Another wouldn't matter.'

'I see,' Miss Campbell said. 'However, as there is no English

235

clergyman it doesn't matter anyway.' She looked again at his empty sleeve. 'Where are you going?'

'To England.'

Miss Campbell looked swiftly up the street and then, putting the large fruit hat round the edge of the invalid chair, down it. The sun gleamed for a moment on the red and black cherries of the hat and on her grey hair and on the grey jowls of her face.

'I think you had better come home and have tea with us,' she said.

Franklin sat in the sitting-room of Miss Campbell's apartment and held a cup of tea in his hand. There was no central heating. The room was cool and not quite dark. 'We have to save light,' Miss Campbell said. She had been wheeled into the room in the invalid chair. 'The heating is cut off, of course. But I will not bore you with that.'

Miss Baker offered a plate of bread and butter. The bread was laid on the plate in rows, very thin, on a round lace doyley. 'Take two pieces,' Miss Baker said. 'I always ask men to take two pieces.'

Franklin balanced his cup on his closed knees and took two pieces of bread and butter and flattened them deftly together.

'Let me take your cup.'

Miss Baker reached out.

'Oh no!' he said. He was very sensitive about it. What world is this, anyway? he thought. He could smell England in the tea. 'I can manage.' The war seemed to him suddenly very far away. 'I can manage.'

'Certainly not,' Miss Baker said. 'Anyway, it's a privilege to help a wounded soldier.'

'Don't be tactless,' Miss Campbell said.

'How did you know I was a soldier?' Franklin said.

'It was a metaphorical remark,' Miss Campbell said. 'I apologize for Miss Baker. But we already decided in the kitchen that you were an airman. Escaping. I hope we were right.'

'Yes,' Franklin said.

'Will you think it a misguided remark if I say I am sorry about the arm?'

'No,' Franklin said. 'It is very kind.' He felt a fool. 'It's not much.'

Miss Campbell drank gulps of milkless tea; it quivered the heavy aristocratic jowls of her cheeks as she swallowed.

'You had better get out of Marseilles,' she said. 'And out of France. Quickly.'

It did not seem to him that either Miss Campbell or Miss Baker, calmly drinking tea and eating their bread and butter, were anything but permanent. He had already told them, in a vague way, about O'Connor. He reminded them now that O'Connor had lost his papers. 'And there seem to be no more in Marseilles,' he said.

'There may be something we can do about that,' Miss Campbell said. 'But you have to get out. Quickly.'

'You said something about a crisis,' Franklin said. 'Was that metaphorical?'

'The British and Americans have landed in Algeria,' Miss Campbell said. 'I wouldn't call that metaphorical.'

'God!' he said.

'This morning,' Miss Baker said.

He sat there feeling very excited. God! It seemed to him that a colossal charge of explosive had gone off under the dormant surface of the war. Miss Campbell helped herself to a fresh piece of bread and butter, folding it calmly.

'Not that it really affects us,' she said. 'We are very old. When you are eighty, revolutions don't scare you.'

'Revolutions?' He grasped wildly at the idea of a revolution in France.

'Yes, of course,' Miss Campbell said. 'It will mean a revolution in France. The French can't make it for themselves. So the Germans will. They'll march in. In any case, the French will begin to behave with that peculiar sheep-like habit of theirs and run round in pointless circles. There's always a crisis point in France when everybody starts running.' The formal and slightly ironical language seemed to belong to another age. 'If you take advantage of that you may get out.'

Hell, Franklin thought.

'May? I've got to get out,' he said.

'Then go to-night. The Germans think very quickly.'

'There's the question of the pass for my friend,' he said.

Miss Campbell again drank gulps of milkless tea, wiping her mouth with her handkerchief afterwards.

'How old is he?'

'Thirty-five.'

Miss Campbell looked at Miss Baker, who had now filled Franklin's cup a third time, and for the first time called her Effie. 'What did we do with the papers we had for Georges?' she said.

'I can find them,' Miss Baker said.

Franklin sat on the edge of his chair. The time had come. Miss Baker went out of the room, and Miss Campbell explained: 'Georges was our man-servant. His name was Georges Leblanc. We were, when France capitulated, going to leave France, and we had all the papers ready. Both for ourselves and Georges. Two days before we were hoping to go Georges had a stroke and died. After that it didn't seem to matter.' She took a deep breath. The change of subject was very abrupt. 'How is England?'

'England was all right when I saw it,' Franklin said.

'I used to live in Dorset,' she said. He expected her to ask about the bombing, but she didn't. 'But we spent most of the late summer in Scotland.' She began a careful reminiscence about a house on a loch; it was fifty years ago and the trout were bright pink, she said. 'I suppose you would call us exiles now.'

By now it was growing darker and he wondered if Miss Baker was coming back. He felt worried for a moment or two, and then she came bouncing as she walked. She was carrying some papers in her hand.

Miss Campbell took them from her. 'I'm afraid I can't see,' she said.

'Perhaps we could have the light for a moment or two,' Miss Baker said.

She went to the door and switched on the light, a single lamp of about ten-watt power, and Miss Campbell looked over the papers. She read without glasses, and said: 'Georges was fifty-five. If you altered the first five to a three it would do quite well.'

'We could do that,' Franklin said.

Miss Campbell gazed at the papers.

'I always thought Georges had something of the appearance of a startled bloodhound,' she said. 'It would simplify things if you could swap the photographs.'

'We could do that, too,' Franklin said.

'All right, then.'

She held out the papers. There was no time to lose. Franklin got up and took them. Large, very old, hugely flabby, so that she did not look unlike an aristocratic bloodhound herself, she smiled at Franklin, showing charming cream teeth.

'If I were you I should go while the going's good,' she said.

'Is the going good?' he said.

'When you are young the going is always good.'

'Very wise,' he said.

'Not at all. It is not until you are old that you realize how good it has been. And then, of course, it is too late to do anything about it.'

He put the papers in his pocket.

'Get down to the station and take the first train for the frontier,' she said. 'Get out the obvious way.'

'What about you?' He seemed suddenly to be doing an extraordinarily selfish thing.

'We shall be here.'

'But you're English!' he said.

'Scots.'

Miss Campbell smiled correctly.

'But anyhow you will be in enemy hands,' he said. It seemed impossible to leave them here.

'On the contrary,' Miss Campbell said, 'I shall be in Miss Baker's hands. And Miss Baker, as long as I have hands, will be in mine.'

He could not answer this god-like simplicity. Miss Campbell smiled again, and once again he could smell all England in the smell of the tea as Miss Baker lifted off the lid of the pot for the last time.

'Another cup before you go?' she said. 'There is one.'

'Thank you, no,' he said.

He shook Miss Campbell's hand: it was large and dog-like, like a cold and friendly paw; and then Miss Baker's: very small and fleshless, with fingers surprisingly warm.

239

'I can't thank either of you enough,' he said. 'I can never thank you enough.'

'Remember us,' Miss Campbell said. 'That will be enough.'

'I will remember you,' he said.

He moved towards the door and Miss Baker, as he said good-bye to Miss Campbell for the last time, said she would come to the street door to show him out.

'It is very dark,' she said in the passage. 'Don't fall.' He felt her cling with her small hands to his empty sleeve. No one had ever touched it before. He felt her pull him along in the dark passage, travelling with tiny steps, until she found the catch of the outer door. 'We first came here in '97,' she said. She stopped. 'Now,' she said. 'There.'

She opened the heavy street door.

In the street outside it was not quite dark. The white after-light of sunset, reflected upwards, lay over the centre of Marseilles and westwards, a pale yellow, towards the sea.

'Thank you again,' he said.

Miss Baker, who had held his empty sleeve until this moment, now let it go.

'Good luck,' she said.

He went down the two steps into the street.

'Thank you,' he said. 'Good-bye.'

'You'd better go,' Miss Baker said. 'There's not much time.'

Moving away and looking back for the last time he saw the light in the sky reflected in her bright icy eyes. No, he thought, there was not much time. She looked unbelievably frail and small. She was smiling a little, but whether to save herself from crying or whether because she was already crying, he never knew.

CHAPTER 23

As they went out of Marseilles that night, himself, the girl and
O'Connor, travelling by train, he sat by the side of the girl, she
in the corner of the compartment by the window, with O'Connor opposite. Above O'Connor's head, on the rack, was the
girl's attaché case, containing all their things. The train, which
was supposed to be very fast, stopped many times at intervals
through the night, and sometimes at these stops Franklin would
lift the window-blind and look out on the darkness of a strange
station, with the ghosts of hurrying people passing to and fro
under shaded lights, the ghostly voluble voices excitedly bab-
bling, or on some remote part of the track where nothing moved
and nothing could be seen except red stars of signal lights in the
blackness, and there was no sound but hollow echoing noises
of shunting trucks and sometimes the wind tuning the telegraph
wires. Occasionally at these stops there came into the carriage
once again the heavy friendly smell of locomotive smoke,
steamy and pungent out of the strange darkness, so that Franklin would remember the night of rowing over the river; but
otherwise there was nothing but the smell of the train, of the
many cheap cigarettes smoked by other passengers, and sometimes the intimate small fragrance of the girl's hair as she leaned
her head on his shoulder.

He did not know at all how long the journey would take. He
hoped simply for darkness at the frontier. It seemed natural that
things must be easier in darkness. He remembered other fron-
tiers, and other trains, in peace-time, and how, as far as he
could recall, there was less vigilance at night. Sometimes, thinking of the girl and O'Connor and not knowing how adequate
the papers of any of them were, he was worried. Then he would
remember Miss Campbell and Miss Baker. At the station in
Marseilles there had been an atmosphere of wild disintegration;
the air was exploding into a million fragmentary rumours; and
it was quite right what Miss Campbell said. Everyone was run-

ning, and it was just possible that there would be a short period when everyone would be too concerned for himself to wonder where other people were running to. If the worst came you could always run in the darkness. It might even be necessary, in fact better, to be separated. He had better face that, he thought.

He sat for some time thinking about this. They had decided, since O'Connor could speak only English, and since his own accent wasn't at all perfect, never to speak to each other in the carriage except when they were alone. They had not yet been alone, and now in the carriage with them there were two sailors and an elderly woman. The sailors, who had smoked heavily all the way from Marseilles, were now asleep. The woman reminded him faintly of Miss Campbell, except that she was very French where Miss Campbell had been very Anglo-Saxon, and she was much younger. But her grey face, as she continually read the book open on her knees, had the same large bland imperturbability. Under the book was a small handbag of food. Now and then she slid her hand under the book and surreptitiously took out something and ate it. The lights in the train were quite dim. She munched the food very furtively, her hand over her mouth, and whatever it was she was eating Franklin never knew.

He got up at last and looked hard at O'Connor and went out into the corridor. He looked up and down the corridor, and the motion of the train swayed him about in the empty darkness. He caught the handrail with his right hand and hung on. O'Connor came out into the corridor a moment later and shut the door.

'Anything up?' O'Connor said.

'No. I just wanted to talk, that's all.'

'What happens at the frontier?'

'That's what I wanted to talk about. I haven't the faintest idea.'

'I wish to hell we were flying,' O'Connor said.

Franklin leaned against the window. In the faint light he could see the faces of himself and O'Connor impressed in reflection on the glass. O'Connor looked disturbingly English still.

'Look,' he said. 'If we get separated.'

'If what?' O'Connor said. 'Don't talk cock. Nobody's going to separate us. Not now.'

'It's more than possible.'

'Nobody's going to separate us,' O'Connor said. He was very firm. 'I'll shoot the bastard who does.'

'You'll shoot nobody.'

'If you only knew how I've been longing to shoot somebody,' O'Connor said.

'I do know.'

'Then you understand my feelings. Nobody's going to separate us now. I'll see to that.'

'All right,' Franklin said. 'Just in case.'

A man came along the corridor, carrying a heavy brown suitcase. He pushed past O'Connor and Franklin, who stopped talking. The man said 'Pardon!' and O'Connor and Franklin pressed themselves against the outer glass so that he could get by.

The man swayed along the corridor, bumping the suitcase against his legs. Franklin and O'Connor watched him go.

'O.K.,' O'Connor said.

'If I should get separated from you,' Franklin said, talking in a low voice, 'take the girl to the French authorities in Madrid. If you get to England take her to my mother. Go and see my mother, anyway.'

'Right. I got the address,' O'Connor said.

'And you?'

'I'll be doing target practice somewhere.'

'Now look.'

'Now look what?' O'Connor said. 'You overruled me last time, and what happened? You got in a hell of a mess and I got in a hell of a mess. The only time you let me arrange things I got you over the river.'

'All right,' Franklin said. 'Ten to one we won't get separated. I just wanted to tell you it doesn't matter much if we do. Each can find his own way.'

'We'll cling together like the ivy,' O'Connor said.

Franklin grinned. 'All right.' There was really no arguing with O'Connor. There never really had been. Better to let him go. 'But for God's sake don't show that revolver. And whatever happens, be nice to her.'

'I'll be nice to her.' O'Connor, a little embarrassed by the effort of saying something tender, stared at his own face in the glass. 'I'll be nice to her. I know how you feel. I'm sorry you didn't find the padre.'

'Thanks. We'll find one,' Franklin said.

O'Connor did not speak. They leaned together against the glass. Franklin, who could see nothing and could only feel the darkness solidly flowing past beyond their reflected faces, felt they were very close together: closer than on any of their trips, closer than in the river with O'Connor swimming him across, closer than at the meeting in Marseilles. This closeness gave him great confidence. O'Connor was one of the imperishable ones who somehow blundered through.

There were no words for this, and he looked up and down the corridor. No one was coming and he said:

'All right. Go back and tell Françoise I want her. Don't talk and, if she's asleep, don't wake her.'

O'Connor looked through the glass division of the compartment.

'She is asleep.'

Franklin looked through the glass. The girl was sitting quite upright. She had closed her eyes, the closed lids slightly paler than the sunburn of her face. It was as if she were not asleep, but really dreamily thinking through the closed lids. She might easily have been praying, too, he thought.

'All right,' he said. 'Go back, anyway. Tell her when she wakes up.'

O'Connor opened the compartment door and went in, and Franklin watched him shut it again and sit down. The girl did not seem to wake, and he turned back to stare at the night flowing beyond his reflection in the sheet of glass.

He stood there for a long time while the train rocked on in the darkness. It did not stop at all as he stood there, and he got the impression of inevitability from its constant speed in the night. Everything had seemed inevitable, really, since the meeting with Miss Campbell and Miss Baker. Everything, after the weeks of indecision and of looking vainly for the padre in

Marseilles, had happened quickly. It was better like that. Almost everything that had happened before that now seemed increasingly confused. It was hard to recall even the most vicious moments of pain. His arm had healed very well; he supposed it was really wonderful. They would let him fly again. They had to let him fly again. It was quite impossible to consider a life without flying, and he would pull every string he knew until they did let him fly. He hung on to the handrail and the train swayed in the darkness, jerking violently, the darkness firing signal lights in a row, like tracer, as they passed a station. He remembered something Miss Campbell had said about being young and not realizing, in youth, that the going was good. He wondered how her youth had been spent; remote holidays in the Highlands, seasons in London, the spring perhaps at Hyères, the summer in Dorset. You could be very young for a long time in those days, and it would not matter if you never knew it, because of the apparent permanence of that gentle world. Now there was no gentleness left, and scarcely any youth at all. You were doing elementary physics one day and bombing somebody to hell the next. The train was smoother now in the darkness, and his face pale and immobile in the glass. He was twenty-two, but he did not feel very young any more.

Miss Campbell wouldn't understand. He thought how admirable and fortunate she was. He would remember Miss Campbell for ever and the smell of tea that was all England. The train lurched again, and then in a moment the compartment door opened and he turned to find Françoise coming out.

She shut the door and smiled.

'Been to sleep?'

'No. Not really.'

'Not really?'

'Half asleep. Just thinking.'

He moved along the corridor, towards the end, the girl with him. It was the middle of the night, and in the compartments most people were sleeping. He held her with his arm in the corner at the end of the corridor and they spoke in low tones.

'Thinking of what?'

'Of what we will do when we are out of here.'

'What will we do?'

'Eat a lot.'

'What else?'

'I will learn English.'

'What else?'

'You will get a new arm. Was there something else?'

'Yes. I will call the arm George.'

'George? Because of what?'

'Because George is the name of the automatic pilot.'

'What pilot? Tell me about him. This George.'

It suddenly struck him that she was talking too much; that her sleep had been really full of truth. It seemed better once again to face the possibility of their being separated.

'Suppose we don't get out of here?' he said.

'We will get out.'

'We may get out and we may be separated.'

'We shan't get separated.' He knew that the moment was coming when he would not be able to argue against it. 'I have faith we won't get separated. I had faith we would get here and we got here. I had faith you wouldn't die after the arm and you didn't die.'

'I shall die after it,' he mocked. 'One day.'

'You shouldn't mock death,' she said.

He held her again in the corner of the corridor, glad that he had said something to make her stop talking. It seemed suddenly as if they were the only people awake on the train: very awake in a darkness unknown to them. Then lights were fired out of the night again, red and yellow and black, and the points of another station crackled explosively under the train. He held her against him and again thought, for some reason, quite inconsequently, of Miss Campbell. The going was very good, after all. It was very good and very wonderful: the night flowing on and themselves the only people awake in it, Marseilles and the uncertainty behind them, and then beyond that, far back, all the difficulties, the nearness of death and the pain. Miss Campbell was quite right. He felt the smooth, warm arm of the girl and wanted suddenly to bury his face in her hair because of the truth of it. Only a little farther, he thought. It can't be much farther. We've come a long way and it can't be much farther. The train swung on in the night, and because of his love and confidence in her he felt himself swing forward before it. For a moment or two he was borne forward on a smooth illusion, and was at last in Spain.

In about half an hour the train stopped at a station. It was not the frontier, and Franklin and the girl went back to their seats. A few people got in and stood in the corridor. In the corner the woman with the book was still reading, and still, sometimes, furtively eating out of her bag.

O'Connor was sleeping in the corner. The girl changed her seat and sat at the right side of Franklin, leaning her head on his shoulder. He put his arm against her and held her there. He looked at O'Connor, the sailors, the woman reading, the attaché case, and persuaded himself for one moment that it was a holiday. Then the train moved on, jerking at first, then smoother and smoother, until the feeling of its inevitability grew on him again. He shut his eyes and wondered how much farther they had to go. It was colder now.

It seemed very cold when he woke and his heart turned over, sick and sour, and he saw the daylight beyond the window-blinds. He knew now there would be no darkness. The sick excitement of the moment, of knowing they were nearly there, made him almost dizzy. O'Connor was still asleep, and the girl was drowsy as Franklin moved her head away from his shoulder and got up. In the corner the woman who resembled Miss Campbell was still reading; she did not look up as he stumbled out into the corridor.

He stood by the window for some time and watched the early day going past: a white farmhouse, with a few vineyards on terraces beyond, and then fields striped brown by ploughing, and then a station house of yellow plaster by a level crossing, and then fields and fields again. The sun was coming uncertainly through grey easterly cloud and he could see a wind blowing the bare trees along the line. The land was rising to the west. Then there was another level crossing, and he saw a peasant and a boy with a brown horse and cart, waiting for the train to come through. Sitting in the cart, the boy had his coat collar turned up, and Franklin could see the mane of the horse tossed suddenly upwards in a wild fringe by the wind.

He felt in his pocket for his papers. It couldn't be long now. Somewhere in the night the train had stopped again, and now the corridor was empty. He had looked at his papers over and over again, putting them to all the tests. It was impossible to think they were not right.

He stood there for about ten minutes, hating the daylight. There were more houses by the track, in ones and twos, and then in small settlements of twenty or thirty, red and white. The vines were all empty beyond them. The fields were empty, and the wind continued to blow fitfully at the empty trees.

He looked into the compartment and saw the girl awake. She was awake and was combing her hair. Seeing him, she smiled and then the black hair fell over her face and for a moment she was lost. O'Connor was awake, too. The blinds on the other side of the compartment were drawn up, and Franklin could see more houses on that side, and then fields, and then beyond them the crumpled faint line of mountains.

O'Connor came into the corridor. He shut the door.

'We're coming to it,' Franklin said.

'Any moment now,' O'Connor said.

'If anything happens act as if you didn't know either of us. We'll do the same.'

'Don't worry,' O'Connor said. 'If I don't get out one way I'll get out another.'

Before Franklin could speak again the train began to slow down. He saw more houses go past, and then a new concrete water-tower, and then the first sidings of a station. He stood rigid.

'Go and sit down and tell Françoise to come out a moment,' he said. 'And remember you're a Frenchman now.'

'Don't insult me,' O'Connor said. 'I might shoot myself by mistake.'

He grinned and went into the compartment, shutting the door. The girl had finished combing her hair and in a moment she came out. The train was going very slowly now.

'We must be there,' he said. 'Are you all right?'

'I am all right.' She smiled. Her hair was smooth and lovely when she had combed it.

248

'There may be some confusion,' he said, 'and we may get separated for a moment. But don't worry.'

'I am not worried.'

He looked up and down the corridor. It was empty.

'Would you kiss me?' he said. 'Here?'

'I will kiss you,' she said.

She kissed him briefly, her lips very warm and steadfast. He felt unsteady.

'Let's go back,' he said. 'I will get the case.'

She did not smile. Her face had the same tense assurance as when he had first seen it, and nothing, he thought, could be more sure than that. He went into the compartment and got down the attaché case from the rack. The two sailors were smoking, and the woman in the corner was still reading. He stood with the case in his hand and looked at the girl and heard the brakes on the train.

In a few more moments the train had stopped and, suddenly, what he had feared and expected and wanted to happen was happening, simply but quickly, in a way that he could not influence nor prevent. He was with the girl out on the platform. He could not see O'Connor. He gripped the case. Some hundreds of passengers seemed to have exploded from the train. For a few moments there was no order among them, and then they were drifting down the platform, and he was with them and the girl with him, and they had their papers in their hands. He was borne forward with them and felt the wind driving coldly down on to the station from the mountains. He saw it blow the dark hair of the girl wildly about her face. It blew into her eyes, so that for a moment she could not see. She brushed it out with her hand. Then he looked back, but still he couldn't see O'Connor, and then the long line of people bore him away from the train, his throat continually tight and dry, until he was in a large office, where men were examining papers and stamping them, and where the worst moment of all his life suddenly slipped past him, unexpectedly simple and brief, before he knew it, and he was walking out again into the cold wind on the station, his papers in his hand. It all seemed so simple that he wondered suddenly if it was purposely simple. He looked wildly about the station for O'Connor. The steam from under the train was blown almost flat along the platform, among the feet of the people. He could not see O'Connor. Walking back towards the coach where they had been he was suddenly torn between the need for finding O'Connor and the fear of losing sight of the girl. He looked back. In the large office behind him the girl was standing at a table. Someone was asking her questions, and he was near enough to see her mouth moving in answer. Her bare head was high up, her hair untidy when the wind had blown it. He thought in that moment how desperately he wanted to marry her. A French curé with long black habit and flat black hat went past him, carrying two bags, and into the crowd, and he wondered why he had never thought of being married in the French church. Then he knew that it could only have complicated things. Now they were almost free and it did not matter. The going is good, Miss Campbell, he thought. Are you thinking of us? We are almost through. We can be married in Madrid.

He thought all this very quickly; it was part of the moments of confusion. He still could not see O'Connor. He turned and looked swiftly into the train, but it was empty. At the far end three or four uniformed men, station officials or perhaps even gendarmes, were getting into the train. He could see their peaked caps above the crowd, and then as he moved back down the platform he saw that they were gendarmes, four of them. They were armed with short rifles.

The crowd on the station had begun to scatter itself; the long queue had been sucked into the office. It was half-past seven. The engine which had brought the train in had been detached and was whistling up the line. He took all this in very swiftly as he looked back for the girl. In that moment he could not see her. Someone else was at the table where she had been. He started wildly towards the office. Then it was all right. He could see her. She was at another table, with another official, answering other questions.

He still could not see O'Connor. He kept midway between the train and the office. The train was still without an engine and there was plenty of time. Then he saw the Frenchwoman who resembled Miss Campbell. She had her papers in one hand and in the other a cake; she was reading the papers and eating the cake at the same time. He wanted to ask her if she had seen O'Connor, but suddenly he could not remember any words of French, and she went on and got into the train.

In the few moments before he went back the girl had disappeared. He could not see her at all now. The desks in the office were occupied by other people, and he knew that she must have come out. He walked wildly about the platform, not seeing her, and then back to the office window, and then about the platform. Down the line the new engine was coming on to the train, and people everywhere were getting back to their seats.

He tried to be very calm. He went back into the train. The Frenchwoman so like Miss Campbell was sitting in the corner of the compartment. She did not look up. Neither the girl nor O'Connor was there.

They must be here, he thought, they must be somewhere. They must be. He walked down two sections of the corridor and then got out on to the platform. The four gendarmes were walking up through the train. It was seven-forty now, and he looked again into the office windows. The girl was not there.

He walked up and down the train for some distance outside it, and then he got into it and walked up the corridor again. It was a very long train and he walked through seven coaches. It seemed to him that there was plenty of time. He wondered where the hell O'Connor could be. He knew that he could go on without O'Connor, but not without the girl. Nothing mattered without her – nothing, nothing, nothing at all. The thought of it filled him with sick panic, and he started to walk back up the train.

The train began to move when he was halfway along it. He knew afterwards that it was a false move; there were many people still on the platform. But he did not know it then, and he began to run. He ran up two sections of corridor, with the train still moving, before he saw O'Connor.

O'Connor was jumping off the train. He was jumping down on to the tracks as Franklin saw him, and then running across them with two of the gendarmes running after him. The train was moving fairly fast as all three of them jumped, and one of the gendarmes fell on his knees. O'Connor was running towards some coal-trucks; he went behind them and then, still

251

running, came out again. The first gendarme was very fast, and was then about thirty yards behind O'Connor. It seemed that he would catch O'Connor very quickly. Then O'Connor made a new line, running hard across open metals between two lines of trucks, gaining a little until he reached the cover of the trucks farther on. Then Franklin saw him stop and press himself against the truck, and wait. He knew in that moment what he was going to do. The gendarme was running up past the truck, between the metals. 'Oh, you bloody fool! You bloody, crazy fool!' Franklin thought. A moment later O'Connor was firing with the revolver. 'Jesus, you fool, you fool!' Franklin thought. He saw the gendarme, about twenty yards back, fall back against the truck. 'You fool, you fool!' Franklin thought. 'You poor idiotic fool! Don't shoot any more! Don't shoot!' and then he saw O'Connor shooting at the gendarme for the second and third and fourth time before running on. He saw the gendarme all the time slowly slipping down until he was almost flat against the truck where O'Connor had shot him.

The train began to slow down and then stopped again as O'Connor and the gendarmes disappeared. Franklin walked sickly back up the train. There were several excited people in the corridor, but no gendarmes at all. He pushed past, looking into all the compartments as he walked, but the girl was not there. He knew that she must be in the compartment where they had always been.

He walked back into that compartment but she was not there. Only the Frenchwoman was sitting in the corner, still reading, but not eating now. Franklin stood vaguely in the compartment, holding the attaché case in his hand, feeling as if he were the centre of the absurd and fantastic mistake. He looked frantically out of the window. The train was just beyond the station, and the wind was blowing pieces of straw and dirty paper down the tracks.

He felt lost and helpless as he turned to the woman in the corner.

'The young woman,' he said. 'The girl. Please! Please! The girl who was here. Didn't she come back?'

The woman looked up. She looked remarkably like Miss Campbell in a younger way.

'Yes. She came back.'

'For God's sake, where is she?' he said. 'Please, please, where is she?'

'She was with gendarmes,' the woman said. 'Her papers were not in order. She came back to tell you that, I think.'

'But what had she done to be with gendarmes?'

Already the train was moving, but he did not notice it.

'I don't know. But I should say not much.'

'What makes you say that?'

'She didn't look afraid.'

The train was moving quite fast now, and on the sidings, among the lines of trucks, there was no sign of O'Connor. He was desperate.

'Did she say anything?' he said. 'A message? Please!'

'There was no time,' the woman said. He was not really listening now. He looked at her wildly and then beyond the windows. A new world was racing past. 'The gendarmes took her out. There was some confusion. One of them jumped out of the train. They were all jumping about and running. Did you see? It was all very confused.'

'Yes, I saw it,' he said.

No, he hadn't seen it. Not that gendarme. Were all the gendarmes running? It did not matter. He walked out into the corridor. It was all over. It did not matter if all the gendarmes had jumped off the train. Nothing mattered. He did not want to talk about it now.

He walked frantically up the corridor, carrying the attaché case. He did not want to talk about anything. He walked through the dark intersection between the coaches, swaying blindly. Then he stood by the window on the other side. The inside of himself was dead. He felt suddenly old, bitterly and vacantly old, in a way that Miss Campbell, herself so very old, would never have understood. After a few moments he felt sick, too, and opened the window and let the wind, cold and violent, blow in on his face. The trees at the foot of the mountains, dark and grey on the sunless side, were leafless. The leaves blown from them looked harsh and dry after the heat of summer. The wind sweeping down the slopes had driven them into great brown drifts in the hollows everywhere.

He stood there for what seemed a long time before shutting the window. The cold wind blowing in so violently from the rush of the train had stung his eyes, and he shut them for a few moments, pressing his head on the glass.

When he opened them he could see the reflection of the girl's face, cloudy and unreal, beside his own in the window. It was for a moment part of the world racing past the train. Her face was very white, and he could not believe in the reality of it, and simply stood there watching it stupidly, as if she were a cloudy memory in the glass. Then he saw her breath forming on the cold glass, forming and dissolving and forming again in a small grey circle before the reflection of her mouth. He heard her breathing very quickly. She was breathing with little gasps of pain, as if she had been running to find him and was frightened, and she began to try to talk at the same time. He heard her say something about her papers and the gendarmes, and then about O'Connor. 'They were taking me off the train when he saw and began to run,' she said. She had never been able to pronounce his name in the right way, and he saw her frightened lips mumbling and faltering as she tried to say it now. 'They began running when O'Connor ran. They all left me and began running.'

'Oh God!' he said. 'Don't talk, don't talk!'

He could not bear the agony of her frightened smile or the agony of knowing what O'Connor had done. He wanted to put his arm about her, but she was standing on his left side and there was no arm there to comfort her. He only stared at her, and then rested his face against her head and watched her bright dark eyes.

She leaned against his empty sleeve and he let her go on crying for a long time, not trying to stop her, and as the train rushed on between trees bare and bright in the morning sun he knew that she was not crying for herself. She was not crying for O'Connor, shooting and being shot at, doing a stupid and wonderful thing for them, or because she was young, or for the terror of the moment or for joy or for the things she had left behind. She was not crying for France, or for the doctor, who represented France, or for her father, shot with his own revolver. She was not even crying for himself. He felt she was

254

crying for something that he could never have understood without her, and now did understand because of her. Deep and complete, within himself, all these things were part of the same thing, and he knew that what she was really crying for was the agony of all that was happening in the world.

And as he realized it there were tears in his own eyes, and because of his tears the mountains were dazzling in the sun.